Invitation to Italy

Victoria Springfield writes contemporary women's fiction immersed in the sights, sounds and flavours of Italy. Victoria grew up in Upminster, Essex. After many years in London, she now lives in Kent with her husband in a house by the river. She likes to write in the garden with a neighbour's cat by her feet or whilst drinking cappuccino in her favourite café. Then she types up her scribblings in silence whilst her mind drifts away to Italy.

Also by Victoria Springfield

The Italian Holiday
A Farmhouse in Tuscany
The Italian Fiancé

Victoria Springfield

Invitation to Italy

ORION

First published in Great Britain in 2023 by Orion Fiction,
an imprint of The Orion Publishing Group Ltd,
Carmelite House, 50 Victoria Embankment
London EC4Y 0DZ

An Hachette UK company

1 3 5 7 9 10 8 6 4 2

A CIP catalogue record for this book
is available from the British Library.

ISBN (eBook) 978 1 3987 1250 8
ISBN (Paperback) 978 1 3987 1251 5

Typeset by Born Group
Printed and bound in Great Britain by Clays Ltd, Elcograf S.p.A.

www.orionbooks.co.uk

To Sham –
at last, a book of mine you haven't read before!

Prologue

The honeymooners were back in the pool again. The girl was swimming breaststroke, holding her head awkwardly. The boy posed on the tiled edge, his golden torso a few shades darker than the day they'd arrived. He ran a hand through his long dark hair, arched his back and dived into the turquoise water. Loretta watched him critically. *Surprisingly well executed. Seven out of ten.*

The boy swam up to his new wife, put his hands around her waist, lifted her up out of the water and tossed her up in the air. She flung her arms and legs wide apart as if doing a star jump and landed back in the pool screeching with laughter. He scooped her up and held her close so that her red bikini and his toucan-print shorts were melded together.

Loretta turned away and began rolling the pool towels into neat yellow cylinders. Her diamanté shoe buckles glittered in the sun; how glamorous they looked. Money well spent even though her calves would be aching by lunchtime.

When she looked up, the couple were no longer canoodling. The girl was floating on her back, her neat toenails sticking out of the water. They were painted shell pink, a nice bridal colour. Loretta's were her usual signature scarlet, shade 26, True Passion, reapplied every three weeks by Flavia at Sempre Bella. Loretta wasn't going to let standards slip just because she'd turned sixty.

'You should come in!' The boy waved an arm at Loretta.

She shook her head.

The boy laughed, as if knowing his suggestion had been absurd. How taken aback he would be if she took up his invitation. She'd step out of her emerald-green chiffon dress and high strappy sandals and execute a near perfect dive – she did not kid herself she could score more than nine these days – into that clear, cool water. She'd hold her breath until she surfaced three-quarters of the way along the pool then power her way to the far steps in a matter of seconds.

Loretta smiled politely. 'I'm afraid I don't swim,' she said. It was what she told all her guests at the Hotel Paradiso. The girl they'd once called *il delfino* – the dolphin – was long gone. Sometimes she hardly remembered her.

Chapter One

Abi closed the lid of her laptop and rested her elbows on the kitchen island. She couldn't wait for Chloe to get back from her dad's so that she could tell her daughter about the trip she'd planned. She had chosen a pretty hotel by the sea with spa treatments and all the activities nearby that a just-about-to-turn thirteen-year-old could dream of. There was even a multiplex cinema and a bowling alley in case the English summer weather let them down, though Abi fervently hoped it wouldn't.

Chloe would have fun; Abi would make sure of that. They'd have a whole week of mother and daughter bonding. Abi would stop obsessing about her ex-husband Alex and his fiancée Marisa, who was pretty, slim, stylish and six years younger than Abi. There would be no rows, no tears. It would be a new start.

Chloe's key turned in the lock. Abi scrunched up her pasty wrapper and empty bag of Maltesers and chucked them in the bin. She couldn't be bothered to cook for herself when Chloe was at her dad's.

'Hi, Mum!'

'Hi, love!' Abi padded into the hall. Chloe stood stiff-limbed as Abi pulled her into an awkward hug.

She could smell garlic and the expensive scented candles that Marisa liked to burn.

'Did you have a nice time?' She made an effort to keep her voice light.

'Yeah.' Chloe dropped her keys into the blue and white bowl on the console table, marched into the kitchen and tossed a pink plastic bag onto one of the chrome bar stools.

'Did Marisa take you shopping?'

'Yeah.'

'And?' Abi smiled encouragingly. She hoped Chloe wasn't going to turn into one of those monosyllabic teens. Or maybe Chloe was just like this with Abi.

'I got this.' Chloe opened the bag and pulled out some sort of all-in-one garment covered in a riot of hot pink blooms and turquoise butterflies. 'What do you think?'

Abi smiled. It would be perfect for the holiday she'd planned. 'It's great, darling. Hold it up so I can see it properly.'

'Marisa helped choose it. She says it makes me look more grown up, but Dad says it looks like a pair of old curtains.'

Abi forced a smile. 'I know it's going to look lovely on you. Now, tea? Orange juice?'

'No thanks. I had a Coke . . . umm, drink at Dad's.'

'So, what did you have for your tea?'

'*Parmigiana di melazane*, it's this auberginey, cheesy, tomatoey sort of thing.'

'Sounds yum.'

4

'It was, but it's not as good as your sausages and mash, Mum.'

Abi felt a little tension ease from her shoulders. 'We can eat that tomorrow night if you'd like, love. Why don't you sit down? I've got something to show you. Could you pass me my laptop?'

'Mu-um?'

'What?' There was something in the way that Chloe dragged out her name that put Abi on her guard.

'Mum,' Chloe repeated. She looked down at the island unit's glossy granite top. 'I need to tell you something . . . ask you something, I mean.'

'What does Alex, I mean Dad, want me to agree to now?'

'Dad and Marisa are going to spend the summer in Italy staying with Marisa's parents.' Chloe paused.

'He told me that a while ago. And?'

'And they want me to go too.'

'That's nice, love, but I can't see how you can go if they're staying out there for weeks. I don't want you coming back on a plane by yourself.'

'They've asked me to stay for the whole school holiday,' Chloe mumbled.

Abi opened her big pink American fridge and unscrewed the top of a half-drunk bottle of Pinot Grigio. She poured herself a glass of wine and took a big sip. She mustn't cry. Chloe had seen more than enough tears.

'But what about seeing your friends? What about Olivia and Precious?'

'I'm not really friends with Precious anymore.' The corner of Chloe's eye twitched. It had done that a lot in the weeks after Alex had left.

'But what about Olivia, you're still friends with her, aren't you?' Abi said. She was aware that her voice sounded unnaturally bright.

'I suppose . . . but she kind of hangs out all the time with Precious these days.'

'Oh.' Abi remembered what that felt like. 'But do you really want to go away for that long? What if you don't like it?'

'It's an Italian island, Mum,' Chloe said slowly. 'Marisa's parents live by the seaside.'

'If they're taking Elsa, it won't be much fun for you.'

'Duh . . . of course they're taking Elsa – she's their kid.'

Abi winced. Alex's second child. The child that he and Abi had always wanted but who'd never arrived.

'What if you don't like the food? There'll be a lot of seafood and fish.' Abi was clutching at straws now. She was glad of the steadying effects of her cold glass of wine.

'I'll just have to live on pizza.' Chloe grinned. 'Anyhow, Dad says Nonna Flavia is a fabulous cook.'

'*Nonna* Flavia?'

'It means grandma in Italian.'

'I know what it *means*.'

'Marisa says Nonna Flavia and Nonno Enzo can be my new grandparents now that Gramps has gone.'

Her lovely dad, Chloe's lovely Gramps. She would have hit rock bottom after Alex left if it hadn't been for him. If only he was still here – he'd know exactly

6

what to say and do. Abi and her late mum had never been that close. It was different with Dad. He'd always understood her. She reached in her pocket for a tissue.

'Please don't cry, Mum. I miss Gramps too. But Olivia's mum says: "substitute grandparents can be valuable role models in a teenager's life".'

Abi sighed; maybe she was being selfish. 'But I thought we might go down to Dorset,' she said. 'Not Bournemouth,' she added quickly. Last year's visit had been an unmitigated disaster. They'd had a massive row when Chloe wanted to go off to the ice-skating rink by herself. Marisa wouldn't stop her having fun, Chloe had said. 'Marisa isn't your mother!' Abi had shouted. 'She doesn't love you – not the way that I do.' And Chloe had burst into tears in the street.

Chloe got up from the kitchen stool. She stood up very straight. 'I want to go to Italy, Mum. You've got to let me. It's the most exciting invitation I've had in my whole life!'

A week in Dorset with boring, spoilsport old Mum or a summer of Italian sunshine and fun – it was a contest that Abi couldn't win.

'Of course, you can go.' Abi forced the words out.

Chloe flung her arms around her. 'I love you, Mum. You're the best mum in the whole wide world.'

Abi buried her nose into her daughter's hair. She caught a hint of the sophisticated Chanel perfume Marisa had bought Chloe for her twelfth birthday.

Chloe stepped back. Reluctantly, Abi loosened her grip. 'Best go up to bed now, Chloe, it's getting late.

If you're not bored with shopping, we could go to Westfield on Thursday night. We could look for a new swimming costume if you like.'

'Brill! Oh, Mum, didn't you want to show me something on your laptop?'

Abi picked up her wine glass. It was empty. 'It wasn't anything important,' she said.

'Okay then. Night, Mum.'

Chloe was singing to herself as she climbed the stairs.

Abi opened the fridge door and reached for the bottle of wine. Out of nowhere she heard her dad's voice. 'The answer's never at the bottom of the bottle, love.' She left the Pinot Grigio untouched, put her glass in the dishwasher and went to lock the front door.

Chapter Two

Abi pressed the doorbell. A blur of bright colour appeared behind the stippled-glass panel. Cherry opened the door.

'Sorry to call round so early,' Abi said. 'I should have messaged.'

Cherry touched her red and green headwrap. 'Lucky I'm up and dressed,' she laughed.

Abi smiled. There was something about her friend's laugh that instantly lifted Abi's spirits. Cherry found joy in everything. It had been the same way ever since school when Cherry didn't have a lot to laugh about, being the oldest of six with her dad working nights and her mum out of the door by five in the morning.

'Come on in, I'll put the kettle on. Tea or coffee?'

'Coffee please.' Abi followed Cherry into her sunny kitchen and leant against the old pine table.

Cherry put two orange mugs on the sunflower-printed wipe-clean tablecloth. She lifted the lid of a large Tupperware box. The heady scent of spices and treacle made Abi's stomach rumble, even though she hadn't long had breakfast. 'Ginger cake? Or are you on your way to the gym?'

'Gym?' Abi frowned. She glanced down at her grey jogging bottoms. It was too hot for jeans and she couldn't do the zip up on her cropped chino trousers anymore. 'Oh, these joggers, I see what you mean. No, I haven't rejoined.'

'Me neither. You won't catch me on one of those running machines.' Cherry gave her trademark guffaw.

'Maybe I should give it another go,' Abi said. 'Chloe's nagging me about it. She keeps telling me that Olivia's mum says, "Exercise produces feel-good endorphins and transforms your energy levels."'

Cherry snorted. 'Olivia's mother? Don't mention that woman to me! She drove me half demented at the last PTA meeting. You haven't changed your mind about joining the committee, I suppose?'

Abi bit into a slice of ginger cake. She wasn't going to join the PTA or a watercolour class or the refreshments rota at Chloe's badminton club or any of the other innumerable organisations people had urged her to try in the years since Alex had left. She didn't want to meet new people. And she definitely didn't want to 'get back out there' and meet a new man, even if there was someone searching for a dumpy, divorced single mum of nearly forty.

'So, how's Chloe?' Cherry asked. She cut another slice of cake and slathered over a generous layer of butter.

'She's fine . . . happy.' Abi took a deep breath. 'She's going to Italy with Alex and Marisa to stay with Marisa's parents. For the whole of the school holidays.'

'What?' Cherry shrieked. 'When did they plan this?'

'I don't know. Chloe only told me last night.'

'Oh, you poor thing.'

Abi looked into her friend's warm brown eyes. She swallowed the lump in her throat. 'I want her to have a good time. Of course, I do. But . . .'

'You think if she enjoys it too much, she'll want to go out there every summer?'

'Alex can work from home now. His office has embraced remote working; he doesn't even have to stay in England. What if Marisa wants them to move back to Italy with Elsa. They could leave London for good; they could take Chloe . . .' Abi made a strange gulping sound. She felt the tears gathering. She swiped her eyes with the back of her hand.

Cherry tore off a piece of kitchen roll.

'Thanks.' Abi blew her nose noisily. 'Sorry.'

'Sorry? I won't take any sorry. What are you sorry for? Loving your child? Anyhow, there's no point fretting, Chloe might hate it. I bet she'll be on that phone begging to come back after a week. Marisa comes from a small island, doesn't she? What's your girl going to do out there compared to all the fun she can have in London?'

Abi pushed Cherry's phone towards her. 'Procida. Google it.'

'How do you spell . . . No, hang on a minute, I've found it.'

Abi waited. An image filled the screen. Sun-drenched pastel-coloured houses cascading down a hillside under a sky so blue it made her blink.

'Now I see what the problem is,' Cherry said. 'Not quite Jamaica, but even so . . .'

Loretta reached up to the high shelf behind the pool bar and took the sky-blue envelope with the Naples postmark from behind the bottle of Cinzano. She was tempted to pour herself a small glass of the vermouth in a bid to still her rapid heartbeat, but it wasn't yet six in the evening. The pool was deserted; all her guests were still out for the day. She couldn't magic up another excuse to avoid opening the letter. Taking a knife from beneath the counter, she slid it under the flap.

Like the first (and perhaps the second, which she'd thrown away unopened), Amadeo D'Acampo's letter was brief. Loretta scanned the page; there was nothing aggressive or sinister about the politely phrased, neatly typed lines, but her breath was tight in her chest, her throat dry. She forced herself to press her damp palms flat against the smooth white surface of the bar and re-read each word calmly and slowly.

Dear Madam,
I write to you for the third and final time for if I do
not hear from you on this occasion, I will accept that
you have, for your own reasons, no intention of
considering my client's interest in the Hotel Paradiso
and I will not trouble you further. I write now only
to reiterate that my client is a man of vision who
desires only to enhance the experiences of the guests of
any property in which he invests. He is a fair man,

who, if choosing your property, would make a more than reasonable offer. It would be a pity if you were unwilling to even consider discussing such a potentially lucrative opportunity.

Yours faithfully,
Amadeo D'Acampo

Loretta wished she had the courage to write back straight away with a brief but polite note: *Thank you for your interest, but please advise your client that the Hotel Paradiso is not for sale. At any price.* If only that were true.

She opened the leather-bound book she'd taken from the reception desk; she still preferred it to the electronic diary embedded in the hotel's rarely used computer. The blank days had multiplied, last-minute cancellations occurring with increasing frequency. Loretta had heard rumours of people booking two or even three different holidays and leaving it to the last minute to choose wherever they fancied or whichever desperate hotel was willing to offer the biggest discount.

Loretta hadn't believed that people would treat a small business like hers in such a way until the day she took a bus to Marina Chiaiolella on the far side of the island and bumped into Signor Martino and his wife, who'd stayed with her the previous three years. They'd cancelled their booking at the last minute, a family matter they said. Loretta didn't know who was more embarrassed. Signora Martino begged Loretta's forgiveness with tears in her eyes. Such a special deal, but such a big mistake! Their new hotel was so impersonal.

There wasn't even a human being to welcome them; they had had to check in on an iPad – imagine that! They would never stay in such a place again. Loretta had expected to welcome them back to the Hotel Paradiso this year but they hadn't returned; perhaps they were too embarrassed.

She knew she might be forced to consider an offer from Amadeo D'Acampo's mystery client, but how could she give up her business? She wished she had someone with whom she could discuss her dilemma but she didn't want rumours spreading that the hotel was in trouble; besides, she had got used to keeping things to herself.

The bells of Santa Maria delle Grazie were chiming six o'clock. She checked around the loungers, picking up the last of the towels, making sure no guest had left their sunglasses, book or phone behind. She closed the leather guest book, tucked Signor D'Acampo's letter inside the drawer under the counter where she kept her personal bits and bobs and locked up the bar.

Chapter Three

The doorbell sounded ten times louder than normal.

'All right, all right, I'm coming,' Abi yelled, rubbing her stiff neck. It wasn't the first time she'd fallen asleep on the sofa since Chloe had gone to Italy. It was so hard to get her seven or eight hours a night; her imagination ran riot in the small hours worrying about what her daughter was doing. She'd tried avoiding blue light and taking long baths; she'd even bought a tin of cocoa to make milky drinks but nothing seemed to work. After a few days she'd taken to coming downstairs at two or three in the morning and reading for a while before going back to bed and trying all over again.

She staggered to the front door. Cherry was standing on the doorstop in a migraine-inducing orange and lime headwrap, skintight cerise leggings and a matching T-shirt with *The Bod Squad* written across her chest.

'Well, what do you think?' Cherry span around. A pair of angel's wings were printed on her ample backside.

Abi blinked. 'Great . . . umm . . . very you.'

'Are you ready?'

'Uh?' Abi wiped the sleep from her eyes.

'Don't tell me you've forgotten.'

'Of course not.' Abi's foggy brain began to piece together the conversation they'd had the night before. She'd phoned Cherry, blubbing hysterically about how Chloe didn't need her anymore. The memory made her cringe.

'I don't know why I agreed to a jog; it'll be more of a waddle,' Cherry laughed.

'And I don't know why I suggested it.' Abi had enjoyed running a long time ago, pounding the pavements early in the morning when the only people out and about were dog walkers and the brewery men tipping great barrels of beer through the hatch in the pavement outside The Duchess of York. Then she met Alex, who preferred pumping iron in the gym during the week – where he could admire his muscles in the full-length mirrors – and lying in bed on Saturday mornings. And then, after nearly two years of trying, Chloe had come along.

'Want to come in? I'll just be two minutes,' Abi said. At least she wouldn't have to get changed; she was still wearing the vest top and pink jogging bottoms she'd fallen asleep in. But she desperately needed a glass of water, her head was banging.

'Sure.' Cherry followed Abi through to the kitchen and leant against the island.

'Water?'

'Thanks.' Cherry mopped her brow. 'It's gonna be hot today.'

Abi held one of Alex's old pint glasses under the tap. A saucepan edged with congealed baked beans was resting in the sink. The papery skin of last night's baked potato was still sitting on a plate by the draining board. She quickly scraped it into the bin. She was thankful she hadn't taken her friend through to the sitting room where empty crisp packets and chocolate wrappers were strewn across the coffee table and the smell of pot noodle hung in the air.

Cherry chugged down the water. 'Ready?' She did a little jog on the spot.

Abi scraped her fine, blonde hair into a quick ponytail, stuck her keys, a credit card and some gum in the pocket of her joggers and slammed the door behind them.

'Can we walk for a bit first?' Abi said. The sun was shining, the heavy leaves of horse chestnut trees casting some welcome shade over the pavement. She inhaled deeply. Maybe some fresh air, even laced with the traffic fumes of South London, would do her good.

'You can't trudge along like that. You've got to power walk,' Cherry said. 'Come on!' She raised her elbows to the height of her substantial breasts, bent her arms and pumped them back and forth as she marched off puffing and panting.

Abi copied her friend, knowing she looked ridiculous. People were turning and staring but Abi could feel a smile forming on her lips. She caught up with Cherry in a couple of strides.

'We'll keep going until we get to the park,' Cherry wheezed.

'Not much further,' Abi said.

Cherry sat down with a thump on the park's first wooden bench. A wilting bunch of carnations with a handwritten note was tied to one of the slats. *Grandad Bert – never forgotten.*

'Life's too short, huh . . . I'm stopping here, got to catch my breath. You jog round, Abi, but just once or twice, it's been too many years since you've run.'

'And you've never run,' Abi said.

'Cheeky! Carry on like that and you won't get any of my roast chicken tonight. You are coming round later – you haven't forgotten that too?'

'Of course not,' Abi said.

'Off you go then.' Cherry leant back, arms behind her head.

Abi had no desire to jog but at least she'd look less daft than copying Cherry's so-called power walking. She set off very gently around the path just inside the black iron railings. It was too late in the morning for any serious runners to be around. A little girl with check dungarees and her hair in bantu knots shot past on her scooter, squealing with delight. Her dad lumbered along behind, a small sleeping child strapped in a sling across his chest. Abi flashed him a sympathetic smile.

Her head was still thumping behind her eyes but as one foot hit the ground then the other, she picked up a little speed. She drew level with the bench where Cherry was sitting. Much to her surprise she wasn't ready to sit down.

'You go, girl!' Cherry shouted.

Abi jogged another lap, the sun warm on her back. It would be hotter than this in Procida right now. She wondered how Chloe was dealing with the heat. When she reached Cherry's bench again, she flopped down next to her friend.

'You were pretty fast second time around,' Cherry said. 'Carry on training and you'll beat Dina Asher-Smith.'

'Very funny,' Abi said.

'Don't know why you ever gave up jogging. Can't see the appeal myself, but you used to like it, didn't you?'

'Not enough time, I guess.'

'Yeah, tell me about it!' Cherry yawned.

Abi felt a pang of guilt. Cherry juggled looking after her two kids with working long shifts at the hospital whilst Abi was a stay-at-home mum with all the time in the world. Once Chloe had started school, Abi could have looked for another office job, but she had put it off, waiting for the time when she'd be pregnant with their longed-for second child. But that day never came. And now Alex was gone.

Cherry stood up. 'Fancy grabbing a drink at that new café round the corner. My treat.'

'Sure,' Abi said.

'They do a great green juice.'

Abi stared at Cherry. The thought of pureed broccoli and seaweed made her feel nauseous.

'Gotcha!' Cherry cackled. 'They do a fab mango milkshake with an ice-cream float.'

'I'll stick to Coke,' Abi said. 'But don't let Chloe know you've seen me drinking one.'

The café was only two minutes' walk away and they managed to grab a couple of seats in the shade. It didn't take long for Abi to finish her drink. She sucked the last of it noisily through the stripy paper straw. 'I'd best get back home; I left my phone on the hall table and Chloe might call.'

Cherry delved around in the bottom of her tall, fluted glass with a long-handled spoon. 'Heard anything from her today?'

Two messages – both replies to Abi's – and one call was all the contact Abi had had with Chloe over the last three days.

'Not yet, but she looked okay the last time she called.'

'You mean that Facetime call with Marisa prancing around in the background?'

'I'd forgotten I'd told you about that,' Abi said.

'You sure did. Showing herself off in a string bikini, that Marisa. Shameless, she is.'

'Hmph,' Abi grunted. She didn't want to dwell on the images in that call, especially not the moment when Alex appeared in the corner of the shot, scooped Marisa up in his arms and ran off down to the water's edge. Alex had been wearing a pair of close-fitting swim shorts that showed off his well-formed legs, a cool pair of sunglasses and an expensive-looking diver's watch. His wet hair was slicked back showing off his sharp cheekbones. The jolt of lust that ran through Abi told her, that despite the five years that had passed since he'd gone, she wasn't over him yet.

'But Chloe seemed happy?' Cherry thankfully interrupted Abi's thoughts.

'She *seemed* happy, but how can I be sure? What if she's putting on a happy face? What if she needs me?'

Abi blinked back the tears that were threatening to come.

'Looks like we need to operate Plan B.'

'Plan B? What was Plan A?'

'The jogging of course, getting those "feel-good endorphins" Olivia's mother promised.'

Abi rubbed her throbbing forehead. 'I must have been desperate to take that woman's advice. But I did feel a bit better whilst I was actually running.'

'Want to go back to the park and go around again?' Cherry had a glint in her eye.

'Only if you do,' Abi chuckled.

'No way! I've done my exercise. That power walking almost killed me. And I've had one of my five-a-day.' Cherry grinned. She used her straw to scoop a minuscule piece of mango out of the remains of her creamy milkshake.

'So, what's Plan B?' Abi asked as they walked back down the street.

'Going to see my friend Nadia.'

'Nadia? Not the one who works for a travel agent in Brixton?'

'You mean the one who's changed firms and now works in that travel agent's right over there?' Cherry pointed to the other side of the street.

'Oh no!' Abi said.

'Oh yes! We're getting you a flight to Italy. You're not going to stay at home wondering about Chloe, you're going out there to find out. You agreed, remember.'

'I said I'd think about it,' Abi protested but Cherry had a grip on Abi's arm and was yanking her across the road as though she were pulling a reluctant dog away from a particularly niffy lamppost.

Cherry flung open the door of Sun and Stars Travel. Nadia looked up from behind her screen. Cherry gave Abi a little push. 'You can't run off now, Nadia's seen us.'

'Hey, Cherry!'

'You remember Abi?'

'Of course I do! Come and sit down, 'scuse the mess.' Nadia swept a pile of brochures to one side of her L-shaped desk.

Abi sat down on one of the metal-legged chairs. The room smelt of newly laid carpet. She glanced at the clock behind Nadia's head; it was shaped like a map of Africa.

'You girls going on holiday?' Nadia said.

'I wish.' Cherry gave a throaty laugh.

'We were just passing,' Abi said.

'Abi's going on holiday, she wants to go to Italy.'

'I don't,' Abi said but part of her was itching to jump on a plane and check Chloe was okay.

Nadia tweaked the edge of her hijab. 'Do you two need to take a minute?'

'I . . .' Abi began.

Cherry gave her a look.

Abi shrugged and fell silent. She wasn't going to sit here and argue in front of Nadia. She'd let Cherry say her piece and had played along but she wasn't going anywhere. She couldn't turn up in Procida; Chloe would have a fit.

'She wants to go to Italy,' Cherry said.

'Any particular part?' Nadia's hand rested on the computer mouse.

'One of the islands off Naples – Procida. She wants to go for a fortnight. As soon as possible.'

Abi smiled weakly but she didn't protest. The sooner she was out of here, the sooner she could go back home and message Chloe. Again.

'You're in luck,' Nadia said. 'I know just the right place. The Hotel Paradiso. I'm sure you're going to love it.' She turned the screen to face the two friends.

'Wow!' Abi said before she could stop herself.

'See, I knew she'd want to go,' Cherry said.

'I do and I don't.' Something was telling her Chloe wanted her there but was it a mother's instinct or just wishful thinking? It wouldn't matter how beautiful the hotel was if Chloe didn't want to see her. And if she did, Abi would happily pitch a tent on the beach.

'Take your time,' Nadia said.

Cherry drummed her fingers on the desk.

Chapter Four

'Passport, purse, phone?' Cherry asked for the third time.

Abi patted the pocket of her white denim jacket and peered into her handbag. 'Yes, yes and yes.'

'Are you sure you don't want me to come with you to help you check in?'

'To make sure I don't do a runner, you mean?' Abi wiped her sweaty palms on the front of her hastily purchased linen trousers. 'I can't believe I'm doing this.'

'You'd better believe it!' Cherry gave a throaty laugh. 'Come here.'

Abi squeezed Cherry tight, inhaling the familiar scent of her vanilla body lotion. 'I wish you were coming with me.'

'Me too, but there's no way I can rearrange my shifts at such short notice and my Candy's got her A levels next year. I need to make sure that lazy girl's doing some studying this summer. Fancies herself as a doctor now – I told her she needs to get off that phone of hers, start looking at some books.'

'Candy's a smart girl, but you're always going to worry like I worry about Chloe. What if she doesn't want me there . . .'

'We've been through all this,' Cherry said gently. 'If Chloe's homesick or bored, she's going to feel much happier having her mum close to hand and Nadia will sort out a ticket and get her on your flight back home. And if she's having a whale of a time, you'll see that for yourself and set your mind at ease.'

'But even if I manage to prise Chloe away from Alex and Marisa for a bit, I'll be alone most of the time.'

'Like you are in London.'

'Hmm . . . I know you're right but I just can't imagine sitting in a restaurant all by myself.'

'You'd rather be at home with a microwaved meal from Sanjay's minimart than eating spaghetti and clams with the sea lapping at your toes? Really? I can taste that Italian food now: fluffy mozzarella, pasta and *zabaglione*, oh my!'

'Zabagli– what?'

'*Zabaglione* – Italian trifle. I had it that time I went to Sorrento with Dwayne years ago and I'm salivating just thinking about it.' Cherry closed her eyes theatrically. 'So, you think of me emptying bedpans whilst you're feeling sorry for yourself lounging around with a fat paperback and a great goldfish bowl of Aperol Spritz.'

'Ouch!' Abi said.

'Got to be cruel to be kind sometimes.' Cherry shrugged. 'Now you get that case checked in. I've got something for you, but you can't read it until you've gone through and you're sitting at the gate.' She handed Abi a small cream envelope and wrapped her in another massive hug.

25

Abi slipped the envelope into the breast pocket of her jacket. 'Thanks, Cherry. I'll message you as soon as I land.'

'You'd better!'

Abi wheeled her case towards the check-in area, her stomach churning with nerves. She followed the instructions on the screen, half hoping some message would appear telling her the flight was cancelled. She heaved her case up onto the belt and watched it slide away. She wandered aimlessly through Duty Free, spraying on perfume samples for something to do, drank a cup of overly milky tea she didn't want from a takeaway cup and she was still at the check-in gate far too early.

She perched on an uncomfortable chair, her carry-on bag resting between her feet, and toyed with her phone. A one-line answer from Chloe to her earlier messages: *Yeah, everything fine*. Did *fine* mean *fine* – or was it reverse teen-speak like 'sick' for 'good'? Cherry was right: Abi wouldn't know for sure how Chloe was if she stayed at home in England. Travelling to Procida might set her mind at rest. She reached in her bag for her book before remembering Cherry's note.

She ripped open the small cream envelope to find a Good Luck card: a purple cat with a wide grin sitting on a four-leafed clover.

Remember when you last got on a plane, Abi? Been a while, hasn't it? And now you're going to Italy by yourself. You're scared. I know. You've half a mind to go back home but your case is on that plane now and you're going with it. I've

*hidden a present in with your clothes and I want – demand!
– a selfie of you wearing it by the pool tomorrow – or else!*

At the bottom of the card, an extra line had been added in purple felt-tip pen: *I was going to write 'it's gonna be OK' but it won't be OK, it's gonna be blinking BRILLIANT!!!*

Abi smiled. She wondered what Cherry had bought her; probably a crazy, colourful kaftan or sarong. Abi could certainly make use of another cover-up. When she'd tried on her old bikini and seen how pale and pasty she looked she'd almost chickened out of the trip. She would have to keep her shorts on to hide her pearl-white thighs. And she'd avoid the beach where lithe, brown bodies like Marisa's frolicked on the sand. Cherry and Nadia had railroaded her into this holiday, but she'd do it her own way.

She took out her phone and typed: *Thanks for your card. You're the best!*

Cherry didn't take long to reply: *I know LOL.*

Abi switched off her phone. They were calling her flight.

Loretta tucked the corner of the white sheet under the mattress and placed the neatly folded scallop-edged quilt at the foot of the bed. She straightened up, rubbed the small of her back and wiped her forehead. It was a warm morning, the lack of breeze intensifying the scent from the bunch of freesias that she'd arranged on the bedside table alongside a fabric-covered box of tissues and a pictorial guide to Procida.

27

She smoothed down her bright red capri pants, stood back and studied the arrangement of scatter cushions in the middle of the bed. The two heart-shaped pink ones would have to go, they were far too bridal. She'd swap them for a couple of rectangular ones with a zingy lemon and lime print. There was nothing like a touch of vibrant colour to raise the spirits.

Loretta didn't know if Abi Baker needed her spirits raising but she knew from experience that a woman spending a fortnight alone in a strange place was a woman with a story to tell. That story might be one they were desperate to share or one that they tried to bury away, unseen but always felt like the pea beneath the princess's pile of mattresses. But whatever the reason for Abi's visit, Loretta was determined to give her a holiday to remember. As soon as the booking had been confirmed, Loretta had juggled things around and upgraded Abi to one of the three garden rooms whose little patios led directly out onto the pool. Now she only needed to fetch those lemon and lime cushions from the spare linen cupboard and the room would be perfect.

She slipped her orange heels back on, straightened up the two small chairs on the patio and went to check on the pool en route. Most of the guests had gone down to the beach but yesterday's new arrival, Bill, was sitting on one of the loungers tapping away on his laptop.

Hearing the click clack of Loretta's heels, he looked up and smiled. He had a nice smile and friendly blue eyes but Loretta wished he would close that computer and relax. Wasn't that what holidays were for? As if reading her mind, he moved the laptop aside and picked up the laminated bar menu. Loretta trotted over.

'May I get you something?'

The Englishman's finger rested on the third item on the menu. 'An Americano with milk please. I guess it's too early for a beer.'

'Whatever you like. You're on holiday, aren't you?'

'I suppose I am, but a coffee all the same *per favore*.'

'Of course.'

'*Grazie*.'

Loretta smiled. Bill's accent was truly appalling but she appreciated his attempts to try and speak her language.

'Nothing else?'

'Not after that wonderful breakfast.'

Loretta vanished behind the counter of the pool bar. She pressed down the freshly ground coffee and twisted the basket into position. She checked her reflection in the side of the coffee machine, tweaked the position of the tortoiseshell combs that helped secure her hair extensions and inhaled the delicious aroma of fresh coffee. Perhaps she'd take ten minutes and have one herself once she'd taken Bill his drink. She needed something to keep her awake; she'd hardly slept last night. The bad dreams had returned, as vivid as before.

Chapter Five

Abi slipped on the white cotton dressing gown left folded on her bedroom chair and opened the sliding door that led to the tiny, paved terrace. The early morning sun was already warm but a gentle breeze lifted the leaves on the lemon trees. The scent of honeysuckle from the trellis that divided Abi's spot from that belonging to the neighbouring room hung heavy in the air.

A sparrow hopped off the arm of one of the two white metal chairs as Abi approached. She sat down and sipped a thick, sweet peach juice from the bottle she'd found in the mini bar, Cherry's gift resting on her lap. Unable to contain her curiosity any longer, Abi struggled with the copious amounts of sticky tape that Cherry had used to wrap the parcel. After a few minutes she admitted defeat and ripped straight through the middle of the shiny foil wrap to reveal a layer of yellow tissue paper. Abi smiled; Cherry never did anything by halves.

She slid her finger under the join in the paper. Would she find a sequin-trimmed kaftan or a heavily fringed rainbow-coloured wrap to ring the changes with the glittery purple scarf she'd already borrowed from her friend? She pulled a swimming costume from the crisp tissue paper and held it up. The top half was turquoise, the lower half peach with side panels of deep sage green. Two wide purple straps formed a halter neck. The low scooped back was finished off with a matching purple bow. She was going to look like a court jester in this kaleidoscope of colours.

She folded up the swimsuit and stuffed it back into its wrappings. Cherry must be joking if she thought Abi was going to put on this comical costume and take a selfie by the pool. Abi's fingers brushed a scrap of paper; she pulled it out but it wasn't the gift receipt she was expecting, it was another note from her best friend.

You've opened this, so Congratulations, you made it to the Hotel Paradiso!!! I searched everywhere for this swimming cossie so I hope you love it. I know you're thinking, "Whoa it's bright!" It's a present from me — what did you expect? — but wait 'til you put it on. That turquoise is gonna make your blue eyes sparkle and that halter neck shape — wow! You'll be Italy's answer to Marilyn Monroe. Send me a pic of you in this NOW, by that pool, not hiding in your room. You go, girl! You're gonna knock 'em dead! xxx

Abi sighed. Cherry would be so offended if she refused to put this crazy costume on. And there was no point putting it off; she might as well sneak a couple of pictures before breakfast whilst no one else was up and around. She stepped back inside her room, sat on the edge of the white scalloped quilt, wiggled her feet through the leg holes and braced herself for the unedifying struggle she'd experienced the last time she'd tried shopping for swimwear.

The costume slipped on surprisingly easily. She stood up and reached behind her neck to fasten the wide purple straps in a double bow.

She picked up her phone from the top of the heavy wooden chest and leant over to pick her dressing gown up off the bed. She was going to wrap it round her very tightly indeed before she stepped outside. As she did so she caught sight of herself in the mirror on the wardrobe door. Automatically she glanced away but not before she noticed something extraordinary. Abi leant closer and looked again. Cherry was right: the vibrant turquoise made her eyes look even bluer. And the sagegreen panels provided an optical illusion that whittled her waist to a size she hadn't seen since her wedding day. She could almost have described herself as sleek if it wasn't for the great big, purple bow on her behind.

She fastened the dressing gown's belt around her waist and stepped back outside, through her small patio and out to the pool. The shutters on the pool bar were closed, the yellow and white parasols still had their cotton ties fastened and the loungers that fringed three sides of the small, turquoise tiled swimming pool were bare. The only sound was the birds tweeting their morning greetings.

She shrugged off her robe and dropped it on the nearest lounger, held the phone at arm's length and took a couple of snaps. Cherry would be pleased with these: the sun sparkled on the inviting blue water and the bright pink bougainvillea tumbling down the brick wall on the far side of the pool added yet another vibrant colour to the hues provided by Abi's swimsuit. The shots were perfectly set up but oh, how serious she looked. It was hard to smile on cue. Her worries about how Chloe would react to her unplanned appearance were written all over her face. She needed Cherry making her laugh or Chloe admonishing her to 'Chill, Mum.'

If Cherry were here, she'd be urging Abi to strike a pose. Abi leant forward and pouted. Eat your heart out, Marilyn! She twisted to the left, raised her shoulders and put one hand on the front of her thigh as if replicating Marilyn's fly-away skirt in *The Seven Year Itch*. Laughing now, she twisted sideways so the camera caught a glimpse of the great purple bow on her backside. She stuck out her bottom, threw back her head and laughed. A genuine laugh.

Abi swiped the screen. These pictures would definitely make Cherry smile and Abi knew she didn't have to worry about her friend plastering them all over her social media. Maybe she'd take just one more snap. She positioned herself right on the edge of the pool, lifted one leg and stretched out her arm like a ballet dancer. She smiled and clicked.

'Would you like me . . .'

Abi's head shot up at the sound of a man's voice. Instinctively, she clasped her hands across the top of her thighs. The man stepped towards her. Abi stepped backwards.

'Watch out!' he called. Too late.

Abi felt her flip-flop skim the edge of the pool. Her arms flailed wildly as she grabbed at thin air. The phone flew out of her hand. She hit the cold water with an almighty splash. She let out a screech.

'I'm so sorry,' the man gasped.

'Ugh, aah!' Abi spat out a mouthful of pool water. She'd landed in the deep end; she kicked her legs to keep upright. 'You idiot! What the hell do you think you're doing, creeping up on me like that?'

She blinked the water out of her eyes. The man's face came into focus. A kind, open face with blue eyes. Very blue eyes.

He descended the metal steps that led into the pool. 'Are you all right?'

'No, umm, I mean yes.' Abi was all right if 'not about to drown' was what he meant by 'all right'.

'Are you sure? Take my hand. I'd jump in but I can't swim.' He stretched out his arm, not muscled up like Alex's, just toned and lightly tanned.

Abi trod water. 'I'm fine honestly, if you could just move out of the way.'

He stepped back. She yanked down the edges of her swimming costume and hauled herself up the steps. Standing on the side, she raked one hand through her long blonde hair, squeezed out a great puddle of water and gave herself a shake. Something bounced against her backside – the great purple bow sewn to the back of her costume.

She edged slowly backwards towards the lounger where her abandoned dressing gown lay, but the man

34

got there first. He scooped it up and held it open for her as if she were a lady in a period drama being helped on with her coat.

'Allow me,' he said.

Cringing, Abi quickly thrust her arms through the armholes, hoping he had not caught sight of the ridiculous bow.

'There you go,' he said.

She turned to face him. 'Umm . . . thanks.'

'I am truly sorry for giving you such a fright, it was all my fault.'

His voice was contrite, but his eyes held a mischievous sparkle. Abi suddenly felt rather warm despite the cool water trickling down her back.

'I don't know why your voice made me panic like that. I wasn't expecting anyone to be by the pool so early,' she said.

'You don't normally pose like that?'

'No, I do not,' Abi said sternly though she felt her lips twitching as she tried to suppress a smile.

He grinned. 'That's a shame. Though if you want to do that again tomorrow morning, I'll probably be the only person around. I like to have a few quiet moments out here before breakfast. If I'd known I'd bump into someone, I would have raked a comb through my hair and probably had a shave.' He ran the back of his hand across the stubble that darkened his jaw. It rather suited him.

'You don't need to . . .' Abi began.

'Don't need to what?'

'Nothing.' Abi pulled her dressing gown cord tighter.

'Nothing?' His eyes roamed searchingly over Abi's face.

'Have a shave,' Abi said, the heat rising to her cheeks.

'Really? I've never felt trendy enough for designer stubble and I can't imagine growing a beard but maybe I should give it a try. Anyhow, I'd better go and have a shower and get properly dressed. I've been sleeping in this.' He plucked at the shoulder of his grey marl T-shirt.

'Same here,' Abi said. 'I mean, I need to have another shower now, thanks to someone making me fall in!'

'I didn't think you meant you slept in a swimsuit.' He bent down and picked up something from the base of a lemon tree. 'Your phone, it looks OK, apart from a bit of dirt.' He blew on it softly.

'Thanks.' She took the still-warm phone and slipped it into her dressing gown pocket.

'Have a nice day.'

'You too.' She stayed by the edge of the pool watching him walk away.

Re-showered and dressed, Abi made her way out onto the breakfast terrace. It was as perfect as the pictures on the computer screen in Sun and Stars Travel promised. Better in fact because for all their pixelated perfection, the images on Nadia's screen couldn't hope to capture the sounds of birdsong, the warmth of the sun on her bare shoulders or the scent of the lemon trees. And the online pictures of the sumptuous breakfast were devoid of the aromas of sweet, sugar-dusted *cornetti* and ripe melon that danced in Abi's nostrils as she waited for the proprietor, Loretta, to fix her coffee.

The man from the pool was already ensconced at his table on the opposite side of the terrace from hers, his face half hidden behind a copy of some business magazine, allowing Abi to study him at her leisure. His worn, grey T-shirt had been replaced by a light blue polo shirt with crease marks as though it were fresh out of its cellophane packaging. His stubble was gone, and his sandy-brown bedhead hair had been tamed, though the odd rogue twist still failed to lie straight. For some strange reason she had the urge to go over and smooth it down.

He looked up and caught Abi's eye. She looked away, busying herself with her mobile phone. The case had an old photo of Chloe printed on it. She looked so proud in her pink leotard and white tutu. Chloe was forever nagging Abi to get a new case. Apparently, the lovely photo was 'so embarrassing'.

How much more embarrassed Chloe was going to be when she found out that her mother had decided to pitch up in Italy. Abi hadn't forewarned Chloe; she hadn't been willing to take the chance that her daughter would freak out and insist that Abi stay in London. Abi had told herself that she would contact Chloe as soon as she arrived on the island but the plane was delayed and the traffic from Naples was heavy and she only just made the late ferry and by the time she arrived, Chloe would have been in bed – she hoped.

And to be honest, Abi wanted to enjoy one night and a leisurely breakfast before she braced herself to make the call. Nearly thirteen was such a difficult age, but weren't all ages difficult when you were a single mum trying to lay down the law whilst an absent dad and his pretty young fiancée swooped in for all the fun stuff?

She finished the last of her cappuccino, stood up and brushed the pastry crumbs off her sundress. She made her way across the terrace. The man from the pool looked up from behind *The Economist*. 'Hello again! Looks like it's going to be a hot one.'

'Yes.' She smiled. 'See you later.'

She popped back to her room, brushed her teeth, put on her sunglasses, handed her key in at the reception desk and set off down the narrow stone steps that led to the Marina Corricella. Glancing back at the hotel, she noticed the man was still sitting alone on the terrace drinking his coffee. He must have seen her heading down the path because he put down his cup and waved. Abi waved back. She couldn't help smiling.

Chapter Six

'What is it, Chloe?' Dad ran a hand through his still-damp hair.

Chloe shifted from foot to foot on the tiled floor. 'Da-ad, can we go to the beach?'

'Not that again, Chloe, I've told you I'm working.'

'But you worked yesterday, and the day before.'

'There's nothing to stop you going with Elsa whilst Marisa's out.' Dad started tapping on the keyboard.

Chloe felt a tugging on her arm. 'Chlo-eee!' It was Elsa. She gave Chloe a big gap-toothed smile; there was jam smeared all around her mouth.

Dad twisted around in the wooden dining chair and put out his arms. 'Hello, my little poopsie. Come here!' He scooped Elsa up into his lap, tweaked her nose and made a funny noise. Chloe didn't want to be treated like a little kid but she couldn't help wishing that Dad's face would light up when *she* came into the room.

Elsa reached for the computer mouse and giggled.

'Ah, no you don't!' Dad said. He put his hands under Elsa's armpits, lifted her up and plonked her back on the floor with an exaggerated *oof*. 'Off you go. Chloe will take you to the beach.'

Chloe plonked herself on the wooden bench in the hall, shoving her feet into her sandals without undoing the straps.

'Ready, Elsa? *Ciao*, Nonna! We're going to the beach.'

Nonna Flavia hurried out from the kitchen. She wiped her hands on her floral housecoat and pressed some coins into Chloe's hand. '*Gelati*, ice-cream, yes?'

Chloe slipped the coins into the front pocket of her shorts. 'Thanks, I mean *grazie*, Nonna.'

'*Gelati! Gelati!*' Elsa leapt up and down.

Nonna smiled. She had a big smile that made her face crinkle up so much that her black eyes almost disappeared. She put one restraining hand on Elsa's shoulder, pulled a lacy handkerchief out of her apron pocket, spat on it and wiped the jam off the little girl's face. Elsa squirmed and wriggled. Chloe patted her back pocket. Her phone should be safe enough.

They made their way down the street past the imposing bulk of Santa Maria delle Grazie. The sun was bright; Chloe was glad of her new sunglasses even though she'd posted a few pictures of them on Instagram and no one in her class had commented on them except Tania, and Tania didn't count because Olivia and Precious said she was ugly, even though Chloe thought Tania just looked normal like most people did.

They turned into the road that led away from the Piazza dei Martiri, walking close to the wall to avoid the traffic. Across the street, a boy leaning against a green moped gave a low whistle and shouted out '*Ciao, bella!*'

Chloe's cheeks burnt, she looked away.

'*Bella! Bella! Bella!*' Elsa sang.

'Ssh!' Chloe said.

'*Bella!*' Elsa yelled at the top of her voice.

Chloe started to walk faster, not caring that Elsa had to half skip, half run to keep up. She didn't slow down until they reached the path that took them to the wide shallow steps leading down to the beach.

She unrolled her striped beach towel and laid back, staring at the sky through her sunglasses. Her phone was digging into her bottom. She pulled it out of her back pocket and began scrolling through her social media accounts.

'Build a wall,' Elsa said. She scraped the edge of her pink plastic spade across the surface of the sand.

Chloe stared at her phone. She'd imagined everyone would envy her summer in Italy, but no one seemed to care. Everyone was too preoccupied with Olivia's posts; she and Precious had been to a music festival with cool bands and slept in a tepee in a field. Olivia had intricate henna drawings all over her hands and was wearing a really short skirt; her legs were long and thin. Precious had a new piercing in the top of her ear; her mum would probably kill her. They were going to have a joint thirteenth birthday party and everyone was going to be there. Except her. It was all so unfair.

A handful of sand landed on Chloe's shin. She sat up and pushed her sunglasses up into her mousy-brown hair.

'I bury you!' Elsa said. She tipped another spadeful of sand over Chloe's legs. Chloe kicked her leg, dislodging the mound.

Elsa glared. A handful of sand flew through the air. Chloe closed her eyes. Too late. She blinked rapidly, trying to clear the painful stinging.

'What did you do that for?' She grabbed Elsa roughly by the arm.

'Let go – you're hurting me! You're horrible, I hate you, Chloe!' Elsa gulped back great tearful sobs. A woman walking past with a parasol tucked under one arm turned and glared.

'Ssh, ssh!' Chloe said. 'Look, we'll dig a big hole, how about that?'

'A really big hole,' Elsa said. 'You dig it.' She threw the spade at Chloe.

'As long as you stop crying.'

Chloe dug the pink spade into the soft sand. Procida was beautiful but she wished she was back home lying on an old beach towel in the garden eating a choc-ice from Sanjay's whilst Mum lolled in one of Gramp's old stripy deckchairs with a book and a big glass of white wine.

Chloe had been away from home loads of times staying with Dad and Marisa in London but she'd never missed Mum before. Mum was just there waiting for her at home, like the wooden coat stand in the corner of the hall or the pair of porcelain ballerinas that had sat on the top of the bookcase on the landing for as long as Chloe could remember. Mum would bombard her with a million questions, a million pointless queries: did Dad check your homework? What did you have for lunch? And Chloe would mumble *yes* and *no* and *dunno* whilst Mum talked on, her words as inconsequential as the TV burbling in the background. But this was different. Dad was glued to his laptop five days a week and Marisa was out and about half the time leaving Chloe with Marisa's parents or babysitting Elsa.

It would be so much better if Mum was here on Procida but she was hundreds of miles away. Chloe was amazed how much she missed her.

Abi stood on the marina taking in all the sights and sounds she'd hardly noticed the night before when she'd bumped her big case along the waterfront and up the flight of steps leading to the Hotel Paradiso.

She strolled along the edge of the water, a row of green, turquoise and white-and-blue boats were tied up to the rough stone wall and beyond that the sea stretched as far as she could see. Small fishing boats covered by tarpaulins rested out of the water just a few paces from a row of cafés whose large cream umbrellas shaded those lingering over their breakfasts. Behind the bars and restaurants, dozens of candy-pink, orange, sky-blue and cream-coloured houses were piled up on top of each other as though someone had tipped a box of giant Lego down the hillside. Above the jumble of buildings rose the clocktower and dome of a huge yellow church with odd, bone-shaped windows that reminded Abi of the dog biscuits she used to feed Dad's little Bobby.

She took out her phone, searching for the best place to take a picture. There! Two little boats in the fore-ground, the rough bark of a palm tree, its green leaves even brighter against the saturated crimson of a little guest house whose balcony was further enlivened with parasols in emerald and the brightest of blues.

It would be so easy to while away the morning wandering around and taking photographs, but the longer she put off FaceTiming Chloe, the more difficult it would be. She wiped her hands on the front of her dress and tapped in her daughter's number.

Chloe's face appeared on the screen. The sun had brought out the freckles on her cheeks and her nose looked a little pink. Abi resisted asking if she was wearing sunblock; she didn't want to start the call with a nag.

'Oh, hi, Mum!'

'Hello, darling, you sound pleased to hear from me,' Abi said.

'Of course I'm pleased. Is it hot in London?'

'What makes you ask that?'

'Your sunglasses and that green, flowery dress you only wear on holiday.'

'Oh, umm, right.' Abi touched the top of her head as if surprised to find her sunglasses there. 'Hot? I don't know really.'

'You don't know?'

'Where are you? Are you with Dad?'

'No, just Elsa, we're on the beach.' Chloe's face disappeared from the screen and was replaced by half of Elsa's. The little girl giggled, a pink plastic spade appeared above her head.

'Oh good,' Abi said. There was a pause. Someone walked past shouting *Ciao, Matteo*! A gull shrieked.

'Mum.' Chloe's face reappeared. 'Where on earth are you?'

'I, uh, don't know quite how to tell you this, love, but I'm here. On the island.'

'Here?' Chloe's head swung around as if expecting Abi to appear out of the sea like a creature from one of the Greek myths she'd been studying at school.

'Yes, here in Procida.'

'You can't be! Move the phone and show me.'

Abi traced an arc through the air with her mobile.

'I thought you were joking!' Chloe said.

'I know you said you're OK, but I wanted to come and see for myself. You're not angry with me are you, Chloe?'

'Oh, Mum, I'm so pleased you're here. Let's meet after lunch and go to the beach. Dad and Marisa won't mind.'

All the tension of the last few days eased away. Chloe sounded happy she was here. *Thank you, Cherry.* Why had she ever doubted her friend?

The steps down to Chiaia Beach were wide and shallow, shaded by palm trees and branches of wisteria overhead. Below them, the beach was dotted with colourful towels and umbrellas. The heads of people swimming bobbed in the water; others stood in the shallows. Abi held her beach bag close to her body, her rolled-up towel under one arm. Chloe carried a leather-handled circular straw bag borrowed from Flavia stuffed with snacks even though they'd not long finished lunch.

'Careful, Chloe, look where you're going,' Abi said.

45

'Mu-um! There's no need to fuss. Even Elsa can walk down here without holding my hand.'

'I suppose she's getting too big for your dad to carry her.' Abi stopped for a moment to readjust the bag on her shoulder.

'Dad hardly ever comes to the beach, he's usually working. He's made some sort of office on the corner of the dining table.'

'Hmm, what does Marisa say about that?'

'Dunno, not much.' Chloe skipped down the last steps. 'Shall we sit over there?'

'Wherever you like.'

They walked a little way along the beach and unrolled their towels on the dark, volcanic sand. Abi rolled up the bottom of her green sundress by a few inches. She didn't fancy revealing the top of her thighs. Had they always been this white? They were nearly translucent! Chloe wedged her discarded sandals under Flavia's bag and pulled her daisy-print top over her head. Her flat-chested figure was unrecognisable beneath the padded cups of a sugar-pink bikini.

'It's new, Marisa helped choose it.' Chloe beamed.

Abi forced herself not to grimace. Why did Marisa have to buy Chloe something like that? Why couldn't she let her stay a little girl for a bit longer?

'There's a shop near the apartment that sells these really cool bucket hats; they've got one in exactly the same pink.'

Abi recognised the wheedling tone. 'Let me guess – you asked Dad to buy one for you and he said no.'

Chloe traced her fingers through the sand. 'Yeah, he said he can't keep doling out money when he's got two mortgages to pay.'

'He was moaning about me not going back to work, I expect.'

'I told him Olivia's mum says you should never bad-mouth the other parent.'

'I bet that went down well.'

'The hat's only ten euros and it's really, really nice.' Chloe gave Abi her sweetest smile.

'I'll treat you, love. We can go to the shop afterwards.'

'Thanks, Mum. You're the best! Let's go for a swim, it's not cold like Bournemouth.'

Abi had only just got comfortable. She stretched out her legs, wiggling her toes. 'OK, but in a few minutes.'

'Dad and I race each other down the beach and he throws himself into the water shouting "Geronimo!" It's so embarrassing but it's the best fun ever! Marisa hides behind her book and pretends she doesn't know him,' Chloe giggled.

'Doesn't she come in with you?'

'No, she lies on the beach getting a tan; I don't think she likes getting her hair wet. But she hardly ever comes here; she's busy helping Nonna or shopping or visiting friends. It's usually just me and Elsa.'

Abi caught her breath. 'Just the two of you?'

'Chill, Mum. The water's not very deep and Elsa's got armbands. We're not going to drown!'

'Can't be much fun for you, babysitting a five-year-old.'

'S'all right. Sometimes she gets on my nerves being

all whiny or wanting to bury me in the sand but sometimes it's fun – like having a little sister.'

Abi looked out to sea. Around the curve of the
bay, the colourful jumble of houses behind the Marina
Corricella was bleached to lighter shades by the bright
sun. Two young children ran past kicking up sand.

'Come on, Mum, let's swim.'

'OK.' Abi wriggled out of her dress.

'That costume's new,' Chloe said.

'Cherry bought it for me.'

'I like it, it looks good.'

'Really?'

'Yeah, it suits you. OMG, you should see what Marisa
wears! Her bikini's got dangly tassels and sparkly bits
and it's real-ly small! When she turns over it disappears
into her bottom like there's nothing there!'

'It doesn't sound very comfortable.'

'I wouldn't want one like that,' Chloe said.

Abi was thankful for small mercies. She stood up
awkwardly. 'Shall we swim?'

'Oh yes, let's!' Chloe ran straight into the sea.

Abi stood on the edge of the water, letting it lap
over her toes. It *was* a lot warmer than Bournemouth.
The days, so far, were sunnier and the couple of meals
she'd eaten were delicious. Chloe was having the time
of her life. Abi was happy for her. Wasn't she?

Loretta bent down to pick up a leaf that was floating
on the surface of the pool. The itch to dive into the
cool depths was still there, somewhere deep within her.

She would never forget the day she had first toddled into the sea when her mother's back was turned, kicked her legs and discovered she could swim as easily as she could walk and run. Young as she was, she knew that she had been born to be in the water. She won her first swimming gala at the tender age of five. When she was in the sea everything made sense – like it did when she was in Giorgio's arms.

How proud Giorgio was the day she completed her first long-distance sea swim. The headmaster, her parents, her friends and neighbours from their little village on Capri all gathered on the shore to cheer her home. Giorgio and his best friend, Salvo, cheered louder than all of the others put together. '*Il delfino* – the dolphin,' Giorgio called her. He watched her compete, he watched her swim, he watched her train. One day, when she was just seventeen, he dropped onto one knee on the sand and presented her with a ring. A beautiful opal. 'It changes colour like the waters in the Blue Grotto,' he said.

She and Giorgio didn't set a date to marry. They would wait until after Loretta had achieved her greatest ambition: to complete the annual Capri to Naples swim, crossing twenty-two challenging miles of open water.

It was hard to spend as much time as she wanted with Giorgio that spring and summer; she had to practise every spare hour she could. She always removed the opal ring before she trained, fearing her wrinkled, shrinking fingers would cause her to lose it in the depths. But after she completed the swim – and surely she would

– she promised Giorgio she would make up for all the time they had lost. How innocently she'd assumed her future was all mapped out.

The mayor waved them off from the Marina Grande. Nine and a half hours later she completed the gruelling challenge. She clambered out onto the Naples seafront, exhausted and exhilarated. Her parents were the first to greet her. And Salvo was next, his red shirt so easy to spot amongst the crowd of family and friends. 'Congratulations!' he cried. But he couldn't meet her eyes. The words 'Where's Giorgio?' died on her lips.

Then she saw them: Giorgio and Adriana. His arms around her tiny waist, the blue shirt Loretta had given him pressed against Adriana's fashionable ruffled blouse, her big, gold hoop earrings glinting in the sun. They were so wrapped up in each other they hadn't even seen her swim those last triumphant strokes.

As soon as they spotted her, they sprang apart. Giorgio rushed up to hug her as if nothing had changed. Adriana stood a little way apart, running her beautifully mani-cured fingers through shiny, dark hair that wasn't coars-ened by sea water, a smile on her perfectly made-up face.

Loretta stood dumbly on the seafront accepting the congratulations of family and friends. She twisted her hands together knowing that her bare finger would never again wear the beautiful opal ring. And it would never nestle next to a plain gold band.

Back home she laid the ring in the black and red lacquer box her nonna had given her, alongside all the swimming medals she'd won. She was no longer

Giorgio's fiancée. She was no longer *il delfino*. She had swum for the last time.

That night she fell asleep straight away but her hard-won rest was marred by her fearful dreams. She was swimming towards the shore but with every stroke the beach was moving further away, the waves were whipping up around her, the currents pulling her this way and that. The dark water was closing over her head. She was drowning. She woke in the small hours, gasping, her body slick with sweat. The relief she felt knowing she was safe on dry land was followed by the raw pain of reliving the moment of seeing Giorgio with Adriana. She lay in the darkness wondering how she could live without him, believing she could never feel lower. Not knowing that the worst was yet to come.

Chapter Seven

Abi put her hand to her forehead to shade her eyes from the late afternoon glare. All the sun loungers were already taken. Except one. And she was far too embarrassed to lie on that one, next to the man who'd caused her to topple into the pool on her first morning. Even if he did have a nice smile and sky-blue eyes.

She turned to go, but it was too late. He'd seen her. He smiled and gestured to the unoccupied lounger. She hovered; it seemed so rude to walk away – and she'd been looking forward to chilling by the pool.

She picked her way past the line of sunbeds, yanking down the edge of her cotton T-shirt dress that seemed to ride further up her thighs with every stride. She unrolled the yellow pool towel, spread it over the vacant lounger, carefully inched the cotton dress over her head and plopped it on top of her beach bag.

The man looked up from his laptop. 'Hi there.'

Abi instinctively tugged at the sides of her swimsuit. 'Oh, hi.'

'Lovely day again,' he added.

'Mmm,' Abi murmured. She searched for something else to say but she felt curiously tongue-tied.

She stretched out on the lounger inhaling the aromatic scent of the lemon trees, glad of the striped parasol that shaded her face from the glare of the unrelenting sun. She picked up *Summer Love at Hollyhock Cottage* and found her place. It was the third in a series she'd been devouring back in London, and as comforting as a pile of buttered crumpets. She turned the page, eager for the next development but for some reason it was hard to lose herself in the trials and tribulations of the rosy-cheeked heroine and her trusty-but-crazy labradoodle. Her thoughts kept turning to what Alex, Marisa and Chloe might be doing. And how much fun Chloe was having without her.

She tossed the book aside and picked up her celebrity gossip magazine. *The bride dazzled in a series of five hand-made designer dresses whilst her billionaire property-developer groom rocked a classic tux in midnight blue.* It was no use; she wasn't in the mood for other people's perfect lives. She stowed the book and magazine back in her beach bag, the beach bag she'd bought in Spain on their last family holiday together – the summer before Marisa came to work at the law firm with Alex and destroyed their happy life. And Abi's chance of finally conceiving her longed-for second child.

'Are you OK?' The man on the lounger was looking at her with concern.

'Fine,' Abi muttered.

'I don't want to pry . . .'

'Then don't.'

A flicker of pain crossed his eyes. 'I'm sorry. I shouldn't have bothered you.'

'No, I'm sorry. It's just . . .' Her voice tailed away.

'Something's happened but you don't want to talk about it. It's okay, I understand.' There was kindness in his blue eyes.

'It's my daughter – Chloe – it's hard to explain.'

He closed the lid of his laptop and pushed it aside. 'How old is she?'

'Twelve, nearly thirteen.'

'I guess that's why I haven't see her with you. Probably lazing in bed half the day, typical tween-ager,' he laughed.

'Chloe's here but she's not staying at this hotel. It's complicated . . .'

'Go on.'

'Chloe's here with her dad, Alex, and Marisa, Alex's girlfriend.' Abi couldn't bring herself to say 'fiancée'.

'They're staying at a different hotel?'

'Marisa's parents, Enzo and Flavia, live on Procida, in the big turquoise apartment building opposite Santa Maria delle Grazie. They invited Chloe and Alex out here to spend the whole of the school holidays with them.'

He let out a low whistle. 'What's that? Six weeks? That's a long time to be without your daughter. I guess she normally lives with you.'

'Yes, Alex left five years ago. Since then it's just been me and Chloe.'

'That's tough.'

Abi fiddled with the woven friendship bracelet Cherry had given her. 'I wasn't supposed to be coming

54

out here but my best friend, Cherry, talked me into it. I expect it was a bit of a shock for them all when I turned up on the island.'

He raised his eyebrows. 'I'll bet it was.'

'When I saw Chloe yesterday, she seemed so happy to see me I was sure I'd made the right decision. But when we met up, all she could talk about was what a wonderful time she was having with Alex and Marisa. This morning, we took the bus over to Ciraccio Beach. The water was so clear, we had a lovely swim and then found this little restaurant with the absolute best seafood spaghetti and wonderful lemon tart, but I couldn't help feeling she was counting down the hours until I'd gone. I'm meeting her again tomorrow morning, but I'm not sure she wants to see me. Maybe I shouldn't have come here. Maybe I got it all wrong.'

'Hey, don't beat yourself up. Kids her age need their mums but they think they're grown up all at the same time. I bet she's happy just knowing you're here on the island, knowing you care. That's a big thing, you know.'

'Thanks,' Abi sniffed. 'Sorry, I don't know why I'm telling you all this stuff. I don't even know your name.'

'Bill,' he said.

'Abi.' His handshake was firm and strong but not in a macho I-can-crush-your-fingers sort of way.

'Glad we're introduced at last.' His eyes lit up when he smiled. They were ever so blue, as blue as the elephants marching across his swim shorts that made Abi smile despite herself. 'I honestly wouldn't worry too much. Trying to work out what's going through a young girl's head is an impossible task.'

'I just want her to be happy,' Abi said. 'And to need me, I suppose.'

'I know how you feel, more than you know.'

'You have children?'

'Two girls, both older than your Chloe. Michelle's nearly sixteen, April's two years younger. So grown up . . .' Bill looked away across the swimming pool. An elderly lady in a yellow swimming cap floated serenely on her back, her eyes closed against the afternoon sun.

'And?' Abi probed gently.

'They're so far away. Gemma – my ex-wife – is Canadian. She took the girls back there after we split.'

'That's terrible.'

'They're healthy and happy, lots of friends, doing well at school and Gemma's a good mum, I can't take that away from her. It's a great life out there for them. Of course I miss them but they're better off with her. I'm so busy with my work.'

'Work's no substitute for a family,' Abi said.

'For me it has to be.' Bill didn't meet her eyes. He picked up his laptop. The conversation was over. Why had she been so blunt?

Abi shifted on the lounger. She turned to the WordSearch at the back of her magazine. She chewed the end of her biro but the answers to her puzzle wouldn't come. Out of the corner of her eye, Bill sat hunched over his laptop tapping away. Abi put down the magazine, laid back and closed her eyes.

56

The blare of 'All About That Bass' woke her with a start. Chloe must have changed Abi's ringtone for a laugh. Again. Abi reached for the phone; Alex's name flashed up. Abi sat bolt upright. Alex never phoned. It must be Chloe. Something must have happened. Something bad.

She pressed her phone right up against her ear.

'Abi?' Alex said.

She felt a tightness in her chest. 'What is it, Alex? What's happened? Where's Chloe . . . What do you mean, you don't know?' Abi's voice rose.

'She's just gone for a walk or something, Abi. I don't know what you're panicking about.' Alex's voice was annoyingly calm and reasonable.

'I'm panicking because you've phoned me!' Abi glanced at Bill, who was diplomatically studying the laminated menu for the pool bar. She stood up and walked over to a patch of shade where she wouldn't be disturbing anyone.

'I'm not phoning because of Chloe. Well, not directly – it's Flavia.'

'Flavia?' Abi repeated.

'Yes, Flavia – Marisa's mother.'

'I know who she is. Is she OK?'

'Yes, Flavia's okay. Chloe's okay. Everybody's okay.'

'No need to be so snappy.'

'Maybe you could just let me talk for once,' Alex said.

'Hmph,' Abi snorted. She forced herself to listen without interrupting but only because she wanted Alex off the phone as soon as possible.

Alex finally drew breath.

'No, Alex,' Abi said. 'I'm not coming over. Absolutely not. No way.'

'Hang on a minute, Abi, that's Chloe at the door.'

Abi waited. She could hear low voices in the background. 'Want to talk to your mum?' she heard Alex say.

'Hi, Mum.' Chloe came to the phone. 'I went for a walk in the marina.'

'That's nice, love, but what's all this about an invitation from Flavia?'

Abi tried to stay calm as Chloe gabbled on.

'Please, Mum,' Chloe said. 'Please say you'll come.'

'Okay,' Abi sighed. 'But I'm only doing it for you. Seven o'clock tomorrow evening. I'll be there. And I'll see you tomorrow morning, you haven't forgotten, have you?'

Chloe paused. 'Of course not! Love you, Mum, see you tomorrow!'

'Love you too,' she said but Chloe had already rung off. She flopped back down on the sun lounger. She was dreading tomorrow already.

'Everything all right?' Bill asked. 'You've gone a bit pale. Why don't you let me buy you a drink?'

'Oh, no, I . . .' Abi began.

'They do a nice glass of white.'

'Oh, okay then. Thanks, that's kind of you.'

'Not at all. I fancy one myself and I prefer to have company. I don't really like drinking alone.'

'Me neither.' Abi felt herself blush.

Bill smiled and waved the menu in the direction of the pool bar where Loretta was perched on a high stool in a purple cocktail frock. Her salmon-pink heels had long ribbons that criss-crossed up her tanned, skinny legs. She hopped down and tottered towards them, a smile on her heavily glossed lips.

'Could we have two glasses of number three, please?'

'You enjoyed that the other evening then. It's very popular.'

Bill turned to Abi. 'The *falanghina* grape is grown on the island.'

'Sounds great.'

'Two large glasses, but I'll bring you the bottle – any you don't finish can go back in the fridge for tomorrow,' Loretta said. She returned swiftly with two large goblets and the wine resting in a cooler.

'Would you put it on my room,' Bill said.

'Of course. Enjoy.'

'Thank you,' Abi said. She took a large mouthful, savouring the blessed feeling that the rough edges of the day were being smoothed away.

'Delicious, isn't it?' Bill smiled. The corners of his blue eyes crinkled.

'Yes. Cheers,' Abi said. She lifted her glass up a little.

'Cheers. So, do you want to tell me about it?'

'The phone call?' Abi took another large mouthful of wine. 'That was my ex-husband, Alex.'

'I thought as much. Your daughter Chloe's okay, isn't she?'

'Yes, thank goodness.'

'Good.' Bill smiled encouragingly.

'Marisa's parents, Flavia and Enzo, have invited me over for dinner tomorrow night.'

59

'And you're not keen?'

'I'm sure they're perfectly nice people but dinner with my ex and his partner – or should I say fiancée . . .' Abi let the expression on her face finish her sentence.

'Ouch! Not fun. When are they getting married?'

'They haven't set a date. They're both so busy at work. Marisa's one of those career girls.' Abi made inverted commas with her fingers. 'Though that didn't stop her getting pregnant straight away. She probably knew it was the quickest way to get Alex to leave me and Chloe.'

'And they've just got the one child?'

'Yes. Elsa, she's nearly five. Apparently, one's enough for Marisa, and Alex agrees.' *At least they aren't going to have the two or three we always talked about.*

'So, one ex-husband, one fiancée, two of your ex's in-laws, your own daughter and a little kiddy – quite an evening. No wonder I need to top up your drink.'

Abi looked at her empty glass. 'Okay, thanks, but just a little.'

'Nonsense. You're on holiday.' Bill gave her a more than generous top-up.

Abi took a sip. She was going to drink this one very slowly. 'I really don't want to go but Chloe was desperate for me to say yes. Apparently Flavia is determined to get to know me. She says now Chloe's part of her family, so am I.'

'And what does Alex say about that?'

'He's probably about as keen as I am but he doesn't want to rock the boat with Marisa's parents, especially as they're putting them up for the summer. Oh, Bill, I'm just dreading it.' Abi put her head in her hands.

'Hey!' Bill lifted her hands away from her face. He had faint freckles scattered across the bridge of his nose; she hadn't noticed them before. 'It may not feel like it now, but this is a good thing.'

'How come?' Abi picked up her glass and swiftly put it down again.

'You came out here because of Chloe, didn't you? To make sure she was okay and to be here if she needed you.'

'I came to see Chloe, not to play happy families with the woman Alex left me for.'

'But don't you see? This is the perfect opportunity to find out how Chloe really is. You'll see the place where your daughter is staying, the table where she has breakfast, even the bed where she sleeps. You'll meet Flavia and Enzo and see what they're really like and if Marisa's parents get to know you, even a little, they're far more likely to let you know if there's ever a problem with Chloe.'

'I never thought of it like that. I just thought how awkward it would be for me. But you're right, you've made me feel so much better. I can handle a bit of discomfort if it means knowing for sure that Chloe's all right. But . . .'

'It's still going to be hard spending the evening with this Marisa.'

'It's going to be so strange.'

'I don't suppose you spend much time together.'

'Actually, we've never met.'

'Not in five years? Surely you must have done.'

'Alex offered to introduce us a number of times. He thought we might even end up as friends. What planet is he on? Us being all pally might make the two of them feel better but why would I want to meet the woman who broke up our home?'

'You're right, it was a stupid thing to say. Relationships aren't exactly my specialist subject.'

'Nor mine.' Abi gave a bitter laugh.

'Well, I wish you luck.'

'I'll need it. A whole evening with pretty, perfect, successful Marisa.'

'I don't envy you but it will be easier to meet her for the first time whilst there's other people around. If you're desperate, I could come with you, give you a bit of moral support.'

'That's incredibly kind but no, I'll manage. Though I'd love to see the look on Alex's face when he saw you. He'd think I'd come on holiday with another man.'

'Or picked one up whilst you're here.'

She folded her arms. 'I can't imagine anyone wanting to chat me up these days.'

'Don't put yourself down. I'm sure you were beating off admirers with a beach umbrella this morning.'

Abi couldn't help laughing. 'Chance would be a fine thing. But what about you? Were hordes of women chasing you around the hotel whilst I was gone?'

'Absolutely not. And I'm glad. Relationships aren't for me. I've been there and done it, tried and failed.'

'That's a shame.'

'It makes life a lot less complicated.' He refilled his glass and gazed out across the pool as if transfixed by the sun shimmering on the turquoise water.

Chapter Eight

The baroque dome and clock tower of Santa Maria della Pietà dominated the seafront.

'Impressive, isn't it?' Abi said. 'Shall we look around inside?'

Chloe scuffed her sandal on the ground. 'That's what old people do.'

'Well, what do you fancy doing?' Abi asked. She'd taken Chloe on a wander down to the main port where the ferries from Naples docked; perhaps it had been a mistake.

'Dunno, I'm thirsty.' Chloe pouted as though she were a lot younger than twelve.

'We'll go to a café if you like,' Abi said. She knew Chloe wouldn't want a glass of water but a sugary drink was a small price to pay for a harmonious day.

'Nonna Flavia says that Da Maria has the best *lingue di bue* on the island.'

'*Lingue di bue*? What are they?'

'It means ox tongues.'

Abi wrinkled her nose. 'Isn't that a strange thing to eat early in the morning?'

'Duh, Mum, they're not real ones. They're pastries filled with lemon cream – you'll really like them.'

'They sound yummy.' Abi was determined to eat more healthily but at least Chloe sounded enthusiastic about something at last.

'Da Maria's just over there,' Chloe said.

Abi chose a table half in and half out of the sun, ordered Chloe's Coke, a coffee she didn't really want and, what the heck, a pastry for each of them.

'*Due lingue di bue.*' The waiter set down their snacks: flaky, golden ovals crusted with sugar crystals.

'These look incredible, do you want to hold one up whilst I take your picture?'

Chloe shrugged. 'If you like.'

'I thought you and your friends liked sharing pictures like this. I bet they're well-jel you're in Italy all summer.'

Chloe rolled her eyes. 'No one says "well-jel" anymore.'

Abi suppressed a sigh; it was going to be a long day.

'Mu-um?' Chloe mumbled through a mouthful of pastry.

'Yes, love.'

'Will you be really upset if we don't spend all day together?'

'Why, have your dad and Marisa got plans?' Abi kept her voice light.

'I made friends with some girls on the beach yesterday. They all learnt English at school so we can talk to each other. Mia is really funny and Rina's teaching me those card games everybody plays.'

'And you want to meet them today?'

Chloe looked down at her plate. 'I don't want you to be lonely, Mum.'

'Me? Don't be daft, love. You go and have fun.'

'Thanks, Mum. Can I go now?' She stuffed down the rest of her pastry and drained her cola. 'See you tonight – Flavia's really excited to meet you!'

Chloe skipped off, ponytail swinging beneath her pink bucket hat. Abi pushed away her half-eaten pastry. Chloe was growing up; it was natural that she'd need Abi less and less. But that didn't make it any easier.

Abi climbed the steps that led from the Marina Corricella to the tiny crumbling church of San Rocco and took the road up past the Piazza dei Martiri to the imposing turquoise apartment building that overlooked Santa Maria delle Grazie. She looked up at the windows of Flavia and Enzo's top-floor apartment. The bells of the yellow church were chiming; she was exactly on time.

She put down the bottle of wine she'd brought and wiped her palms on her skirt. It had been hard to choose what to wear knowing she would never look as good as glossy, gorgeous Marisa so she'd settled on an old favourite: a blue and white short-sleeved shirt dress that covered all the untoned bits she didn't like to look at. It was a little faded but looked fresh and crisp after Loretta had insisted on steaming and pressing it herself when Abi asked to borrow an iron.

She was about to press the doorbell when she noticed someone had left the front door ajar. She rang the bell anyway, pushed open the panelled door and entered the dark hallway. Voices came from the top landing followed by the sound of feet scurrying down the stairs.

'Mum, you came!' Chloe leapt down the stairs two at a time. The dim light in the stairwell made her look even browner.

'I said I would.' Abi tried to take a step forward but a small, curly-haired child had tumbled down the last few steps and was clinging to her leg.

'Aunty Abi, Aunty Abi!' The little girl gazed up at Abi from under her long lashes. She had Alex's eyes set in Marisa's pretty heart-shaped face. Abi had only met Elsa once before, with Alex. Who on earth had told the little girl to call her 'Aunty'? As if sensing Abi's hostility, Elsa's lip began to tremble. She stuck her thumb in her mouth.

Abi forced herself to smile. None of this was Elsa's fault. She crouched down to Elsa's level. 'Hello, sweetheart. What a pretty dress!'

Elsa smiled; she had a big gap between two of her front teeth. 'Come and see my toys!' She let go of Abi's leg and proceeded to use her chubby arms to help haul herself back up the stairs.

Abi followed Chloe and Elsa up to the top floor. The scent of fried garlic was wafting down the stairs; her stomach grumbled. An old lady in a brown smock patterned with pink spriggy flowers was standing in the open doorway. Her face was etched with deep lines, her kind eyes dark as currants.

'I am Flavia. *Piacere*, pleased to meet you. Welcome to our home, Abi.'

'Thank you.' Abi's reply was muffled by Flavia's embrace.

67

'Umm, hello, Abi, shall I take that wine?' Alex said. He ran a finger around the inside of his shirt collar. Why did he have to look so ridiculously handsome? Behind him stood Marisa in a simple, sleeveless ruby-red dress. Her long glossy, black hair was clipped back with two silver barrettes. She was even prettier than she looked in her photographs, but her beauty had a brittle quality and her elegant dress looked more suited to a board meeting than a relaxed family dinner.

'Pleased to meet you,' Marisa said at last. She fiddled with the jewel-studded bangle around her slender wrist.

'And you.' Abi forced the words out. She handed her bottle of wine to Alex.

'*Fiano di Avellino* – very nice,' Alex said. 'I'll put it in the fridge.'

Marisa twisted awkwardly on one foot. Her eyes darted from side to side as if she might suddenly make a run for the door.

Chloe tugged at Abi's arm. 'Come and see my room.'

'Of course. You'll excuse us a moment, won't you?'

'I'll fix us all some aperitifs,' Alex said. 'Is an Aperol and soda okay?'

Abi nodded. Anything would help.

'This way, Mum.'

She followed Chloe down the dimly lit corridor.

Chloe flung open a heavy wooden door and threw herself onto a bed covered by a floral quilt and a pile of green and pink crocheted cushions. 'Isn't it pretty!' A stack of Chloe's books and some Italian magazines shared the bedside table with a wooden lamp with a fringed silk shade. Abi's eyes were drawn to a garish glass clown sat on a high shelf.

'Nonno Enzo brought that back from Venice years ago – it's Murano glass,' Chloe said. She bounced back off the bed and skipped across the room. 'Look, if I stand on tiptoe, I can see the sea!'

'Oh yes, you can.' Abi stared through the window trying to calm her breathing. If only she could stay here all evening watching the sky shifting colour as the sun set. But she had to go and face the others. 'We'd best go and join the throng.'

'It's okay, Mum. Don't worry.'

'Worry? What would I be worrying about? I'm sure your Nonna Flavia has cooked something delicious.' Abi rubbed her hands together.

Chloe beamed. 'Her cooking is yum.'

'Great!' Abi put a big smile on her face. At least the food would be good and it was only one evening – she could cope with that, couldn't she? As long as she had the aperitif Alex had promised to rustle up.

'There you go, Abi, one Aperol and soda.' Alex handed her an old-fashioned cut-glass tumbler as she and Chloe walked back into the lounge. She took a sip of the orange liquid; it reminded her a little of some medicine she'd had as a child. Across the room Marisa was perched on a couch upholstered in plum brocade, her knees pressed together, tracing the top of her crystal tumbler with her forefinger.

'Abi, you must meet my husband, Enzo,' Flavia said.

'Of course.' Abi had been so distracted by Marisa's presence, she'd failed to notice the old man in the corner who was now slowly levering himself up from his brown armchair. Enzo was small and wrinkled with wire-framed glasses like an illustration of a grandfather in a child's story book. He straightened up slowly, adjusted his olive-green knitted waistcoat and coughed twice.

'*Piacere*,' he murmured, pulling Abi towards him so that her nose was buried in his wisps of tobacco-scented grey hair.

'Pleased to meet you. *Piacere*,' she repeated.

He held her at arm's length, his soft brown eyes scanning her face through his slightly smudged lenses. He nodded, as if satisfied, and cracked a smile. 'Sorry, speak no English.'

'Speak no Italian,' Abi quipped.

He gave a wheezy laugh, sat back down and picked up his drink, cradling it in both knobbly hands.

'I learnt to speak English dealing with all the tourists who visit our salon,' Flavia said. 'Enzo looks after the business side, so he had no need of it. Now I only work a few hours a week for some regulars who still ask for me but they are all Italian so I speak very little English now. Some words, I forget.'

'You speak very well,' Abi said.

'You are too kind.'

Marisa smiled. She'd already drained her drink. Alex sat next to her, legs sprawled apart, studying his fingernails. Nobody spoke.

'Mum liked my room,' Chloe piped up.

'You have a beautiful home,' Abi said. The brocade couches, lacy curtains and heavy wooden furniture weren't to her taste but she could tell from the spotless surfaces and polished mirrors that the apartment was Flavia's pride and joy.

'Thank you. *Molto gentile*, very kind.'

'Have you always lived here?'

Flavia glanced at her daughter.

'When Marisa was young, we lived in another place.'

'Another house,' Marisa said. She twisted her fingers together, unable to meet Abi's eyes.

'Marisa loved growing up by the sea, didn't you, Marisa,' Alex said.

'A little mermaid,' Flavia said. Her features softened. 'Long days at the beach. Such happy children.' Her eyes strayed to the framed photograph of two children on top of the sideboard. The young Marisa had a wide smile and her hair was secured in two big bunches tied with pink bows.

'Such a pretty child,' Abi said. She could hardly say otherwise. 'And that must be your son.' Alex had only mentioned him once.

'Yes, that's Marisa's younger brother, Nico,' Flavia said.

'And does Nico live on Procida, too?' Abi asked. She wasn't remotely interested in Marisa's brother, but it seemed like a fairly innocuous topic of conversation.

'No, he lives a long way from here,' Flavia said. Her hand strayed to the garnet and silver cross on a long chain that dangled over the shelf of her bosom.

'Shall we have the *antipasti*? Mamma makes delicious *bruschette*,' Marisa said. She was already on her feet.

'The tomatoes here are the best – it is the taste of the volcanic soil,' Flavia said. 'Let us go and sit at the dining table. Alex, you could pour some wine, perhaps.'

'Sit next to me, Mum,' Chloe said.

'Thanks, love.' Abi sat in the proffered seat wishing she hadn't landed up sitting directly opposite Marisa.

Alex pulled out a chair. He held up a hefty hardback copy of *À la recherche du temps perdu*. 'Yours, I believe, Marisa. You've a habit of leaving books lying around in the strangest places.'

'That looks like it's written in French, not Italian,' Abi commented.

'Yes, I prefer to read in the original language when I can – it adds more nuance.' Marisa took the book and laid it behind her on the corner of the sideboard.

'Marisa speaks several languages,' Alex said.

'Oh,' Abi said. Of course she did.

'Mum likes reading too, don't you, Mum?'

'Umm, yes, I suppose so,' Abi muttered.

'She's always got a book on the go,' Chloe added.

Marisa put down the fork she was fiddling with. 'Really? What are you reading at the moment?'

'Oh . . . sorry, I've forgotten the title.' Abi pressed her foot hard against Chloe's ankle, but her daughter failed to take the hint.

'It must be one of the Hollyhock Cottage series,' Chloe said. 'Mum loves those.'

72

'What's it about?' Marisa smiled encouragingly. It seemed as though she was finally beginning to unwind.

'Well . . .' Abi shifted on the upright dining chair. 'The main character, Jessie, she's restoring this old rambling cottage in a sweet English village and she's got this crazy rescue dog who's half Labrador. Jessie is always trying to matchmake the villagers. It's a sort of romance, I suppose.'

'It sounds very relaxing,' Marisa said.

Abi smiled blandly; she could guess just what Marisa was really thinking.

'It's just escapism,' Alex snorted.

Abi took another swig of wine. Had he always been so dismissive of her?

'Sometimes it's nice to read something that takes you away from all the troubles in the world,' Marisa said.

'Hmm,' Abi said. All the troubles in the world, indeed. What did Marisa with her perfect life know about troubles?

'You should try reading one – Mum says they're really good,' Chloe said.

'Thanks, I might just do that. Hollyhock Cottage, did you say?' Marisa beamed at Abi.

Abi fiddled with the stem of her already empty wine glass, willing Alex to top it up.

'Another *bruschetta*?' Flavia asked.

'Please, they're fabulous,' Abi said. She crunched into the tasty tomato and garlic-topped bread, glad to have an excuse not to talk for a short while.

'I was going to make my spicy *spaghetti poveri* with anchovies for the first course, but I had a piece of luck when I met Claudio – he's the fishmonger I like to use,' Flavia said. 'He buys straight from the boats each morning. He told me that his cousin had been diving for *ricci* today over at the Capo Bove.'

Marisa's face lit up. '*Linguine ai ricci di mare*? Sea urchin pasta – what a treat! Do you need any help, Mamma?'

'No, you sit there,' Flavia said. She bustled out to the kitchen.

'Sea urchins?' Chloe looked doubtful.

'You'll have to watch out for the spikes, they tickle your tongue,' Alex said.

Chloe paled. 'Are they really spiky, Dad?'

Abi inclined her head towards Alex. He took the hint and refilled her wine glass.

'Dad?' Chloe repeated.

'Do you know what a sea urchin looks like, Chlo-bo?'

'Not really. I could go and get my phone and look.'

'No phones at the table,' Marisa said.

Chloe acquiesced meekly. Abi felt a surge of resentment. Why did Marisa get the good behaviour? Abi had been fighting a losing battle against Chloe's mobile ever since Alex had bought it.

'Do they really tickle your tongue?' Chloe said.

Marisa tutted. 'Of course not, you open them and extract the pulp . . . Do you enjoy cooking, Abi?'

'Yes, there's nothing like a home-cooked meal,' Abi said, relieved that Chloe was now talking to Alex and therefore unlikely to wax lyrical about Abi's legendary fish finger sandwiches on sliced white bread and her enthusiasm for adding extra cheese to supermarket lasagne.

'I love Italian food, though of course I'm biased, but I do think the English have cold-weather cooking down to a fine art. All those pies and casseroles and steamed puddings are delicious,' Marisa said.

Abi looked at her sharply; she was sure that the skinny-minnie had never eaten a steak and kidney pie or a jam roly-poly in her life.

'Chloe's loving all the pizzas and ice-creams,' Abi said. 'I expect you and your brother enjoyed those when you were children. It must have been heaven living here with all the wonderful gelaterias.'

Marisa's eyes flickered towards her father, who was using his forefinger to dab at the last crumbs of *bruschetta* on his plate. 'Yes . . . umm, of course we loved them.' She pushed back her chair. 'The *linguine ai ricci* must be ready by now. I'll help Mamma bring it in.'

To Abi's – and Chloe's – relief, the linguine was a slippery tangle of pasta without a spike in sight. Abi reached for the spoon Flavia had kindly provided; it was tricky to master the art of twirling the long strands around her fork.

'It tastes of the sea,' Chloe said. She pushed aside the garnish of flat-leafed parsley.

'But so delicate,' Abi added.

'And next, we have the *branzino*,' Flavia said. 'What do you call the fish?' She turned to Marisa.

'Sea bass, just simply grilled. Mamma likes to serve it with *zucchini alla scapece* – courgettes prepared with a white wine vinegar, garlic and mint dressing.'

'Are you sure you don't need any help?' Abi made to get up.

'Just sit down and chill out, Abi,' Alex said. He leant across the table to top up her wine. She moved her hand across the top of her glass. The rough edges of the evening had been smoothed away and she didn't want to make a show of herself in front of Marisa, who spent more time fiddling with the stem of her wine glass than she did drinking from it.

'Are you okay, Mum?' Chloe whispered.

'Yes, I'm fine.' She was surprised to realise she was. She was beginning to relax; the wine – and Flavia's kindness – had seen to that. Even the awkward conversation about books no longer seemed to matter. Bill was right. Seeing the place where Chloe was staying was putting her mind at rest. She couldn't help wondering what would have happened if she'd taken up Bill's jokey offer to accompany her this evening. Alex's face would have been a picture. The thought made her smile.

Chapter Nine

Abi pushed open the door of the Hotel Paradiso. The scent of furniture polish and fresh flowers mingled in the air. Chloe's flip-flops made a flapping sound as they crossed the glossy tiled floor to the door leading to the garden.

'Are you sure the lady who runs the hotel won't mind me having a swim?' Chloe said.

'Honestly, it's fine. Loretta's lovely. As soon as she knew you were staying nearby, she told me you were more than welcome to come over whenever you want.'

'That's so nice of her.'

'You can get changed in my room if you like or just leave your stuff by the pool. You've got your swimming things on underneath, haven't you?'

'Yeah, I don't need the room, I'll be all right out here.'

'That's Loretta over there.' The hotel's proprietor was busy tying up the umbrellas; at this time of the afternoon there was no longer any need to shade her guests from the intense heat.

'Shall I go and say hello?'

'No need, she's coming over.'

Loretta picked her way past the loungers, a vision in peacock blue and tangerine. 'Good afternoon, Abi. And this must be Chloe!'

'*Salve*!' Chloe said. Abi smiled. She wasn't sure what Chloe got up to when the two of them weren't together but she was pleased that her daughter was picking up some of the language.

'*Ciao*! How nice to meet you! Please treat the Hotel Paradiso as your home. I'll move a couple of loungers around.'

'No need.' Bill was already standing up and rolling up his beach towel. 'I'll move to that spot over there by the palm tree. You can sit here, Abi, and let your daughter have this other one.'

'Oh no, I can't have you squashed in that corner over there,' Loretta said. 'But if you wouldn't mind helping me move this parasol out of the way we could easily wheel that spare lounger over to this side.'

'No, I'll move. I don't want to intrude,' Bill said.

'No, please don't move, not on account of us, there's plenty of room,' Abi said.

'If you're sure. In that case, where exactly do you want this umbrella, Loretta?'

'Just there. That's perfect. Thank you.'

'I'll move this for you. Glad to help.' Bill wheeled the spare lounger into position.

'Thanks so much,' Abi said. 'Chloe, this is Bill and Bill, as you guessed, this is Chloe, my daughter.'

'Delighted to meet you. Had a nice day? I hear you and your mum have been out and about exploring the beaches.'

'My dad and Marisa – that's his girlfriend – usually go down to the same old beach but I like trying all the different places,' Chloe said. She undid the metal buckles on the straps of her cut-off dungarees and tossed her cropped, stripy T-shirt onto the lounger.

Chloe walked to the edge of the pool, held her nose and jumped in with a splash.

'Not joining her?' Bill said.

'We swam at Posto Vecchio this morning. That was enough for me.' Abi stretched back, luxuriating in the warm afternoon sun.

'Isn't that the beach they call the postman's beach after they filmed *Il Postino* there?'

'That's the one. It's very atmospheric, sheltered by these great tufa cliffs. But there's no road down, so we went over by bus to the cemetery and then we had to take the steps. It doesn't get as much sun in the morning but that suited me. It's too hot to be on the beach at midday.'

'Mad dogs and Englishmen and all that.' Bill grinned.

'My dad used to sing that ditty. Noel Coward, wasn't it?'

'That's right. So, what's on the cards for you two tomorrow?'

'Oh, no plans. Chloe's spending the day with Alex. He's finally taking a break from work to spend the whole day with her and Marisa and their little girl Elsa.'

'I was thinking . . .' Bill began.

'What?' Abi asked.

'If you would like to, umm . . .' Bill opened his sunglasses case then snapped it shut again.

79

'Wondering what?' Abi said.

'I was just, uh, wondering if you'd like a cup of tea?'

'Ridiculously English, but who cares? I'd love one. I'll see if Chloe does too, but she'd probably prefer something cold and fizzy.'

'Prosecco?' Bill grinned.

'Don't even joke about it. She's growing up far too fast already. Sometimes I wish I could stop time.' Abi sighed. It seemed only yesterday that Chloe was sporting frilly white ankle socks and wearing her hair in bunches secured by her favourite red plastic bobbles.

'Hard, isn't it?' Bill frowned.

'I feel bad complaining when your two girls are so far away.'

'Yeah. I'd do anything to see Michelle and April messing around in that pool right now.' He blinked and looked away.

Abi turned to watch Chloe moving through the water. The halter neck ties on the pink bikini revealed two white strap marks on her back made by the more substantial tankini Abi had helped to choose on their trip to the shopping centre.

'I think I can hear a distinctive click, click, click,' Bill said. His usual smile had returned.

'Loretta? I don't know how she manages in those strappy shoes all day. Hey, Chloe! Do you want a drink of something?'

Chloe swam over and rested her forearms on the side of the pool. 'I don't suppose I can have another Coke?'

'Okay, but only because you're on holiday.'

'Did I hear something about a Coke?' Loretta said. She flashed Abi a bright red smile. Her lips matched the silky blouse she'd teamed with white capri pants and a fetching red and white spotted scarf tied at the neck just so.

'Yes, one Coke, please, and two pots of tea.'

'Allow me?'

Abi put up her hand. 'No, Bill. Today's my treat, I insist . . . On my room please, Loretta.'

'Of course.' Loretta paused by the side of the pool where Chloe was powering up and down. 'She swims well, your daughter.'

'Yes, quite the little fish,' Abi said.

Loretta's smile didn't quite meet her eyes. 'I'll be right back,' she said. Halfway towards the pool bar, she stopped, bent down and rubbed the back of her ankle.

Chloe flung herself on the lounger, spraying Abi with tiny droplets of water. 'I'm so dying for that Coke.' She put her hand to the back of her head. 'Ugh, my ponytail's turned into a rat's tail. Got a comb, Mum?'

Abi plonked her bag on the end of the lounger and rummaged around. 'Here you go. What are mums for, eh?' She moved her bag back onto the floor as Loretta approached with the tray of drinks. 'Thanks, Loretta, that's lovely.'

Chloe took the mini bottle of cola. It made a crackling sound as she poured it over the ice in her glass. 'Thanks, Mum. You're the best.'

'You won't be saying that when I make you drink water instead when we get back home.'

'Nag, nag, nag!'

'My daughters are never allowed fizzy drinks,' Bill said.

Chloe gasped. 'Never!' She glugged down half her drink as if fearful that Bill would snatch it away.

'They live in Canada with their mum. She's really strict – so they tell me.' He winked at Abi.

'Are you on holiday by yourself then? Have you got a girlfriend?'

'Chloe! You can't ask questions like that.'

Chloe pulled a face. 'You're always telling me to take an interest in other people.'

'No, no girlfriend,' Bill laughed. 'I'm too busy with work for all that.'

'Dad's always working. He's a lawyer but he's got a girlfriend and they had a baby, though Elsa's nearly five now.'

'Sounds like a busy man. Well, I haven't got either, so I guess that's why I'm on holiday by myself.'

'Mum's never been on holiday by herself before. Her best friend Cherry made her come.'

'Chloe!' Abi gave her a warning glance.

'My mother made *me* come,' said Bill.

Chloe giggled. 'Don't tease.'

'No, seriously. I've been coming out to Italy on business for years but I don't know when I last took a holiday. I'm not very good at relaxing.'

'I guessed that.' Abi inclined her head towards Bill's laptop.

'A couple of weeks ago I made the mistake of telling my mother I was going away on yet another business trip. Before I knew it, she had booked me into this hotel for a "proper long holiday afterwards" in her words. I knew I should never have given her that iPad for Christmas! Lucky I could change my flight, but you'd think she'd have stopped worrying about me. I'm forty-three, not fourteen.'

Abi laughed. 'Once a mum, always a mum, I guess.' She poured out some more tea and automatically gave Bill a top-up. 'And your boss was okay about you taking holiday at such short notice?'

'I don't have to worry about that. I run my own business – I guess that's why it's hard to switch off.' He rapped the lid of his laptop. 'I think I need to start going out and about though. I've tried my hardest but lying here by the pool all day just isn't me.'

'Posto Vecchio Beach was really nice, wasn't it, Mum?'

'I'm sure it's great but I'd feel a bit strange sitting on a beach by myself. I thought I'd go and explore the Terra Murata tomorrow.'

'I've heard of that. Isn't it the oldest part of the island?' Abi said.

'Ancient. It's the oldest and highest part. I'm planning on heading out early, when it's not too hot, straight after breakfast.'

'Mum'll go with you.'

What?! Abi coughed and spluttered.

'Are you all right, Mum?'

'Tea went the wrong way, excuse me.' Abi coughed again. Her nose was burning.

'How about it?' Bill said. 'Fancy a walk round the Terra Murata?'

'Oh no, I couldn't.' It was nice of Bill to ask her but he couldn't really want her to come along; he seemed quite content in his own company.

'Yes, you can,' Chloe said. 'You love all that old historical stuff. Remember when we used to go to Spain and you insisted on taking me and Dad round all the sights.'

'Hmm.' Abi remembered it well. Alex moaning and dragging his feet like a schoolboy. He'd never been interested in exploring the old Spanish heritage. In fact, he never wanted to do anything other than go to the beach, yet somehow he'd succeeded in making her feel like *she* was the boring one.

'Do you really like history?' Bill said. 'I wouldn't want you to say yes just to be polite.'

'I haven't said yes yet.' Abi smiled.

'She will say yes though, won't you, Mum? Honestly, she loves all those crumbling buildings and windy old lanes. Dad and I used to call her Dora the Explorer.'

'You did say you didn't have any plans.'

Abi was cornered. 'Okay, it's a date.'

'It's a date,' Bill repeated, his eyes twinkling. Abi felt herself redden. She hadn't meant *that* sort of date. Had she?

84

Chapter Ten

Abi was getting impatient. Chloe was walking at a snail's pace, apparently entranced by the sight of an old man sitting by a small rickety fishing boat stroking a skinny white cat. Honestly, her daughter was as bad as Dad's old spaniel, Bobby, who stopped and sniffed at every lamppost.

'What's so interesting?' Abi said.

'Nothing.' Chloe kicked a pebble away. 'You don't have to walk me back to the apartment, you know.'

'I don't have to, but I like to, you know that.'

Chloe grunted.

'I expect you'll have a fun day with Dad tomorrow.'

'I guess so. And so will you, Mum, going for a walk with that guy from the hotel.'

'I'm not sure that's a good idea, Chloe. Poor Bill is probably desperately thinking of an excuse to get out of it.'

'He seemed happy to me.'

'He always seems pretty happy. I'm sure if he wanted some company, he could have found someone to go on holiday with.'

'But he only booked a holiday because his mum made him.'

Abi laughed. 'I'm surprised he confessed to that. Not many men would.'

'That's because lots of people pretend to be something they're not.'

'Sounds like one of Olivia's mother's comments.'

'Tania said it. She puts these quotes and pictures and stuff on Instagram.'

'Tania? I don't think I've heard you mention her before.'

'She's just some girl in my class who's been liking some of my pictures lately.' Chloe shrugged.

'That's nice.'

'I suppose so.' Chloe rammed her hands into the pockets of her shorts. 'We'd better speed up. Nonna Flavia's making spaghetti with tomato sauce tonight and Dad said if I'm late he'll eat mine.'

Abi refrained from pointing out that *she* hadn't been dawdling.

She waited on the doorstep of Flavia and Enzo's home until she was sure Chloe was safely inside the top-floor apartment, crossed the road and retraced her footsteps down to the Marina Corricella. The restaurants and bars were beginning to fill up. Great round goblets of jewel-coloured drinks and flutes of sparkling wine were being set before the drinkers and diners outside La Pentola. Sounds of laughter and the clinking of glasses competed with the shriek of a gull.

A waiter brushed past her carrying a loaded plate of golden *bruschette* topped with bright red tomatoes; they smelt as good as the ones Flavia had made. Abi hesitated.

She'd enjoyed a large lunch with Chloe; she shouldn't eat anything else. Stealing herself, she turned away from the tempting empty tables. She'd distract herself from her rumbling stomach by taking a few pictures of the colourful boats moored along the marina's edge.

She dug out her phone. Cherry had sent two pictures: the first a microwave meal, the pierced film half rolled back revealing something lumpy and brown; the second a family pack of crisps. *Tonight's tea at the nurses' station, send me a picture of yours so I can dream xxx.*

Sometimes Abi felt Cherry was actually watching her. She smiled at the waiter from La Pentola who was passing with a tray of used dishes. 'Table for one?'

'*Certo*!' He flung his arm in the direction of a small table.

She soon devoured a plateful of fresh anchovies marinated in a tongue-tingling blend of lemon, garlic and chilli pepper and lingered over a plate of pasta scattered with velvety mixed beans and plump pink mussels all washed down with a cold glass of house white. She nursed a tiny cup of dense, bitter espresso, feeling quite content. How had she ever made a meal out of a pre-wrapped pasty and a family packet of chocolate buttons?

She paid the bill and picked her way carefully along the edge of the harbour and up the steep steps to the Hotel Paradiso. The sounds of the drinkers and diners grew fainter. Below her the warm glow from the old streetlamps cast long trails of light over the dark sea.

She stopped to catch her breath by the array of potted cacti outside the entrance to the hotel. The reception was deserted. Abi waited a few moments but Loretta didn't appear. She leant over the front desk and took her key from the rack on the wall and pushed open the door to the garden. Small lights set into the side of the pool illuminated its turquoise water. She took the path between the lemon trees, well lit by two lanterns and the lamps that shone from some of the other guests' rooms.

Something moved on a sun lounger in the darkest corner of the garden. Abi froze; her fingers gripped the top of her handbag. There was definitely someone sitting there, hunched up with their arms around their legs and their knees drawn up to their chest. A familiar pair of dangly earrings flashed in a chink of light. Abi exhaled in relief.

'Loretta?' she called softly.

Loretta turned. She looked at Abi as though she wasn't quite sure who she was.

Abi stepped towards her. 'Are you okay?'

Loretta stood up, her usual radiant smile back in place. 'Oh, good evening, Abi. Yes, I'm fine, thank you.'

'I think you may have dropped this,' Abi said. She bent down and retrieved a blue envelope that was lying by the lounger.

'Thank you. How was your evening? Did you go out to eat? Anywhere nice?' Loretta said. She slid the envelope into the back of the leather bound book that usually lay on the reception desk. A sheet of matching blue paper was poking out from between its pages.

'I stopped off at La Pentola. They had this really unusual pasta dish with beans and mussels.'

'I know that dish – delicious! I've sometimes wondered about opening a restaurant here myself.' Loretta's eyes strayed back to her guest book.

'Are you sure you're all right?' Abi said. 'That letter – it's not bad news, is it?'

'Perhaps it may turn out to be good news,' Loretta sighed.

'Want to talk about it?'

'I couldn't possibly bother you – you're a guest. You're here to relax, not listen to my troubles.'

'My dad used to say: "a problem shared is a problem halved".' A lump caught in Abi's throat. After two years his loss still had the power to hit her when she least expected it.

'I appreciate that, Abi, but I find it hard to share my problems.'

'Sometimes it's easier to talk to a stranger, someone you're not close to. I guess that's why people confide in their hairdressers.'

'That wouldn't work in a small place like Corricella.' Loretta gave a wry smile. 'But perhaps you are right. Will you take a drink of limoncello with me? Not here, let us sit in the little office behind the reception desk, that way I can keep an eye on anyone coming and going.'

'Of course. I'd be delighted.' She followed Loretta back down the path. Two minutes later she was perched on a rather hard office chair sipping an intensely lemony digestif from a shot glass.

Loretta chewed the side of her lip. She rubbed her thumb and forefinger together. 'You like this limoncello?'

'Yes, delicious.' It was a good thing for her liver that Sanjay didn't stock this in the minimart. 'But what's wrong? Is it something to do with the hotel? You've owned it a long time, haven't you?'

'Just over forty years.'

'Forty years? Goodness, you must have bought it when you were about twelve!'

'That's very sweet of you.' Loretta smiled. She patted one of the tortoiseshell combs that secured her abundant black hair. 'Actually, I was only just twenty.'

'That's still incredibly young.'

'It's a long story.' Loretta glanced down.

'I'm not in a rush.'

'You're sure you want to hear?'

Abi nodded. 'Go on.'

'My parents owned a hotel on Capri; I'd helped out there ever since I was a child and started working there full time after I left school. It was expected that I would work my way up until one day, when my parents retired, I might take it over.'

'But you weren't happy with that?'

Loretta shifted in her chair. 'I was at first; I couldn't imagine any other life but then something happened. I had to leave Capri, at least I felt I had to. There was a boy, Giorgio, my fiancé back then . . .'

Abi waited. 'It's okay. You don't need to tell me the details.'

'I haven't spoken about it for so many years. He . . . he met someone else. I couldn't stay, not in such a small place, not with everybody knowing and pitying me.'

'Believe me, I know just how you feel.'

'I felt that you might,' Loretta said. 'I could sense that sadness when you first arrived.'

'Sometimes I wanted to run away too, after Alex – my husband – left me, but Chloe needs to see her father. And I was lucky – the judge in the divorce settlement awarded me our beautiful house. Alex can afford to pay the mortgage – he earns plenty of money at his law firm so there was no incentive for me to up and leave.'

Loretta nodded. 'Unlike you, I had no reason to stay. I left Capri and took a job working in a hotel in Germany for an old friend of my father. My parents understood, and besides they felt the experience might benefit our family's hotel. Perhaps they expected me to come back after a few months but afterwards I went to England to a country house hotel in the Lake District. I was a trainee manager there. It was a good job but I missed Italy. I came back here and tried to settle in Milan, but it wasn't the Italy I knew. I yearned for the rugged beauty of the islands, the scent of volcanic soil and to see Vesuvius once more. I knew that I must return to our island and I accepted that one day I would bump into Giorgio. I knew it would be hard, especially as I heard he had married the other girl, Adriana, by then.

'I'd gone to the port in Naples to get the ferry home, half wanting to return to Capri, half dreading it. One of the workers was shouting out "This way for Procida". On a whim, I bought a ticket and joined the queue to get on the boat. I decided I would spend a week or two here, I still had my last month's wages. Anything to put off going home to Capri a little longer.'

'And you never left?'

Loretta put down her empty limoncello glass. 'That's right. Fate brought me to the Hotel Paradiso. I'd found a room near the main port where the ferries now dock. One day I got up early and took a walk up to Santa Maria delle Grazie then down here to the marina, where I could watch the fishing boats come in. I saw a flight of steps and wondered where they might lead. I never imagined they would lead me here. Oh, Abi, your heart would break if you could see the pitiful place it was back then! The roof full of holes, vegetation growing in the window frames and the pool tiles cracked. But the view across the pastel-coloured houses and out to sea, it took my breath away. I knew at once that I wanted to awaken this sleeping beauty and create the hotel the architect must once have dreamt of.'

'How had it got into such a state?' Abi asked.

'Greed, pure and simple. The hotel was established by a local man whose family had amassed wealth in the fishing business. It's a poor, hard life on this island for many, but a man with a big modern boat could make himself rich. It seems that he built the hotel to fuel his ego; he never ran it himself and he paid the staff so little that they did not care about the place. By the time his son inherited it, the place was ruined and the boy was glad to sell it cheaply.

'Of course, no young girl could afford such a property, even in the condition it was in, but when my dear parents heard of it they agreed to use their savings to fund the restoration, telling me to treat it as an early inheritance. And I was glad I accepted, for when my papa passed away we discovered that a long-time employee, who he trusted with his life, was in league with Papa's accountant and the pair had been embezzling him for years. When all the debts were cleared there was nearly nothing left.'

'How terrible!' Abi instinctively touched Loretta's bony brown arm.

'It could have been a catastrophe, but I had this and I've poured my heart and soul into the place.'

'It's so beautiful and peaceful.'

Loretta smiled. 'Thank you, I'm so glad you think so. Buying this place healed me and I believe it sometimes has that effect on others too. But things have been difficult for a while. And now I have received this . . .' She took the letter from the guest book.

'What is it?'

'An anonymous buyer is interested in the hotel and I fear he is going to make me an offer I cannot afford to refuse. I'm not getting any younger, Abi.'

'Nonsense!'

'No, it's true, true of us all. But without this hotel to run, I'm not sure I'll know who I am anymore. What would I do with myself? I'm still young in my heart. I can't imagine a life of leisure, lounging around in a tracksuit all day.'

Abi laughed. 'I can't imagine you doing any such thing. You always look so elegant – look at your nails!'

Loretta turned her hands over. The tiny emerald gems embedded in her long fuchsia nails glittered. 'Thank you. Maybe it's vain but having my nails done is one thing I would hate to give up. It was such a relief when Flavia took over the old beauty salon when she and Enzo moved to the island.'

'What a coincidence! Flavia and Enzo are the people that my Chloe is staying with. It's their daughter, Marisa, who is engaged to my ex, Alex. But I thought they'd lived on Procida all their lives.'

'No, Marisa was quite grown up when the family arrived. I couldn't tell you where they lived before; Flavia's not one to talk about herself.'

'Marisa hasn't told me much about herself either but that's probably my fault. Last night when Flavia invited me over for dinner was the first time we'd actually met.'

'And how did that go?' Loretta smiled. She seemed much more relaxed now she was no longer talking about herself.

'Not as badly as I feared, but I can't say I enjoyed the experience – apart from Flavia's wonderful cooking. It's hard not to compare myself to someone so perfect. Marisa's so beautiful, all long legs and glossy dark hair, a tiny waist and golden skin. She's a successful lawyer and speaks three languages. She makes me feel so dumb and ordinary.'

Loretta looked Abi in the eye. 'Believe me, you're neither of those things.'

'But Marisa's got everything: she's smart, sexy, even her parents are both alive and well. She could have had anyone but she had to take my husband and my child.'

'I thought Chloe lived with you.'

'Yes, Chloe does live with me but Marisa's so young and fun I'm scared that one day she'll take her away from me.' *But I didn't mean Chloe, I meant Alex's second child who should have been mine.*

'Oh, Abi!' Loretta exclaimed. 'You're Chloe's mum, nothing can change that. Of course, you'll have your ups and downs, which mothers and daughters don't? But Chloe could never love Marisa the way she loves you. I've seen the two of you together. Besides, Marisa will have found out that the things you gain at the expense of others are bittersweet – they don't make you truly happy.'

'She seems happy enough to me.'

'Perhaps she seems happy now, but our deeds have a way of catching up with us,' Loretta said. 'Shall we have one more drink?'

'Yes, please, just a little.'

Loretta topped up the shot glasses.

'*Saluti*!' Abi said.

'*Saluti*!' Loretta raised her glass. It was good to share a little of what had happened the day of the Capri to Naples swim. The pain of a lost love was something other people could understand. But she would never talk about what happened the day after. She was still too ashamed.

Chapter Eleven

Stripes of light fell across the floor tiles from the half-opened shutters. The day was already warm. Abi pulled on her pair of cropped linen trousers, picked up a white puff-sleeved top and put it down again. Twice. She didn't know why she was faffing about so much this morning. All she needed to do was put on something comfortable; Bill wouldn't care what she wore. Most men didn't notice women's clothing. Unless they looked like Marisa.

She forced herself to decide on a yellow sleeveless shirt patterned with tiny swallows. She knotted Cherry's purple scarf edged with silky tassels and tiny silver bells around the strap of her small cross-body bag just in case she needed to protect her pale shoulders from the sun. It was too early for breakfast but the anticipation of spending the day with Bill and the bright light barely filtered by the thin, silky curtains that screened her room from its small patio garden had led her to leap out of bed at an unusually early hour. And to her surprise she felt remarkably rested.

She closed the door to her room quietly and was at the side of the pool in a matter of strides. No one was around, the pool bar still closed up and the reception area unmanned. She pressed the button that unlocked the front door with a loud click and took the steps down to the Marina Corricella. A single wisp of cloud smudged the cerulean sky. She would need her sunglasses today.

She picked her way along the edge of the marina, stepping up and down at each of the slipways, carefully avoiding the ropes that secured the small pleasure craft to the harbour wall. The scent of warm pastries and coffee drifted over from the locals enjoying a morning breakfast outside La Pentola where she had dined the night before. A waiter greeted her with a loud '*buongiorno*'. Further along the front, two men were standing on the deck of a large fishing vessel, easing out the knots and tangles from a huge net, too intent on their task to notice her. A yellow-beaked gull perched on a heap of fishing tackle watched them, a smoky-grey cat prowled nearby. She could have happily whiled away the morning if Chloe hadn't persuaded her to accompany Bill on his walk. And her stomach told her breakfast was calling.

She took the steps back to the peppermint-green Hotel Paradiso. Bill was already on the terrace, frowning down at his phone as he tore the end from a flaky brown *cornetto*. Abi's usual table was already taken; her eyes flicked around the terrace.

Loretta was by her side in an instant. 'I've swapped you with that Swedish couple over there – they were complaining there wasn't enough shade though why you come to Italy in July if you don't like the sun, I don't know. I've put you over there, next to Bill. I hope you don't mind.'

'No, of course not.' Abi pulled out a cane-backed chair at the table by his.

Bill looked up. 'Oh, you swapped tables.'

'Loretta had to move some people around.'

'And there I was thinking you wanted to sit next to me every morning.' Bill grinned.

'I don't . . . I mean, I do . . .' Abi felt her face burning. She picked up the drinks menu even though she knew Loretta was already fetching her usual cappuccino.

'Just kidding. It's great to have a new neighbour; once I've said *god morgon* I'm clean out of Swedish.'

'But I don't want to interrupt your work.'

Bill pushed his phone to the far corner of the green and white tiled tabletop. 'Bad habit to work over breakfast. It's a good thing you've interrupted me. I'm really looking forward to our walk this morning.'

'You're sure you wouldn't rather go by yourself? Chloe did twist your arm somewhat.'

'I'm glad she did. I'm relying on you to transform me from workaholic to adventurer.' Bill's blue eyes twinkled. Their little gold flecks seemed to reflect the sun.

Abi laughed. 'Transforming you could be a tall order, though I could start by making you lock your phone in the safe.'

Bill grimaced and clutched his arm. 'You can't! I'd feel like I'd lost a limb!'

'So, what's so fascinating about your work? I haven't asked what you do.' Abi tore open a sachet of sugar to stir through the cappuccino that Loretta had discreetly placed by her elbow.

'I'm in ceramics, importing them to the UK from Europe, mainly from Italy. My company mostly supplies independent shops but we sometimes get orders from the big department stores.'

Abi cut into her custard-filled *cornetto*. 'So, is that what you're doing here?'

'I've got no suppliers on Procida, they're over on the mainland. I usually spend a few days at Vietri sul Mare on the Amalfi Coast – that's where a lot of the biggest and best manufacturers are based.'

Abi nodded. 'That must be interesting.'

'To me it is. Not so much to everyone else. I tried to interest my ex-wife in coming along on my trips, just for a couple of days of factory visits and taking in the sights.'

'But that didn't work out?'

He raised his eyebrows. 'You could say that. But I won't bore you talking about my work. What time do you want to meet for our walk today?'

'According to my guidebook, this is Antonio Scialoia, a nineteenth-century politician, economist and man of letters,' said Bill.

Abi gazed up at the bronze figure on the plinth. They were standing in the Piazza dei Martiri, not far from Flavia and Enzo's apartment. 'Very distinguished, isn't he.'

'The tails and waistcoat help. It would be hard to look so impressive in some of the outfits people wear today.' Bill inclined his head to a couple dressed identically in voluminous shorts and orange baseball caps.

Abi giggled. 'And his posture is so upright, you can't imagine him ever slouching around in a tracksuit. But he's got sad eyes, don't you think?'

'Perhaps he's thinking of the Procidan martyrs commemorated on that memorial over there.'

Abi walked over and stood in front of a set of railings enclosing a stone monument. There was nothing atop its plinth, just an inscribed marble plaque fixed to the dark stone.

'Rather stark, isn't it? It can't be something to do with the war – it's a lot older than that . . . 1799, I wonder what happened then.'

'Some sort of uprising.'

Abi turned away from the memorial to the sweeping belvedere overlooking the sea. 'I can't imagine anything bad happening here.'

'The island has quite a bloody history. It was often under attack – that's why they built the Terra Murata up on the highest point to defend it. But you're right, it's hard to imagine a battle on a day like today. Beautiful isn't it, and what a view! You can see right across the marina – look, that's our hotel.' Bill pointed towards the mint-green building.

Abi leant against the low wall. 'Oh yes, I can see it – and there's the straw parasols that belong to Arturo's Bar. Chiaia Beach is in the other direction, I think that's where Chloe's gone today.'

'I can see a few people dotted in the water. It looks very inviting – if you can swim.'

'Oh, I'd forgotten you don't swim.'

'I never learnt how.'

'Really? My best friend Cherry never learnt either.'

'The one who sent you on holiday? She sounds like a great friend.'

'She makes me laugh too.' Abi's lips twitched, recalling Cherry's last message.

'I must meet her sometime.'

'We're not likely to bump into her here, I'm afraid.'

'No, umm . . . of course not. Shall we walk? We could take a peek inside Santa Maria delle Grazie on the way.'

Abi turned away from the sea. Ahead of her loomed the church's yellow and white bell tower and big baroque dome. Three golden mosaics of the Holy Family sparkled on its yellow façade.

'We'll cross the road after that green truck,' Bill said.

Abi nodded but she wasn't concerned about the rattling vehicle heading towards them, her eyes were fixed on an elderly woman emerging from the entrance to the church. Abi blinked in the sunlight. She was right – it was Flavia. The old lady was looking downwards, her gait slow. She stepped into the road without looking. The truck swerved and hooted. Flavia reached the opposite pavement, oblivious. She trudged the few yards up to her front door and stood on her doorstep rooting in her boxy handbag for her key. A young woman came out from the building; Flavia entered. The door slammed shut behind her.

They crossed the road, stepped around a parked moped and entered the church Flavia had just left. A handful of people were sitting in the pews, heads bowed in prayer. Abi's top wasn't skimpy, but she was glad she had wrapped Cherry's purple scarf around her shoulders. Bill stood beside her; she was conscious of the firm line of his jaw, the rogue twist of hair by his ear that wouldn't lie flat and the subtle citrus aroma from his sun-warmed skin. He made an occasional quiet remark as they wandered around the cool interior and back out into the street. How different he was from Alex who would have seen no reason to lower his voice.

'Ready to walk up to the top?' Bill said.

'Is it far?' The sun was high and Abi's hair felt damp against the back of her neck.

'No, but it is getting hot.' He shrugged off a small red, canvas rucksack. 'Here, have a drink . . . is that all you want? Have a bit more.'

Abi took another dainty sip; she could gladly have chugged back the whole bottle. 'Thanks. I won't have any more, we'll need to save some for later.'

'Have as much as you want. We'll refill it at that fountain on the corner over there.' Bill pointed to an elderly man bent at an awkward angle drinking from a plume of water running from the mouth of a cherubic white face crowned with ceramic grapes.

Abi held out Bill's bottle but no water came. 'How strange. It was working a minute ago.'

'Abracadabra!' Bill said. Water flowed.

'How?' Abi said.

'There's a tap on the side.'

'Oh!' Abi flushed. Sometimes she wondered how she'd failed to inherit a shred of her dad's practical nature.

'I think that's full now, Abi,' Bill added.

'Oops, thanks.' Water was pouring down the sides of the bottle. She wiped her wet hand on the front of her trousers.

'This way.' Bill strode on; he looked cool and comfortable in a short-sleeved white shirt and loose khaki trousers. He was lucky; despite his sandy hair he had the sort of skin that tanned easily, unlike Abi whose complexion went shiny and pink at the first sign of summer.

She followed him up the sloping street. 'That's where Chloe's staying.' She pointed out the turquoise apartment block. An old lady was resting her arms on one of the balconies watching the comings and goings in the street but the green shutters of Flavio and Enzo's apartment were closed tight.

She could feel a stretch in the back of her legs as the road climbed. She was terribly unfit; she would definitely have to go jogging with Cherry again once she got back home. Thankfully after a few minutes Bill stopped at a large, paved area.

'This is the Belvedere of Salita Castello, also known as the Belvedere Dei Cannoni on account of these two monsters.' He patted the rough surface of one of the two huge iron cannons that faced out to sea. 'I love this old stuff. History was my favourite subject at school, it's what I would have studied if I'd ever gone to university. How about you?'

'Art was the only thing I was ever any good at. I would have chosen that if I'd carried on studying, but I went straight into an office job.' Abi frowned. She still remembered the disappointed look on Mrs O'Brien's face when Abi told her she wasn't going to apply to art school. There hadn't been any point; she knew all she wanted to be was a wife and mother. She'd signed up with the local temping agency who sent her to help with the filing at a city law firm. And on the very first day she met Alex.

'I thought you looked a bit arty,' Bill said.

'Me?' Abi was astounded.

'The colours you wear: that purply scarf with the yellow top. There's something about that combination.'

One of Mrs O'Brien's lessons came flooding back. 'You're right. They're complementary colours, opposite each other on the colour wheel, but I'd forgotten all that; they just looked nice together.'

'See, you're naturally artistic . . . hey, don't look so embarrassed. I can't help noticing. I look at designs all the time.'

'For your ceramic business?'

'Yes. I'm not artistic myself, I couldn't design anything to save my life, my business partner does that, but I've got an eye for the patterns and colours that might sell.'

'So, what is your role?'

'All the practical, business side: finance, logistics, that sort of thing. But you won't want to hear about that. Come on, let's take in the view. This is the narrowest part of the island; you can see all the way across from one side to the other.'

Beyond the weed strewn, rough cliff, the island stretched away from Abi in a gentle curve. Below her were the colourful buildings cascading down to the Marina Corricella and the two rows of boats lined up along its edge. A small yacht was sailing in, a streak of white marking the water behind it. A gull swooped low, screeching loudly, perhaps hoping for some scraps left on the deck of one of the larger fishing vessels moored further from the shore. Above the stacks of ice-cream-coloured houses rose the dome of the church they had just visited and behind that, the top floor of Enzo and Flavia's turquoise building obscured her view of the main harbour on the far side of the island save for the edge of the breakwater stretching into the rich blue of the sea.

'It must be even more beautiful at sunset,' Bill said.

'Yes, I imagine it must be.' Abi's heart sank. The belvedere was so romantic, she was sure Alex must bring Marisa here. They would watch the sunset in each other's arms planning their dream wedding. She blinked back a tear. Life was so unfair.

'Would you like me to take your picture here?' Bill said. 'Hey, Abi, are you okay? What's the matter? You look like you're about to cry.'

'It's just so beautiful here, it's made me all emotional.' Abi sniffed. 'Look, why don't I take a picture of you first? Prove to your mum you aren't spending all your time working.'

Bill laughed. 'That's not a bad idea. Where should I stand?'

Abi waved her hand towards the railing. 'Just over there. I'll be able to get in the church and a lot of the harbour. Shall I take it on your phone?'

Bill reached into his small rucksack, took out his phone and frowned. 'Hold on a moment; I didn't realise I still had these websites open.' He quickly swiped at the screen before handing it to Abi.

Abi turned the phone sideways to capture the panorama. 'And now for your close-up.'

Bill groaned. 'If you must. It won't be a pretty sight.'

She moved the screen to bring Bill's face closer into focus. 'Say cheese!'

'Cheddar!'

It was the same silly thing Abi's dad used to say. She swallowed the lump in her throat. 'Shall we walk on?'

The sky was a cloudless blue, the sun warm on her back. She was glad of the occasional patch of shade cast by the oleander trees whose pretty pink blossoms enlivened the route to the top of the island. Above them a small white church clung precariously to the very edge of the cliff.

She followed Bill across dark, volcanic paving slabs and under a tall archway into a rather gloomy vaulted passageway; black crosses were embedded in its rough, sloping stone walls.

Emerging into bright sunlight they headed for a pair of wide ridged columns supporting a carved stone architrave, topped with a white statute of the Virgin Mary. The entrance opened onto a wild, neglected courtyard. Vegetation grew up the walls and out of the windows of the bleak, crumbling palazzo. An inscription told them they had reached Palazzo d'Avalos, the old prison.

'Imagine being sentenced and taken here, looking through a window out to sea, knowing you would be locked away for years. It's like something out of *The Count of Monte Cristo*.' Abi pulled Cherry's scarf a little tighter.

'Apparently it was originally built as a castle, then used as a royal palace and a military college. It wasn't turned into a prison until the early eighteen hundreds. You can take a guided tour but perhaps you'd like to visit somewhere a bit more cheerful.'

'Yes please, this place is a bit creepy.'

'We'll head to the very top of the island, then.'

The atmosphere immediately lightened as they left the decaying prison behind for the sloping, cobbled street of San Michele. High on the warm peach-coloured wall a small glass-fronted nook held an intricate white carving of a winged figure raising his sword.

'I guess that's St Michael,' Abi said.

'Yes, that's him, the patron saint of the island.'

'Tell me about him.'

'What am I, your tour guide?' Bill joked.

'You've been doing a good impression so far. Go on, tell me a story about him.'

'All right, but I'm not putting on different voices like I used to do for my girls! Now, once upon a time the seas were full of danger with pirate ships plundering the island. The people of Procida sought refuge in the high points of the island and called on the Abbot of the abbey for help. He placed a silver statute of St Michael on the abbey's loggia and called upon the faithful to pray alongside the replica of the saint. As the pirate ships came nearer, the islanders prepared for battle. And then . . .'

'Then what?'

'I thought you'd appreciate the dramatic pause.'

'I do,' Abi laughed.

'Thunder clapped, lightning scorched the sky and St Michael himself miraculously appeared surrounded by bright lights. The terrified pirates fled and the island was saved. Legend has it that on a clear day the pirates' anchors and chains can be seen at the bottom of the sea where they were abandoned in their rush to leave. There's a painting that tells the story in the abbey. Would you like to go and see it?'

'I'd love to. It's been years since I did anything like this.'

'Why's that?'

'Alex and I used to go to Spain and Portugal.'

'But there's so much history there, too.'

'Alex said holidays were for relaxing on the beach not "tramping around" as he put it and he couldn't see the point of walking unless it involved eighteen holes of golf and a pub at the end of it. Then when Chloe came along, we would choose somewhere with a kid's club, an all-inclusive, that sort of thing.'

'I get that. Happy kids make happy parents, but Chloe's older now and you've been on your own for a while.'

'I've had a couple of weekends away with Cherry but she doesn't like leaving her kids with their dad for long and her job's so exhausting she just wants to flake out with a cocktail. Chloe and I went to Bournemouth last year but everything went wrong. That's why I was so concerned about her coming here with Alex and Marisa. I knew she'd have a far better time with them than she did with me.'

'I'm sure that's not true.'

'Last year's holiday was a total disaster.' Abi shook her head.

'Don't beat yourself up, Abi. Being a parent can be hard.'

'I guess,' Abi murmured. Marisa and Alex didn't seem to experience the problems with Chloe that she did. 'Let's go and look around the abbey,' she said quickly. She needed to focus on exploring the island and get Alex and Marisa out of her head. And the strange warm sensation she felt when Bill's sincere blue eyes met hers.

Two minutes later they were admiring the abbey's creamy yellow and white façade. An elegant clock tower with two old bells formed a silhouette against the cloudless blue sky. Behind the clock tower rose a beautiful, curved dome and in the archway above the door was another statue of St Michael, raising his sword.

Abi pointed to a short flight of white marble steps lined with terracotta planters brimming with red geraniums. 'That seems to be the way in.'

'Careful on those steps, they look a bit slippery,' Bill said.

Before she had chance to tell him she could manage quite well, he had taken her arm. The touch of his hand on her bare flesh made her catch her breath. She turned her head away in case he caught the smile that spread across her face from feeling him so near.

Chapter Twelve

Abi put on her sunglasses and stepped out of the abbey into the bright light.

'Did you enjoy that? I thought it was rather splendid,' Bill said.

'Oh, yes, very much. That gold–coiffured ceiling was amazing.'

Bill put up one hand to shield his eyes. He reached into the red rucksack and fished out his sunglasses' case. 'Just one last little detour en route to lunch if you don't mind,' Bill said. 'I'd like to take a look at part of the village that's still inhabited. It's easy to think of the Terra Murata as just a tourist attraction but there are plenty of people still living up here in some of the old houses.'

'Okay, you're the tour guide.' Abi grinned.

'Good thing I've got my virtual flag.' Bill thrust his arm in the air. A young Japanese couple turned and stared.

Abi giggled. She followed him into the via Guarracino.

'This was just what I was looking for,' Bill said.

Archways curved over the front doors of apricot–yellow–pink–and–white walled houses decorated with pretty wrought-iron balconies. Terracotta pots filled with dark green leafy plants and succulents sat at the base of steep external staircases leading to the upper floors, their windows shaded by colourful shutters or striped awnings. Cars and mopeds were parked haphazardly in the piazza below.

'It's so atmospheric!' Abi watched an old woman rolling out pasta dough on a makeshift table set up in the shade, her face as brown and lined as the bark of one of the island's palm trees. Two doors along, four children squabbled over a game of cards under the watchful gaze of a green parrot in a domed cage. 'I wonder how old these houses are,' she mused.

'I don't know, I'll have to look it up.'

'What sort of tour guide are you?' Abi laughed.

'A hungry one! Ready to get something to eat? We could stop off at the belvedere with the cannons on the way back down?'

'Sure,' Abi said though she hadn't noticed anywhere to eat when they'd stopped there earlier.

They strolled along side by side; the walk was much easier coming back downhill and they reached the belvedere sooner than she expected. Bill sat on one of the benches and undid the drawstring on his rucksack.

'Oh, have you brought lunch with you?'

'I wasn't planning to, but as soon as Loretta knew we were going out exploring together she insisted on packaging up this picnic for us.'

'That's so kind of her.'

Bill began unwrapping several white paper packages. The aroma of oregano and grassy olive oil hit Abi's nostrils.

'Mmm, looks like mozzarella in those wraps – they smell amazing!'

'And so does this. It's some sort of cake – very lemony.'

'I fancy some of that focaccia stuffed with prosciutto but it's huge.'

'Luckily Loretta packed a knife.' Bill cut through the bread's golden salty crust. His hand brushed against hers as he passed over half the sandwich. A pleasurable little shiver ran through her again.

He looked at her curiously. 'Are you all right, Abi? Would you like some water? I think there's a drop left.'

'Yes, thanks.' She chugged back the water and forced herself to concentrate on Loretta's delicious offerings. They ate in companiable silence interrupted only by the shriek of a gull and the happy laughter of a small boy being lifted out of his buggy to sit astride one of the large cannons.

'You know what I'd like now?' Bill said. 'A cold beer. We could stop off at one of the bars in the marina.'

'That's a fantastic idea.' A nice glass of crisp white wine would settle her nerves. 'Let's go.' She brushed the crumbs off her lap and stood up.

They made their way back down the sloping road. As they drew nearer to Santa Maria delle Grazie, Abi looked up at the apartment where Chloe was staying. This time she did spot Flavia, out on the balcony bending over one of her prized potted herbs. Perhaps she was picking some basil leaves for the spaghetti with tomato sauce that Chloe enjoyed so much. Abi waved but Flavia was lost in her own thoughts.

They entered the marina by the shady steps and emerged by the cane tables and chairs outside Bar Arturo. A couple was just leaving; a waiter clearing away a pair of small white coffee cups waved them towards the now-empty table.

Bill pulled out a chair. 'You sit in that one, enjoy the view.'

'Thanks.' Abi sat down. The aroma of garlic and fresh herbs was drifting over from the next table where a sad-eyed man was sitting alone winding linguine around his fork, staring out towards the sea. Abi undid her purple scarf and knotted it around the handle of her bag so she wouldn't forget it; she didn't need it now that she was shaded by one of Bar Arturo's straw parasols.

The waiter placed two menus on the table.

'We'd just like drinks,' Bill said. 'A Peroni for me. What about you, Abi?'

'A glass of white wine, *per favore*.'

'Of course. May I recommend this *biancolella* from the island?'

'Yes, a glass of that please.'

'Very good.' The waiter whisked away the menus.

'You've got a visitor,' Bill said.

'Who?' Abi looked around expecting to see Chloe.

'This big chap.'

A plump, smoky-grey cat was striding purposefully towards Abi. It let out a small miaow and began rubbing its soft, plush head against her bare ankle.

'You're out of luck, kitty-cat, we're not eating.'

'They might bring a dish of those crunchy Tarallo snacks with our drinks.'

'I hope not − I can't resist them.' Abi patted her stomach. 'Do cats eat things like that? I don't suppose they should.'

'This one looks like it eats anything and everything.' Bill leant down to give it a stroke. 'Some people used to call Procida the island of cats, there are so many of these fellows padding about.'

'I saw a really small skinny white one lurking around one of the piles of nets the other day but I haven't seen it since. I hope it's okay, poor little thing.'

'Maybe you should keep a few of these in your pocket in case you see it again.' Bill plucked a snack from the dish of Tarallo that had just appeared alongside their drinks.

'Please, keep those away from me.' Abi gave the glass dish a little push. She picked up her drink.

'How's the wine?'

'Mmm. Cold and much appreciated.'

'As is the beer.' He grinned.

She took another sip of wine. Delicious. But she would stick to the one glass − she was feeling strangely light-headed. Perhaps she was still affected by their walk far above sea level, the way some sailors suffered from *mal de debarquement* once back on dry land.

'It's so nice to sit here and just chill,' she said. 'I'm going to do nothing but put my feet up for the rest of the day, give my legs a rest before tonight.'

'Why, what are you planning?'

'Nothing too adventurous, but I booked a table for dinner over in the main harbour, where the ferries come in. Loretta recommended a place called La Vecchia Barca.'

'You're joking! She mentioned that place to me the other day and I've booked for tonight as well.'

'Not eight o'clock?'

'A quarter to.'

'I'll give you a wave when I arrive,' Abi joked.

'Or you could join me.'

'Oh no, you must be sick of me by now.' She took a large mouthful of wine, forgetting her resolve to take dainty sips.

'Why would I be?'

'Oh, prattling on about cats and nonsense like that.'

'I like cats. And believe it or not, you'll be doing me a favour. Even I draw the line at taking my laptop to dinner so I've spent every night sitting in a corner reading my guidebook.'

'So that's why you know so much about the island.'

'Believe me, Abi, I must have read each chapter at least twice. I need rescuing.'

'In that case, how can I refuse?' She was surprised how steady her voice sounded.

'I'm looking forward to it.' Bill smiled. The little golden flecks in his blue eyes gleamed.

Abi's heart gave a strange little lurch. She must get a grip. They were two hotel guests sharing a table. That was all. Bill wasn't looking for another relationship and she definitely wasn't ready for the hassle of dating another man. Or the inevitable heartbreak that followed.

Chapter Thirteen

The sheet lay in a tangled heap on the tiled floor. Loretta's silky negligee clung to her damp body; her heart was racing. The hands on the alarm clock glowing green in the darkness confirmed it was not yet five in the morning. But she dreaded falling asleep again. The bad dreams had returned as vivid as before: little Marco thrashing around in the water; his mother Maria screaming for help; the small white dog drifting further and further away. Water swirling around her, the sand turning into wet concrete beneath her feet, pinning her down. Reaching to try and save Marco before he slipped away from her. Next: laughter, cruel and raucous. Maria and Marco's faces red and twisted, the dog laughing too, its gums stretched back in a grotesque smirk, gold hoop earrings swinging from its hairy white ears. The waves closing over her.

Loretta fumbled for the water on her bedside table. The glass was cool; she held it with both hands and drank greedily. Gradually, her breathing returned to normal. Her eyes became accustomed to the darkness, the shapes of her dressing table, her oval mirror and the small curve-legged stool becoming clearer. She was safe in her room, in her beloved Hotel Paradiso but part of her was back in her childhood bedroom, the day after her Capri to Naples swim. Exhausted, she had spent most of the day in bed, sometimes sleeping, sometimes pretending to sleep, listening to the voices of her parents drifting through the open window as they dealt with the well-wishers who had dropped by their hotel to congratulate them on their daughter's success. She hadn't wanted to greet anyone, knowing they would have heard the news that Giorgio was now with Adriana.

Hours later, she'd ventured down to the beach, imagining she would be alone under the dark night sky. The wind was strong, carrying the scent of the sea. A dog barked, alerting her to the presence of two figures on the sand: Maria, who worked in the *pasticceria*, and Marco, her youngest child. Loretta's thoughts were so wrapped up in Giorgio she was barely aware of the unfolding drama, until she heard Maria's screams. Marco was flailing in the water, his mamma calling in vain; his beloved pet dog, now a light patch of fur bobbing far from the shore, swallowed up by the black sea.

So many years had passed but the dreams returned in the still of the night, taking her back there, the sounds of the sea and the wind pounding in her head. And the voices whispering in her ear: 'coward, coward'.

Loretta laid back, staring up at the fluffy white clouds and chubby pink cherubs above her head. The frescoes still delighted her more than ten years after she'd commissioned a local artist to decorate all the bedroom ceilings. Heartbreak and self-loathing had paved her path to the Hotel Paradiso but she was proud of how she'd rescued the neglected property. She dreaded the day she would finally sell up and leave.

The hotel was half the size of the one her parents had owned but ten rooms still required a great deal of work. People rarely comprehended the sheer physical graft that went into lifting catering packs of coffee onto high shelves and turning hefty mattresses. And neither she nor dear Ada were getting any younger. Loretta often toyed with the idea of taking on an extra member of staff but her profit margins were tight and where would she find someone as reliable as Ada, who bent on creaking knees to scrub the grout between the bathroom tiles and made the beds so fastidiously that not a wrinkle remained?

Today, it was Ada's turn to serve breakfast. Loretta knew how much Ada loved the mornings when she swapped mopping floors and folding laundry for busy-bodying about the terrace and the kitchen as if she owned the place, but it was hard for Loretta to relinquish control, especially on a morning like this when the chatter on the terrace would help to calm her whirring mind.

She could no longer lie still. She swung her legs out of bed, got dressed and made up as quickly as she could; even at this hour she wouldn't dream of facing the world with a freshly scrubbed face. Her lotions and potions and overflowing make-up bag were vital tools, as necessary to her as a fisherman's net and buoys. Quietly she exited the hotel and took the steps down to the Marina Corricella. A faint smell of fish mingled with the fresh scent of the sea. She inhaled deeply, feeling that she was filling her lungs with life itself.

It was early for Loretta to be up and about but only a few moments passed before she spotted an old acquaintance rowing across the harbour. Aldo kept his hands on his oars but he acknowledged Loretta's wave with a nod of his head. There was no point in either of them calling out *buongiorno*; they would not hear each other above the cacophony of the seagulls swooping over the deck of the *Mamma Lucia* as Aldo's small blue and white boat drew alongside the big fishing vessel.

The crew on the *Mamma Lucia* were a little too far from shore for Loretta to easily make out their features but there was no mistaking Ada's brother's unusual flaming red hair nor old Fortunato's battered blue cap as the men stood on board sorting their fish and preparing to come ashore.

Aldo's rowing boat was soon joined by one belonging to the owner of La Pentola. Loretta could tell from their gestures that the two men were exchanging a bit of banter as they waited to collect their daily fish.

Loretta kept walking. Crockery was being laid on rush mats on the tables outside a small guest house but most of the restaurants were still shut, their umbrellas tied up and the tables bare. She picked her way carefully in her red high heels, past the trolleys loaded with fishing apparel. Old Angelo was sitting in his usual seat; he had hooked part of his fishing net over the post of an adjacent chair and was carefully easing out the knots. One day she would be as old as him, she supposed.

She reached the boat repair shop at the end of the marina, turned around and began to retrace her steps, stopping only to admire the pink flowers cascading from the old fishing boat on its high plinth and to cross herself as she passed the statue of the Virgin Mary.

Most of the crew of the *Mamma Lucia* had now left their trawler moored in the harbour and were chugging back to shore, half a dozen of them crammed into the small tender, each with his own bag or cool box of fish balanced on his lap. Some still lived down in the traditional fishermen's dwellings by the sea, able to identify their own house from a distance amongst the multitude of colourful buildings on the shore, as others had done centuries before. Night after night they sailed out into the dark and sometimes treacherous sea to bring back their catch. The men had modern technology to help them now; the *Mamma Lucia* even had a big red crane to draw up the nets but it remained a hard and dangerous job. It was never taken for granted that each morning they would return.

Life on Procida wasn't always easy, sometimes it was tragic, sometimes exhilarating, but it was raw and real. How had she once thought she could thrive in a slick city like Milan with its traffic fumes, flashy boutiques and the smell of a million people? She needed to live on this rugged volcanic island she now called home. Even if, one day – perhaps soon – she had to sell the Hotel Paradiso, she would stay on Procida to see out the rest of her days.

The bells of Santa Maria delle Grazie were ringing out. Loretta turned away from the shrieking gulls swooping over the deck of the *Mamma Lucia* and picked her way back to the steps that led to her hotel.

Breakfast on the terrace was still in full swing. Loretta went to pick up a couple of empty cups but Ada waved her away.

'Sit over there, Loretta. I'll bring your breakfast. Fruit and a *cornetto ai cereali* with your coffee as usual?'

'Yes, *grazie*.' Loretta couldn't resist a pastry in the morning, but she felt a little better for choosing the healthier oat bran and barley croissant rather than her favourite filled with sweet and sticky *marmellata*.

She sat down at a newly cleared table.

'*Buongiorno!*' Abi said. 'I just wanted to tell you what a wonderful time I had last night at that restaurant you suggested; the crab linguine was just superb. And you wouldn't believe it – Bill had booked the very same place, so we ended up eating together.'

'What a coincidence!' Loretta tried to feign innocence.

'We had a lovely meal,' Bill added.

'I'm so pleased,' Loretta said. 'And what have you got planned today, Abi?'

'We're taking a boat trip around the island.'

'That's a good idea. I'm sure Chloe will enjoy that.'

'Actually . . .' Abi twisted her napkin. 'It's umm, me and Bill.'

'I've fancied taking a boat trip since I got here and luckily I've persuaded Abi to come with me.'

'Luckily? I'm not sure about that.' Abi laughed.

'I'm sure you'll have a wonderful time,' Loretta said smoothly.

Once the two guests had departed, she allowed herself a satisfied smile. It was nice to think there could be a chance that others might find the lasting love which had eluded her. She shook her head as if that would dispel the image of Giorgio's face that appeared unbidden. After all the years that had passed, it still had the power to hurt her.

After breakfast she perched on her stool behind her desk, proudly surveying the reception area. The floor was shining, the cushions on the sofas plumped up and the scent of a huge vase of fragrant orchids perfumed the air. Guests waved goodbye as they headed off to the beach; others were happily ensconced by the pool. Ada had reluctantly relinquished her position on the terrace and was preparing one of the smaller rooms for their new guest, a Signor Ricci whose late booking had been added to the guest book in Ada's spidery hand. Loretta sipped a glass of chilled fizzy water and began her morning tasks: turning her attention to the week's bookings, the laundry list and the orders for the *pasticceria,* the fruit shop and the minimart. The soothing strains of Franco Battiato crooning '*Il cielo in una stanza*' came from the speakers in the corner of the room.

She took a call from a potential guest enquiring about Christmas. Yes, she would be open this year. A man ringing with a special deal on professional vacuum cleaners was dealt with politely yet swiftly. A dinner reservation was made for the couple in room six.

It was only the sound of suitcase wheels on the tiled floor that roused her from her work. A man was walking towards her. She stood up.

'*Buongiorno*.' The man's voice was unmistakable although age had made it a little deeper, a little croakier.

Loretta gasped. It seemed as though all of the oxygen had been sucked out of the room; the light coming from the pink and blue chandelier was too bright. The zigzag patterns on the overstuffed sofas seemed to be moving; the walls of the reception area were closing in. Her legs were as weak and gangly as a newborn giraffe's. She gripped the edge of the desk to stop them from slipping under her.

Chapter Fourteen

'I think the boat tours set off from over there – isn't that their red and white banner?' Abi said. She and Bill were standing on the quay beside the statue of Christ the Fisherman, a wooden crucifix mounted upon a dome of rough lava stones atop a pedestal studded with majolica tiles, enclosed on all four sides by decorative metal railings.

'We're not booked on that tour,' Bill said. 'Our boat is further along the front. Though I'll pop into that shop over there first if you don't mind. I'd like to pick up a baseball cap on the way – I left mine at the hotel.'

'That makes sense; it'll be hot out on the water.' Abi touched her wide-brimmed sunhat. She suspected it made her look a little eccentric but she knew she'd be glad of it later.

They crossed to the other side of the street where the restaurants, bars, offices and shops were topped by apartments with open archways sheltering balconies looking out towards the sea from which fishermen's wives once watched their men return. Washing was strung along some of them, wafting in the gentle breeze bringing life to the crumbling colourful façades.

A man leant from an upper window bellowing into a mobile phone. The pavement was wide but they had to pick their way around and between tables and chairs, parked mopeds and oleander trees laden with pink blossom.

Abi waited outside the *pasticceria* inhaling the delicious vanilla-scented aromas that filled the air whilst Bill swiftly purchased a blue basebell cap from the shop beside it. A green Ape delivery truck with a dented bumper rattled past.

'All set.' Bill appeared with a smile. 'That's our one, *Dina D*, over there.'

The glossy white motorboat was tied to a chain secured to a long, narrow wooden jetty. Two rows of bench seating, shaded by a cream canopy, faced each other across its wide varnished boards. A young man with several days' stubble and tiny shorts was fitting white leather mats onto the sun deck. He saw Bill and waved.

Abi was conscious that her jaw had dropped open. 'This is ours?'

'Sure is.' Bill grinned.

'But how . . .'

'I thought it would be nice to hire our own boat, stop off at the Marina Chiaiolella, have lunch somewhere, take our time. Francesco, our skipper, will stop at some places for swimming.'

'I didn't bring much money,' Abi said. She hated to think how much the outing was going to cost them. She hoped Francesco would take a credit card.

'This is my treat, Abi. No, don't try to argue. It wouldn't have been nearly so much fun doing this by myself — I'm so lucky you agreed to come with me.'

Abi was glad she was wearing her sunglasses; she wasn't ready for her eyes to give away how lucky she felt too. Bill was a nice guy; she didn't want to give him the wrong idea. She wasn't willing to open her heart again, no matter how attractive he was. She and Bill were becoming good friends. And that was all.

'Let's cross the road, but careful, wait for those two e-bikes,' Bill said. He put his hand on her arm.

Francesco put down a pile of bolster cushions as they approached. '*Ciao*, Bill. You are Abi, yes? I am Francesco. Welcome to the *Dina D*. Once you are aboard, if you would put your shoes in here.' He gestured to a woven basket. 'Now, *signora*, rest your hand on my shoulder to steady yourself as you get in.'

Abi stepped gingerly into the boat, sat down and removed her shoes.

'You can lie back and lean on these cushions here, if you like,' Francesco said.

'Bill?' Abi said. Bill hadn't come aboard; he was poised with one foot on the edge of the boat and one on the paving, staring at something across the street.

'Abi, isn't that your Chloe over there?'

'Chloe? It can't be. She said she was going to the beach with Alex and Marisa today.'

'There on the bench,' Bill said. 'I'm sure it's her.'

The girl on the stone bench was looking down at the floor. Her shoulders were slumped, a curtain of mousy brown hair half covered her face. Abi didn't need to see the girl's face or recognise the familiar floral jumpsuit to know that Bill was right. She jumped up, grabbing her sandals from the woven box, wobbling slightly on the deck.

Francesco frowned. 'Is okay?'

Bill stepped into the boat. 'Here, Abi, grab my arm, I'll help you get out. Would you wait five minutes, Francesco?'

'No problem.' Francesco shrugged.

Abi stepped onto dry land and stuffed her feet into her sandals. 'Chloe!' She strode towards the bench. Chloe looked up. Her eyes were wet with tears. 'Chloe, what on earth's happened? What are you doing here? Why aren't you with Alex and Marisa or Elsa?'

Chloe shifted on the bench, unable to meet Abi's eyes. 'Dad's busy working and Marisa's gone out. Nonno Enzo goes to the café every morning to play cards and Nonna Flavia's busy cleaning the house again even though nothing needs doing, then she's going to make pasta with Elsa.'

'Making pasta? Didn't you fancy that?' Abi sat down next to her.

'Not really. I was supposed to meet my new friends Mia and Rina this morning but they weren't there and I don't want to sit on the beach all by myself.'

'Of course, love, I understand,' Abi said, though she was surprised that Chloe looked so upset. Back home her daughter was quite happy to take herself off to the park with a book or wander about the local shopping centre spending her pocket money on plastic hair slides and tat. Perhaps it was different in a foreign country.

'I don't know what to do.' Chloe sniffed.

'We'll spend the day together,' Abi said brightly.

'I don't want to mess up your plans,' Chloe snuffled. She rummaged in her pocket and blew her nose on a scrappy bit of tissue.

'Don't be silly, love.' Abi pulled Chloe into a hug, her nose wrinkling at the unfamiliar scent of Flavia's shampoo. She looked over Chloe's shoulder. 'Sorry, Bill,' she mouthed.

Bill nodded. He began talking to Francesco. Abi prayed he'd be able to get a refund for the trip.

'I'm so glad you're here,' Chloe said in a squeaky little voice. Her stiff body relaxed a little in Abi's arms. Abi had been right to fly out to Procida. Chloe needed her. Despite her protestations of maturity, she was just a little girl.

'I love you, Mum,' Chloe said.

They were the words Abi lived for. Whyever had she thought Marisa could steal her daughter away?

'I love you too,' Abi said. But as she saw Bill shaking hands with Francesco and preparing to walk away, her heart sank.

Chapter Fifteen

Loretta stared up at the frescoed ceiling. Sunlight was dancing on the chandelier's glass droplets. A man's voice was repeating her name.

'Where am I?' she began. Then she realised: she was lying on the floor behind the reception desk. Tentatively, she reached to the back of her hair, feeling the familiar ridges of the tortoiseshell combs that secured her hair extensions. Someone had wedged a cushion between her head and the cool floor tiles.

'It's okay, Loretta, you're safe. I caught you. Do you think you can get up?'

'I don't know,' she murmured. If she laid here and closed her eyes, would he go away?

'Here, let me help you.'

'No!' Loretta jerked up into a sitting position. 'I'll manage.'

But she allowed him to take her arm and help her stand. She wiggled her feet back into her stilettos; she needed those extra few centimetres to take command of the situation. She gripped the edge of the reception desk tightly. How cool and reassuringly solid it felt.

'Loretta?' His voice was hesitant now; one of his eyelids twitched rapidly.

Loretta studied the man now standing on the other side of the desk, glad of the glossy white barrier between them. His once jet-black hair had turned to salt and pepper, the soft, boyish face now showed the lines and marks of sixty-odd years. Loretta felt a thrum in her temples, a tension headache wrapping a steel band around her head. After more than forty years, she was going to have to confront the past. And the feelings she had buried for so long.

Reluctantly, she acknowledged him: 'Salvo Ricci! After all these years!'

His face softened. 'So, it really is you, Loretta! I can hardly believe it!'

'But what are you doing here?'

'Doing here?' He reached for the handle of his suitcase and wheeled it slightly nearer to the desk. 'Why, staying here of course – on holiday.'

'A holiday?' she repeated.

'I am truly sorry that I gave you such a shock but I thought perhaps you would recognise the name on the booking.'

'The booking?' Loretta knew she was in danger of sounding a little dense. She lifted the hotel diary onto the reception ledge and ran her forefinger over the name and phone number under today's date. 'I have only the last name.' It was the booking Ada had taken. If only Loretta had answered the phone that day, she would have recognised the name and Salvo's voice. She could have pretended the hotel was full and saved herself this pain.

'Ricci is a fairly common name, I suppose.' He smiled.

'And after all these years I did not . . . well, what brings you here?'

'Just a change of scene, but dear Loretta, would it be terribly rude to ask that I might freshen up before we talk any further?'

Loretta stood up a little straighter. How unprofessional she was being. Salvo Ricci was a guest at her hotel. For better or worse. He must have his room key and be allowed to unpack before she quizzed him on his motives and plans.

'Of course. Room four. It is one of our smaller rooms. If I had known . . .' She handed him the key.

'The room is up the stairs, that way? Please don't get up, I shall find it easily I am sure, and afterwards, perhaps we might take a coffee.'

'That would be nice,' Loretta said. She would make hers a caffè corretto – a coffee 'corrected' by adding a shot of grappa.

She reached into the drawer under the counter for her spare powder compact, pressing the pink sponge across her forehead and over her nose. She reapplied her glossy lipstick. There was no need to reline her lips, she used the type of liner that lasted all day. Satisfied that her four coats of waterproof mascara needed no attention she walked out to the pool bar, switched on the coffee machine and waited for the water to heat up. It would be nicer to have their drinks outside. She found the chirping of the sparrows and the scent of the citrus trees calming. And today she would need all the help she could get.

Loretta frothed the milk for her cappuccino. She'd decided that the shot of grappa in a *caffè corretto* was a bad idea — it was barely midday. She never usually drank cappuccino after breakfast but she would be able to toy with the milky drink for longer than a few-sips-and-gone espresso. She spooned over the milk carefully and amused herself by drawing a leaf in the foam. It came out wonky; her hand was trembling.

'*Un caffè macchiato, per favore.*' It hadn't taken Salvo long to unpack and track her down.

'Of course.' She smiled. Forty years later and he was still taking his coffee the same way: a shot of espresso and just a dash of milk to 'dirty' it. Had his life changed at all? Or was he still living on Capri? Was he still best friends with Giorgio? Part of her dreaded finding out, part of her was curious to know. She turned back to the coffee machine and twisted the basket into place.

Above the hiss of the steam, she heard the sound of a stool scaping back. Salvo would expect her to join him, perching at one of the bar's high aluminium tables. Still feeling slightly dazed, she placed his small white cup and saucer and her larger cup on a round tray along with a glass cube filled with packets of sugar and sweeteners. She took his cup and saucer and placed them on the shiny tabletop.

'*Grazie*,' he said. 'No sugar, though, thank you.'

She was not surprised to hear that he had given up his two-sachets-a-cup habit; his physique was remarkably slim for a man in his sixties. Did he have a wife to cook healthy meals for him? She could see no signs of a ring. She stirred her sweetener. Waiting.

Salvo picked up his coffee, took a sip and replaced the cup. His hand looked too large for the dainty china. He nodded, apparently satisfied. 'A beautiful place.' He closed his eyes for a second. 'Aah . . . the aroma of the lemon trees.' The leaves cast a dappled pattern across their table. 'And this is all yours?'

'Yes, I own and manage the Hotel Paradiso.' The feeling that her world had grown soft and wobbly at the edges was beginning to subside. Talking about her beloved hotel, she felt on safer ground.

'I wasn't sure.' He paused. 'Believe it or not, it was pure coincidence that brought me here.'

Loretta nodded. She took another restorative sip of coffee.

'This place was recommended to me by my niece. She stayed here recently on her honeymoon.'

'A young couple?'

'Yes, my brother was widowed and remarried. His second wife is the mother of my niece Graziella. A beautiful girl.'

'Her new husband was Orlando?' She cast her mind to the handsome boy making his near-perfect dive into the pool.

'The very same.'

'But they lived in Turin, not Capri,' Loretta remembered. Perhaps all Salvo's family had moved away from the island.

'Yes, as does my brother now, so the islands off Naples are a novelty for Graziella and Orlando. By coming to Procida they could call in on some of our family's elderly relatives on Capri without having to stay with any of them, thrilling one relative whilst perhaps inadvertently snubbing another.'

Loretta smiled. She knew how complex families could be. 'And do you still live on Capri?'

'Yes, I never left. I got a position at the Blue Parrot, as a porter at first. I've stayed there for my whole career, working my way up gradually.'

'To management?' Loretta felt it was a safe enough assumption. At school Salvo had been a dedicated and hardworking pupil.

'General manager.' He smiled shyly.

Loretta clapped her hands. 'General manager of the Blue Parrot – a five-star hotel! That's some job. *Complimenti*! And yet you holiday here, and your niece too?'

'Of course I suggested my niece stay at our hotel for her honeymoon, but she is an independent girl, unwilling to holiday under the watchful eye of her father's elder brother. And the Blue Parrot is not stuffy I hope, but perhaps a little formal for the tastes of such young folk. I cannot imagine anyone feeling intimidated here.' He glanced around at the cheerful yellow and white parasols, the Danish guest floating in the pool on a hibiscus-print lilo whilst her husband lounged nearby engrossed in a brick-sized Jackie Collins novel.

'Intimidated – I should hope not!' Loretta said. 'I remember Graziella and her new husband. I believe they had a pleasant stay.'

'Yes, they loved the pool especially. It must be heaven for you, swimming here.' Salvo's eyes softened. He remembered her as *il delfino* – the dolphin – of course he did.

Loretta's chest felt tight; her throat constricted. She forced out the words: 'I don't swim.'

His eyes widened. She waited for Salvo to ask the questions she dreaded. She didn't want to talk about those fearful dreams that still sometimes conquered her nights. Sharing a little of her past with Abi had been enough. Abi was a stranger who knew only what Loretta chose to tell her. Salvo knew too much. She shivered despite the warmth of the day.

Salvo was quiet; he seemed to understand. 'I'm sorry . . . that was clumsy,' he began. He rubbed his forefinger over his neat moustache.

Loretta sat up a little straighter. 'Please, there is no need to apologise. I am busy with the hotel, that is all. So, your niece enjoyed her honeymoon on Procida, I am glad. And she recommended this hotel to you?'

'It may seem strange to come here on holiday when I live on Capri.'

Loretta gave a little shrug. She did think it rather odd. People from the larger island saw no reason to come to its tiny neighbour, a place that was barely a kilometre and a half at its widest point.

'To tell the truth, I had no desire to go on holiday at all. I didn't want to leave Capri but I had to force myself to put some physical distance between myself and the Blue Parrot. I am due to retire soon; the role has become a little too much for me and I wish to make a smooth transition to my deputy, Giuseppe. But to tell you the truth, I cannot imagine retirement. The hotel is my life. And without it . . .' He spread his palms upward on the table. 'When Graziella spoke so highly of the Hotel Paradiso, I mentioned it to Giuseppe in passing. He practically begged me to come out and stay here.'

'At such a busy time of year?'

'Yes. I was horrified. How could I leave the hotel in July? But that was Guiseppe's point. He is an experienced manager, but he has never had to run a five-star hotel at its busiest. With my devotion to the hotel – some might say obsession – he is concerned that he might inherit the hotel without his capabilities being fully tested. With me out of sight but just here, a short ferry ride away, he could take the helm for a fortnight and we would both have peace of mind. If I stayed at home on Capri, I would not be able to resist slipping into the hotel bar for an aperitif.'

'And checking up on him,' Loretta said.

'Yes.' Salvo gave a wry smile.

'So, that is why you are here.'

'Not entirely, I confess. I considered a spa hotel on Ischia. I have a little arthritis and I thought I might take a cure but when Graziella mentioned the proprietor of this place was called Loretta, it piqued my curiosity. Of course, I dared not hope it might be you, not after so many years. I saw you only once on Capri, after you left.'

'I came rarely, just to visit my parents.'

'I understood perhaps that you did not wish to see anybody else and that is why I did not make myself known to you. Though when I saw your red jacket with the checked lapels crossing the street, I wished to run up to you.'

'That red jacket. I had forgotten about that though I was very fond of it for a while. I'm surprised you remember seeing me, it must have been a long time ago.'

'I would never forget seeing you, Loretta.' Salvo leant further forward. She caught the aroma of his oriental cologne, warm and gingery. 'You and I were friends once long ago. Or perhaps you just tolerated me because I was a friend of . . . someone else.'

He left Giorgio's name unsaid.

'Tolerated?' Loretta shook her head. 'No, no. Salvo, you were a good friend. It is not your fault what happened. It was Giorgio's fault, no one else's. You were his best friend; you were loyal to him. And you were kind, you picked me up and took me home that day.'

And she had rewarded Salvo by never speaking to him again, never having anything to do with any of her old schoolfriends, leaving Capri to travel as soon as she could, then settling here on Procida. She felt Salvo's eyes on her. They were full of pain. Had he been living with guilt, thinking she somehow resented him? She had never meant that. She picked up her coffee but it was cold. The cup rattled as she returned it to the saucer. With a trembling voice she continued: 'It wasn't up to you to tell me about Giorgio and . . .

her. Words wouldn't have helped. It was already all over for us, although I didn't know it. And I heard afterwards that it was not long until they got married.'

'I heard so too.'

She looked at him quizzically. Surely he would have been Giorgio's best man, but it sounded like he hadn't even gone to the wedding. Had Giorgio snubbed him too? She didn't want to cause this kind man any distress so she changed tack.

'And you, did you marry?'

'No, there was no one. Perhaps I was too devoted to the Blue Parrot, some might say I was married to my job.'

'Oh. I thought perhaps Gina.' Loretta remembered her schoolfriend. Gina's father worked with the little tourist boats at the blue grotto. 'She was nice. I remember she liked you.'

'She was lovely. Perfect, but . . .' Salvo shrugged. His eyes drifted towards the pool.

'More coffee?' Loretta filled the silence.

'Yes, please.'

She cleared away the empty crockery and dropped the cups into the mini dishwasher under the counter. She repeated the rhythms of clicking, twisting and pressing levers, inhaling the nose-twitching aroma of the hotel's signature coffee beans, glad of a few minutes to gather her thoughts. Looking over at the pool to make sure that none of her other guests was waving for her attention, she returned to her stool carrying Salvo's macchiato, a small glass of water for him and her own blood orange juice.

He accepted the drink with a smile. 'You have created a warm and welcoming environment here, Loretta. A far harder task than most can imagine. It's not about the walls, the floors, the beds, lighting, flowers and scents, not even the choices of cakes at breakfast and fine wines at night. A leading hotelier must create something greater than the sum of the parts.'

'An ambience.'

'Yes, and more than that. They must master the art of alchemy, turning base metal into gold. A general manager such as myself must be a magician, the hotel his stage. The guest to be surprised and delighted, unaware of the science behind each trick. Like so . . .'

He reached across the table and plucked something from behind Loretta's ear. He placed his fist on the table, slowly turned it over and opened his fingers. A fragile pink hibiscus blossom lay quivering on his palm.

Loretta gasped. 'How did you do that?'

'Magic.' His brown eyes twinkled. 'Like the magic that is all around us in a fine hotel like this.'

He handed her the flower. She tucked it into her hair behind the ear where Salvo had pretended to find it.

'Thank you, for the flower and your kind words.'

'My pleasure.' He picked up his coffee and smiled. 'And your plans, now you are here on the island?'

'To try and switch off. It is hard to stop looking around each day for tips and tweaks, little bits of inspiration to take back to the Blue Parrot. I need to think about my own next step. I have been thinking more and more of owning and running my own hotel, something small, certainly no larger than this. But whether I should take on such a challenge, I'm not sure. But firstly I must try to force myself to holiday like an ordinary guest.'

'You will find that hard. But perhaps you might take a stroll along the marina then return here later for a cocktail by the pool.'

'Thank you, Loretta.' He drained the rest of his coffee. 'I will take your advice: a short walk by the sea then perhaps up to the Piazza dei Martiri. I am told there is a most attractive belvedere with views all along the coast.' He got down from the stool and pushed his hands into the pockets of his knee-length khaki shorts. 'See you later. Though I may need you to cast a spell as well as bring me a cocktail if I am to fully relax.'

Loretta laughed. 'See you later, have a nice time.'

Salvo walked away towards the door that led through to the reception then out of the hotel. He had a slight stiffness to one knee that made his gait a fraction uneven. Loretta removed the flower from behind her ear and turned it over in her hands. For so long she had dreaded meeting Salvo or anyone else from those long-ago days, fearful that they could rip away the frayed and feeble sticking plaster across her heart.

She'd almost stayed lying on the floor behind the reception desk, eyes closed, hoping that Salvo would go away. Only her professionalism and devotion to the Hotel Paradiso had forced her to rise to her feet. And yet, her conversation with Salvo just now had acted like a cool breeze across the heat of her pain. Salvo instinctively seemed to understand her hurt, to know how much to say and how much to keep in the past, unsaid. And he understood exactly what the Hotel Paradiso meant to her. This morning, to her surprise, she had regained an old friend.

Chapter Sixteen

'We'll do something really fun today,' Abi said. Her voice sounded overly cheerful even to her own ears but she was rewarded by Chloe's wan smile. Across the road, Bill was still standing by the *Dina D* talking to Francesco.

'We could go back to Ciraccio Beach,' Chloe said. 'I reckon I could swim right around the stacks of rocks this time.'

'And we can have lunch at that place with the amazing *torta limone*.' Abi smacked her lips for emphasis but the thought of eating the delicious lemon dessert didn't lessen her disappointment. 'I'll just say bye to Bill first.'

'Bill?' Chloe blinked. 'I didn't know Bill was here. Oh, there he is by that white boat. Were you supposed to be doing something together?'

'Nothing that we can't do another time,' Abi said.

Bill left Francesco by the boat and strolled towards them. 'Are you ready to go?' he said.

Abi stiffened. Bill could see how upset Chloe was and he had two daughters of his own. Did he really expect her to leave Chloe in the lurch for a day gadding around on a boat?

'Where are you going?' Chloe asked.

'Everywhere. All round the island.' Bill pointed to the *Dina D*.

'On that boat? Wow!'

'Wanna come?' Bill smiled.

'Oh, no, Bill . . .' Abi began. She was sure Chloe's presence was the last thing Bill wanted and she certainly couldn't expect him to pay for both of them.

Bill ignored her. He turned to Chloe. 'Francesco's got no problem with taking a third passenger. It's not as if you're going to weigh down the boat! Come and take a look – what do you think, Chloe?'

'We can go, can't we, Mum?' Chloe tugged at Abi's arm just the way she'd done as a little girl. 'Ple-ee-ease!'

'Are you're sure you're okay with this, Bill?'

'More the merrier. Hop aboard, Chloe, then it's shoes off and in the basket.'

'Everybody ready now?' Francesco said. His ready smile hadn't faltered.

'Abi?' Bill took her arm and helped her aboard.

'Towels are here, cold drinks in the cool box,' Francesco said. He undid the rope and took his place behind the chrome steering wheel. Abi and Bill sat opposite each other on the white benches. Chloe lolled back on the leather mats, her head resting on an orange towel which she'd rolled up and rested against one of the bolster cushions. They chugged away from the shore. Chloe held up her phone taking picture after picture.

'The first place we will pass is La Lingua Beach,' Francesco said.

The boat swung to the right past a small pebbly beach with a motley collection of sun loungers and folk in various states of undress sprawled on their towels.

'That beach is stony rather than sandy but we will come to a wonderful place for a swim.'

'We're not swimming here at the beach?' Chloe said.

'No, we won't stop just yet,' Bill said. 'That's the joy of sailing; we can reach a place these beachgoers won't. We'll find somewhere private just for us.'

The boat navigated around a spur of land. 'This is the Punta Lingua, where you can swim,' Francesco said. 'You are in luck. You do not often see these birds.' He pointed to a group of cormorants perched on an outcrop of lava rock drying their wings in the sun. They looked slightly sinister all lined up in a row watching them.

'Won't we disturb the birds?' Abi asked.

'No, I think they will be okay,' Francesco said. 'It is a nice spot to swim, just use the ladder at the back.'

Chloe's smile was back. She was already shrugging off her floral jumpsuit.

'Want me to take a picture of you both swimming?' Bill asked.

'Can you do it on my phone?' Chloe said.

'Sure.'

'Catch!'

Bill dived to grab the phone before it hit the wooden deck.

'That was a bit silly, Chloe,' Abi said. 'Now be careful on that ladder, hold onto both sides.' Oh dear, she did sound like a nag.

'Come on, Mum!' Chloe called. She was already swimming away from the boat.

'The water is variable here. If it is too cold you can just swim a little bit and you will meet a warmer patch,' Francesco said.

Abi clutched both sides of the steep ladder and lowered herself into the water. It wasn't at all cold. She swam a few gentle strokes, keeping her eye on the shore.

'I'm going to swim the whole way round the boat,' Chloe called.

Abi flipped over and floated on her back. She gazed up at the imposing buildings of the Terra Murata where she and Bill had walked the previous morning; the sky was a cloudless blue. Every so often she caught sight of Chloe circling the boat. Her daughter looked so happy. A feeling of contentment washed over her.

Chloe swam over and trod water next to her. 'Mum, my fingers are going all wrinkly.'

'Maybe it's time to go aboard, we'll get the chance to swim again.'

Abi let Chloe go up the ladder first. She didn't want anyone seeing her bottom wobbling up the steps, not even her daughter. Bill tossed them both a towel. Abi covered herself up as quickly as possible. She sat down next to Chloe, her hair dripping on the white leather mats. She dug into the bag she'd brought with her and pulled out a comb.

'Can I borrow that after?' Chloe said.

The next stretch of coastline needed no introduction. The colourful sugar-cube houses of the Marina

Corricella were instantly recognisable. They looked even lovelier viewed from the sea.

'There's our hotel,' Bill said. It was easy to spot the mint-green building. The view from the upper floor must be stunning, Abi thought, though she was quite content with her garden room with its easy access to the swimming pool.

'Santa Maria delle Grazie.' Francesco pointed towards the big yellow church.

'That's Nonna and Nonno's apartment, up there behind it. It makes you realise how high up they are,' Chloe said. 'Do you think they might see me if I wave?'

'It's worth a try,' Abi said. She had to suppress a smile as they both waved and Bill joined in.

'Chiaia Beach, one of the most popular beaches on the island,' Francesco commented as they skirted the next part of the coastline where regimented rows of blue and white umbrellas and loungers faced the sea.

'This is where I come with Dad and Marisa and Elsa,' Chloe said, 'but we don't go to the expensive pay bit, we go to the public beach. We have the best fun ever.'

Abi winced. She tried not to let it matter. Chloe was here with her today, her eyes shining, all her earlier melancholy vanished.

Francesco looked over his shoulder. 'You are all enjoying your stay on Procida?'

'Yes, especially the last day or two,' Bill said. He smiled at Abi.

'You're lucky to live here, Francesco. It's such a beautiful, peaceful place,' Abi said.

'It looks tranquil, but appearances can be – how you say – deceptive. Under this clear, calm sea there is a deadly buried ring of raging fire. On this round-island trip we will sail over three undersea volcanoes. We will sail over the top of one in a moment.' He turned the steering wheel so that the boat cut a path further away from the dark row of jagged, volcanic rocks.

'Is it going to erupt?' Chloe asked.

Francesco chuckled. 'Someday, but not today.'

'That's a relief,' Abi joked. Despite Bill's stories of martyrs and marauding pirates, she still couldn't imagine anything frightening or unpleasant happening on the picturesque island.

Francesco turned his head back towards the horizon. Abi adjusted the bolster cushion against her back, stretched out her arms and legs and frowned. One of her fingernails had chipped; perhaps she'd knocked it against the ladder on the boat. She'd painted them a cheerful mango colour but she hadn't thought of bringing the bottle for touch-ups. But it was only a tiny irritation on what was turning out to be a perfect day.

The boat swayed gently as they crossed the clear water.

'Francesco, is that Ischia over there?' Bill asked.

'Yes, that's right. You can see Mount Epomeo, the highest point of the island.'

'Ever hiked up that?'

Bill and Francesco chatted away easily; Chloe took photo after photo. Abi lay back admiring the view of the rugged island. The coastline was growing more barren, the sandy-coloured cliffs etched with deep vertical markings.

Francesco seemed to read Abi's mind. 'These cliffs are made of tufa, a soft volcanic rock; the ridges show the different eruptions that have occurred. I love this part of the coastline. Sometimes in the early morning and evening you can spot small dolphins here, following the tuna. But not at this time of the day, I'm afraid.'

'That's a shame,' Abi said.

'Yeah. Dolphins would make the best photos ever,' Chloe said.

'Photographs are nice to look back on,' Francesco said. 'But the best camera is your eyes. In a few minutes we'll come to the harbour at Chiaiolella, so you can take a stroll and stretch your legs.'

The sweep of the Marina Chiaiolella was quite a sight, filled with the tall masts of classic sailing yachts. Abi could see the concentration in the set of his shoulders as Francesco steered the *Dina D* through the narrow entrance into the gracious, curved harbour. She slipped her dress back over her swimsuit, which was now nearly dry, and reached for her straw hat. With a helping hand from Bill, she alighted on the wooden pier.

Chloe made a face. 'You're not really going to wear that hat out here are you, Mum. It's so embarrassing.'

'I don't want to get burnt.' Abi glanced at her reflection in the window of a nearby yacht. She didn't look too bad, did she?

'I think your hat looks charming,' Bill said.

'Embarrassing,' Chloe muttered.

'You don't know what embarrassing is,' Bill said. He deftly removed Abi's hat and switched it with his own baseball cap. Bill pushed Abi's hat further down on his head but it was too small and popped back up again. 'Let's go!' He strode along the marina past the rows of pleasure craft. Abi walked by his side, shoulders shaking with mirth.

'OMG! You two are SO embarrassing!' Chloe looked so mortified, Abi couldn't resist flipping Bill's blue cap around so that the peak faced backwards. 'Mum!' Chloe shrieked.

'Oh, darling, I'm only teasing.' Abi removed Bill's cap from her head.

'But I'm not. I think this rather suits me.' Bill adjusted Abi's hat at a jaunty angle.

Chloe's face paled. She stared at Bill open-mouthed. Bill's lips twitched.

'He's not being serious . . .' Abi began. But Chloe was already laughing. Laughing so much her body was heaving with strange hiccup-like noises.

'Your turn, Chloe,' Bill said. He plonked Abi's hat on Chloe's head.

Chloe giggled. To Abi's surprise she kept the hat on for a few strides before giving it back. Abi and Bill swapped hats and, much to Chloe's relief, Bill put his baseball cap on the right way round.

The three of them continued to walk along in front of the row of restaurants facing the water. The sound of clattering pans and a tinny radio playing Paolo Nutini came from the open door of one of the kitchens. Masses of orange lantana cascaded out of wooden planters; the aroma of fresh roasted coffee drifted over from a café. Abi took a swig of the ice-cold water she'd taken from the cool bag on the boat; the bottle was slippery in her hand.

'Can I have some, Mum?' Chloe reached for the cold drink.

'Of course.'

'This is a great trip. Thanks so much for letting me come along,' Chloe said.

'My pleasure,' Bill said.

'It's been fantastic,' Abi added.

It was wonderful to see Chloe looking so happy, Francesco was an interesting guide and the sun was high in the sky warming Abi's back. But when Bill smiled at her, she suspected those weren't the only reasons she was enjoying the day so much.

Chapter Seventeen

'You'll need to put Benedetta down, *carina*,' Flavia said. 'You don't want her to get dirty.'

'Benedetta wants to make pasta.' Elsa pouted. She held Marisa's old rag doll tightly.

Flavia bent down. She heard her knees creak. 'Benedetta has an allergy; the flour makes her sneeze.'

'Poor Benedetta.' Elsa ran her fingers over the doll's chain-stitched nose.

'She can watch us. You're never too young to learn to cook,' Flavia said.

'But Benedetta's really old,' Elsa said. Sometimes she was too smart, Flavia thought.

'She's forgotten how to make *mezzelune*.' Flavia gently prised the doll from Elsa's grasp. 'Let's put Benedetta here where she can see better.' Flavia leant the doll against the back of the middle shelf of the wooden dresser; her white cotton legs poking out either side of a turquoise jug painted with sunflowers.

'Now, please pay attention!' Elsa waggled her finger at the doll's flat, impassive face.

'Can you climb up on that chair?' Flavia said. Elsa was rather too heavy to lift.

Elsa scrambled up. Although Flavia had put two cushions on top of each other and secured the ties around the ladder-back chair, the little girl could barely see over the table.

'What do we do first, Nonna? Are we making *mezze-lune al cioccolato*?'

'Not chocolate filling today.' Flavia gave Elsa's chubby cheek a squeeze. 'Today, ricotta and sage.'

'Not *cioccolato*?' Elsa put on a wheedling voice.

'No, not today,' Flavia repeated. 'First, we sift the flour. Do you know what I mean by that?'

Elsa shook her head. Her dark curls danced.

Flavia took a sieve that was hanging on the wall. 'Like this. See how it comes out like a fine powder.'

Elsa's eyes widened. 'Fairy dust!'

Flavia smiled. 'Yes, light as fairy wings.' She took a large metal spoon from the narrow rack hanging above the sink. 'Now we scoop out a well in the flour like this to make space for the eggs. No, Elsa, we have to crack them first. Take that egg out. Do you want to try?'

'Please, Nonna!'

That's the joy of being a child, Flavia thought. Even cracking an egg is new and exciting. 'Watch, Elsa. Break it carefully into this yellow dish then we catch any pieces of shell.'

Elsa bit her lip, her face screwed up in concentration. Flavia opened the door of the small freestanding fridge and placed a tub of ricotta on the tiled work surface next to the small wooden chopping board heaped with sage leaves plucked from the terracotta pot on the balcony.

She rubbed a velvet, silvery leaf between her fingers, savouring the aromatic scent.

'Look, Nonna!' Elsa stuck her forefinger into the dish of eggs.

'Well done. Only two pieces of shell. We can fish those out. Now can you carefully measure half a teaspoon of salt?'

The telephone was ringing. Flavia turned down the radio. 'Wait a moment, Elsa.'

She hurried into the hallway and picked up the phone. '*Pronto*!'

There was silence at the other end of the line. Behind the dining-room door, she could hear Alex on one of his interminable virtual meetings: 'I think you'll find that Clause 23.4, not 23.2, clarifies that point.'

'*Pronto*!' she repeated. 'Sono Flavia – it's Flavia.'

Still silence. Frowning, she replaced the receiver.

In the kitchen, Elsa was holding up a spoon proudly. 'Half a teaspoon of salt, Nonna.'

'Oh, yes, good girl. Now the oil, and we mix everything together.' Flavia measured out a tablespoon of golden-green extra virgin olive oil. She wrapped her hand over Elsa's as they used the handle of a wooden spoon to gently stir the mixture. Could Elsa sense how hard and fast Flavia's heart was beating?

The shrill ring of the telephone started up again. She patted Elsa on the head. 'Excuse Nonna, sweetheart.'

Her hand trembled as she lifted the receiver. Could it really be him? Could it really be her beloved son, Nico? She hardly dared hope.

'*Pronto?*' Her voice was shaky.

A long pause. Her dress was damp under her arms and around its high neckline, even though she was standing in the cool, tiled corridor. It felt as though a giant ball of pasta dough was lodged in her throat. Silly to be so nervous when she longed so much to hear from him.

A man's voice came down the line. An automated voice. *You are entitled to a special discount on our new windows . . .*

She didn't even listen to the rest. Cold callers had to make a living; they couldn't imagine how her hopes were raised and dashed every time she picked up the phone. Clutching the silver and garnet cross around her neck she murmured: 'Oh Holy Mother, please show Nico how to forgive.'

Nico had lost touch with his friends when they moved to Procida, he'd struggled in his new school, his grades had suffered. But they'd all made sacrifices. It hadn't been easy to pack up their old life and start again. She wished Nico would see that and make his peace with them, but he'd packed his bags and left for a new life in the north. His monthly phone calls did little to compensate for his absence; in a way they made it harder to bear, reminding her of what she'd lost. Each day she prayed she'd find her son standing on the doorstep. She dreamt of putting her arms around him and telling him face to face how much he meant to her. One day Nico would come home. She had to believe that.

She walked back into the kitchen. Elsa removed her thumb from her mouth. 'What do we do now?'

Flavia composed her features into a big smile. 'Nonna's going to show you how to knead the dough.'

'*Saluti!*' Loretta raised her glass of wine.

'*Saluti!*' Salvo echoed her toast.

'This is such a treat. I can't think when I last went out for lunch and didn't have to rush back.'

Salvo's eyes twinkled softly. 'The pleasure is all mine. Now, I want you to promise to relax and enjoy yourself and not fret about what's going on back at the hotel.'

'I promise,' Loretta said. She took a nice big mouthful of crisp white wine as if sealing her intention. 'Besides, I can trust Ada to keep an eye on the place for a few hours.'

'She looks as though she enjoys playing your role when she gets the chance.'

'Yes, she likes the opportunity to take over. It makes a nice change from laundry and sweeping up, I suppose.'

'As long as she doesn't change all the locks whilst you're out,' Salvo joked. He opened the menu. 'Have you any idea what you'd like to eat?'

Loretta ran her finger over the short list of starters. 'Perhaps the *insalata di limone* to begin.'

'And then the spaghetti with mussels, lemon pesto and mint?'

'However did you guess?'

'It used to be your favourite. I remember they served it at your sixteenth birthday celebration at your parents' hotel.'

'You're right. Mamma asked the chef to decorate the edge of the plates with edible flowers and no one was quite sure whether they should eat them,' she laughed.

'I remember that night so well. You wore a lovely sea-green dress.'

He was right. She had felt beautiful that night. And oh, so proud to be with Giorgio. 'Yes, I loved that dress. But how on earth do you remember?'

'Sometimes it is easier to remember an event from many years ago than something that happened yesterday.'

'That seems truer the older one gets,' Loretta said. 'But I often wish it were the other way around.'

Salvo blinked. 'We all have things we'd rather not remember. Life throws up plenty of regrets. But we cannot change the past, Loretta, no matter how much we might wish to, or know what the future holds. All that truly matters is today.'

His melancholy tone surprised her. For a moment she didn't know what to say. She was relieved when Salvo's old sparkle returned as he bantered with the waiter as he took their order and returned with a basket of bread.

Salvo held his wine glass to the light. 'The taste is sublime but also this colour is so pure. We don't serve any Procidan wines at the Blue Parrot; perhaps our sommelier should take a trip over here to visit some of the vineyards.'

Loretta tapped him lightly on the arm. 'You're not supposed to be thinking of work.'

'I consider myself scolded, but to tell you the truth, since I've been here I have allowed myself to relax and think of other things. Meeting you again has brought back so many memories. Remember that school trip to Pompeii? I hadn't thought of it in years but I found myself chuckling about it whilst I was unpacking.'

'We were terribly badly behaved.'

'We played hide and seek in the ruins. You were one of the ring leaders.'

'Don't remind me!' Loretta put her hand to her face.

'It was fun though, wasn't it?' He sighed. 'Great days.'

'The *insalata di limoni, signora*?' The waiter interrupted them. He was hovering with a plate in each hand.

'Please,' Loretta said. The dish of sweet Procidan lemons dressed in extra olive oil, garlic and chilli pepper was placed in front of her.

'You have made a good choice,' Salvo said. 'And so have I.' He cut into his tuna tartare.

They ate their first few mouthfuls in contented silence broken only by the clatter of cutlery and snatches of conversation from the tables around them. In the distance a small white yacht rounded the volcanic rocks into the marina and nosed its way into a gap next to an old fishing boat. Four young people, dark-haired and bronzed, jumped ashore, the boys in shorts, the girls wearing loose shirts with the sleeves rolled up shrugged over their bikinis. They looked to be in their twenties, no older than Loretta had been when she had bought the Hotel Paradiso. For years she'd wished she could go back in time and do things differently but today she could watch them without envy. The sunny day, delicious food and Salvo's pleasant company was contentment enough.

The next course arrived. Loretta twisted her fork into the fragrant heap of spaghetti. She savoured every mouthful as Salvo talked eloquently about his years managing his hotel. They had so many experiences in common they couldn't help sympathising or laughing at each other's stories.

Every so often the conversation turned to the times before Loretta left Capri. For so long she'd avoided anything or anyone that reminded her of those days. The Capri to Naples swim and its aftermath had defined her youth – her whole life distilled into two terrible days. The moment when she emerged from the sea, her triumph turning to shock, the pity in the eyes of her family and friends as Giorgio's duplicity was revealed; the next night, watching Maria, Marco and their little dog on the beach – those events had overridden everything that came before. To her, the young Loretta was frozen in time like an ash-preserved person found at Pompeii, condemned to combing their hair or walking their dog for ever.

It amazed her how much of the past Salvo remembered, how many different stories and events, both happy and sad. And as they reminisced, there was no pity in his eyes but the warmth of a dear friend whose friendship she'd thrown away. As they finished their wine whilst waiting for desserts – Salvo insisted and Loretta would diet tomorrow – she discovered through tentative questioning that Giorgio and his new bride had moved away to run an *agriturismo* in Umbria and that for reasons she didn't probe, Salvo and Giorgio ceased to be friends after Loretta had gone.

They carried on talking as the tables around them emptied, lingering over tiny cups of dense, bitter coffee and then sharp shot glasses of limoncello that gave her a warm and fuzzy feeling. Salvo insisted on paying the bill.

Loretta stood up. She allowed Salvo to drape her turquoise ombre chiffon scarf over her shoulders and they walked across the marina to the sound of the chimes of Santa Maria delle Grazie ringing out. As they climbed the steps to the hotel it felt natural for Salvo to take her arm in his.

He pushed open the door from the street. 'Glad to see the place is still standing,' he joked.

Ada came out from behind the reception desk with some reluctance. She'd done a grand job: the cushions on the couches were plumped to perfection and judging by the tiny drops of water on the surface of the leaves, she'd even changed the water in the exuberant bunch of gladioli on the glass table beneath the Venetian mirror on the far wall.

'Thank you again for lunch,' Loretta said.

'No, thank you for joining me.' Salvo paused for a moment as if he might say something else.

'Your key,' Loretta said.

'Thank you, I almost forgot.' He took the stairs to his room.

Loretta walked out to the pool, all her guests seemed settled, no one waiting for a drink. She took her seat behind the reception desk, checking through the post that had arrived that morning. There was no further correspondence from Amadeo D'Acampo. His previous letter still lay unanswered in the bottom drawer. Perhaps she would show it to Salvo; with all his experience in the hotel business he might be able to give her some advice. The thought made her feel a little lighter.

'I guess it's time to get back to the boat,' Bill said.

Abi reluctantly dragged her eyes away from the shimmering golden mosaic above the door of a marsh-mallow-pink church.

'Yes, come on, Mum!' Chloe skipped on ahead, her ponytail swinging.

'Enjoy Chiaiolella?' Bill asked. He walked next to her, near enough for her to catch the faintest waft of his fresh, citrus cologne.

'Yes. It was nice to get over to another part of the island and seeing the coastline from the boat has been magical. I could sail all day,' Abi said. She couldn't remember when she had last felt so relaxed.

Francesco waved from the bow as they approached. Abi was glad, the boats did all look rather similar. She let Bill help her back on board and slipped off her sandals.

'Going to sit at the back on the sun mats with me and Chloe?'

'Why not?' He sat down in a rather awkward cross-legged position.

Abi laughed.

'What's funny?'

'You look like you're about to do some yoga.'

'Cheeky! I wish I was that bendy. You wait until you're a forty-something, you won't be so smug then.'

'Mum's thirty-nine. She's forty in a couple of months.'

'Thanks, Chloe!' Abi did not like being reminded.

'Thirty-nine? I would have said twenty-nine!' Bill's eyes sparkled.

'Who's cheeky now?' Abi said, though she couldn't help smiling.

Bill untangled his legs and stretched them out straight as Francesco carefully nosed the *Dina D* out between the lines of rocks, manoeuvred the boat to the right and began to follow the shoreline.

'The sea is less calm on the eastern side of the island because the sirocco winds blow this way. Today it is not so windy but on other days the waves are rough,' Francesco said. 'See those great gaping holes in the tuff rock – they are caused by the waves wearing it away. A little of the land is lost every year.'

'The sea's smooth today,' Abi said. A yellow-beaked gull was bobbing gently just yards from the boat.

'Today is pretty perfect but you will notice more surf and undulations as we travel along to the next bay. We can stop for another swim here if you like. You'll be swimming right over another underground volcano.'

'This one isn't going to erupt either, is it?' Chloe said.

'Not today.' Francesco turned his head and winked. He stopped the boat. 'Careful on the ladder.'

Chloe stood up, held her nose, and before Abi had chance to intervene she'd jumped clean off the side of the boat. Abi clamped her hand to her eyes.

'I can't believe she just did that!'

'It's frightening being a parent. I hate to think what my girls get up to that I don't know about,' Bill sighed.

'Coming in this time?' Abi asked.

'I don't swim, remember.'

'How silly of me, I completely forgot. What a shame!'

'Can't swim, goes on holiday 'cause his mum tells him to: I'm not doing a very good job at impressing you, am I?' Bill joked.

'Friends don't have to impress each other,' Abi said.

A cloud crossed Bill's face. 'Friends?'

Abi felt herself colouring. Had she been too presumptuous? She and Bill were just fellow guests at the hotel, thrust together by circumstance but she thought they'd developed a genuine rapport.

'I did like to think we were,' she said quietly.

Bill's smile returned. 'Friends. Of course we are.'

'Mum, are you coming?' Chloe shouted from the water.

'Wait a moment, take these goggles and a pair for your daughter. You will be able to see some fish.' Francesco tore off a small chunk of bread and threw it into the clear, green sea. 'The fish, they will come soon.'

Abi strapped the goggles round her head, they pressed hard against her nose. She slowly descended the ladder, holding out the other pair to Chloe. She trod water, helping her daughter to adjust the head strap.

She swam a little further away from the boat, took a deep breath and submerged her head. Colourful fish darted here and there in the clear water. For a few moments she was lost in wonder at the variety and colour of the world beneath her. Running out of puff, she surfaced.

'Did you see those, Chloe?' But Abi didn't need to ask, she could see from Chloe's wide smile. It was a shame that Bill wasn't able to join in.

'Going to look again?' Chloe asked.

Abi inhaled a lungful of air. Her second peek beneath the surface was just as rewarding as the first. It was almost an anti-climax to swim around the boat afterwards but even so she circled the boat several times before pulling herself up the ladder back on board.

'There's a shower attachment on the boat if you want to rinse off the salt water – we won't be stopping to swim again,' Francesco said.

'Can you reach?' Bill asked.

'Yes, I'm fine, thanks,' Abi said. She wasn't sure she could cope with Bill angling the flow of water over her semi-naked body. She showered quickly, wrapped a towel over her costume, threw back her head and let the sun warm her face.

Chloe held up her phone and took more pictures as they passed under the narrow bridge linking Procida to the nature reserve of Isola Vivara. They sailed on past the two ridged, twisted stacks of pale grey rock between Ciraccio and Ciracciello beaches where she and Chloe had swum on their first outing together. Despite the heat of the day, rows of daytrippers were toasting themselves deep bronze in the afternoon sun. Abi looked over her shoulder. The island of Ischia was receding into the distance.

'You get a good view of the castle at Ischia Ponte from here,' Francesco said. 'It is a good place to visit if you take a day trip from Procida to that island. But for me, I have no need to visit Ischia or Capri. For me, Procida has all that I need.'

Abi smiled at the pride in Francesco's voice. Chloe's happy face, Bill's sparkling eyes. Procida had all she needed too.

'Now we round the Punta Serra to Posto Vecchio, also known as the postman's beach after the famous movie filmed there. You will see now that the sea is less smooth,' Francesco said.

Abi could feel it too. The water was growing choppy and the waves were crashing against the tufa cliffs, streaking the sea with white foam.

'They have landslides here,' Francesco continued. 'See the netting on one side of the beach where they try and prop up the cliff. Some people, they bring their towels and lie right there. Crazy!' Francesco's face was turned towards the prow of the boat but Abi could not mistake his serious tone and the shake of his head.

The boat turned away from the beach. Something curved and black was moving through the blue-green water.

'Is that a seal?' Abi said.

'Where?' Bill craned his neck in the direction Abi was looking. 'Looks like it could be one. What do you think, Francesco?'

Francesco carried on looking straight ahead. 'Sorry, I am afraid we have no seals here.'

'I can see it,' said Chloe, pointing. 'That dark patch on the water.'

'No, impossible!' Francesco looked around. 'Ah, no. It is a diver. He must be collecting sea urchins over there off the Capo Bove.'

'Oh!' Abi said, although she didn't quite believe it – until a man's head wearing a diving helmet appeared above the surface.

'Never mind, Abi, it was a nice idea,' Bill chuckled.

Chloe sighed. 'It would have made such a cool picture.'

'Thanks for letting me come on the boat today,' Chloe said.

The three of them were nearly at the top of the road leading up from the port. The lowering sun was shooting rays of white light across the mosaic of Mary and the baby Jesus above the entrance to Santa Maria delle Grazie. Outside, a stooped old woman in an orange and brown smock leant on two sticks. Abi pulled Chloe into a great big hug, pressing their faces so close together that her nose was full of the scent of the Factor 30 she'd insisted on slathering all over her daughter.

'We're so glad you came along,' Abi said.

'Yes, my pleasure,' Bill added.

'You're sure you're all right if we leave you now, love?'

Chloe adjusted her sunglasses and hitched her beach bag higher up on her shoulder. 'I'm fine. I'm not going to get lost, am I?' She inclined her head towards Flavia and Enzo's apartment. 'Oh, Mum! I almost forgot. Nonna Flavia told me to ask you to ring her. She wants to offer you a manicure or pedicure or something at the salon.'

'Oh, there's no need.' Abi tucked one hand into the pocket of her dress, trying to conceal her chipped polish. She twisted the end of her sparkly scarf.

'Nonna said she'd do it personally. I think she'll be really insulted if you say no.'

'It's very kind of her; I suppose I can't refuse.' Abi took her hand from her pocket and examined her nails as if seeing the chips for the first time. 'Maybe they could do with a freshen-up. I could touch them up myself, but I don't suppose I'd find this unusual orangey colour in the local pharmacy.'

'You will call her, won't you?' Chloe said.

'Okay, I promise, as soon as I get back to the hotel. See you soon, love.'

'Bye, Mum.'

Abi wanted to give Chloe another kiss but she was already skipping up the road.

'Looks like I'm not going to get out of that one,' Abi said.

'Isn't a manicure supposed to be nice?' Bill said. 'I'm sure Gemma took April to the salon for a birthday treat.'

'It just seems a bit weird having Marisa's mother doing my nails.' Abi splayed her fingers and frowned.

'It's a nice gesture.'

'I suppose so.' Abi shrugged. She felt a bit ungrateful, but she really wasn't looking forward to it.

★

Half an hour had passed since Loretta had taken Abi and Bill their cold drinks, after they'd returned from their trip. She couldn't hear her two guests' conversation, her stool behind the pool bar was too far away, but she couldn't fail to notice the way that Abi leant closer to Bill as he spoke, the way she threw back her head and laughed and the way he, just occasionally, lightly touched her arm.

'They look like they're getting on well,' Salvo said, folding away his newspaper.

'Yes, don't they.' Loretta dried the last of the clean glasses and put them on the shelf behind her.

'I think you deserve a little break,' Salvo said.

'I guess I could spare ten minutes.'

Loretta came out from behind the counter and lifted herself up onto the stool opposite him. She rested her elbows on the round, aluminium tabletop; her pink stilettos dangled several inches from the floor. He was just an old friend so why was she so conscious of his warm, oriental cologne and the broad shoulders beneath his smart navy-blue shirt?

Over the years she'd wondered how she'd feel if she ran into Giorgio again. She'd never imagined that Salvo would be the one to unlock the door to her past.

Chapter Eighteen

Abi spread a yellow towel out over her sun lounger. Her phone was beside her; there was nothing from Chloe today, just a message from Cherry checking up on her. But Cherry had nothing to worry about. Abi lay back, savouring the aroma of the lemon trees. Droplets of water clinging to her legs refracted the sunlight, making tiny sparkles across the top of her thighs. Her swimsuit was wet from the pool, but it would dry soon enough in the hot morning sun.

Bill stirred on the lounger beside her. 'Another perfect day,' he said. 'Too early for a beer, I suppose. Maybe I'll order a coffee, it'll stop me nodding off.'

Abi yawned. She stretched her arms over her head. 'I think I'll join you. It's hard to keep awake sometimes, it's so relaxing here.'

'We had a good long walk yesterday,' Bill said.

'Wonderful. I'll never forget those views.' Abi smiled. Since their round-the-island boat trip, she and Bill were spending more and more time together. It felt natural to chat together over breakfast and to choose the lounger nearest to him if he was sitting by the pool. And it was daft to chow through a plateful of pasta whilst scrolling down her phone when the two of them could be sharing a leisurely evening meal.

Yesterday they'd gone exploring with a map of the island, hand drawn by Loretta, leaving behind the churches and shops and piazzas to wander high paths along the clifftops. The day was hot but ancient pines provided patches of shade and the air was fresh. White houses clung to the hillside; in the distance the island of Ischia and the two humps of Vesuvius on the Italian mainland were clearly visible. They peered through great iron gates guarding grand villas overlooking the sea, passed lemon groves and rows of tomato plants like the ones Abi's dad used to grow. The crunch of their trainers on a narrow path disturbed sleepy lizards who scattered in all directions at their approach; birds tweeted, their song no longer masked by the sounds of human activity. As they marvelled at sculptural prickly pears, Abi peeked out of the corner of her eye at Bill and once or twice she caught him looking at her too. And when they got lost, doubled back on themselves and ended up in the middle of someone's vineyard, Bill just laughed instead of tutting and grumbling the way Alex would have done.

When they made it back to the hotel, both rather rumpled and overheated, neither of them had suggested that they spend the next day together, but somehow they'd ended up on two adjacent loungers whiling away the morning.

'Seeing Chloe later on?' Bill asked.

'We're going to grab a quick ice-cream this afternoon, but I don't think I'll be seeing much of her over the next couple of days what with these new girlfriends she's palled up with and all the time she wants to spend with Bibi.'

'Bibi?'

'Chloe and Elsa found a stray cat with a sore paw down in the marina the other day and insisted on rescuing it. I don't know where they got the name from but I've seen a photo of the little thing and Bibi does seem to suit it. The girls love her but Alex can't wait to see the back of it, he says its mewing is interrupting his Zoom meetings.'

'He's not an animal lover then?'

'Far from it, but Flavia and Enzo agreed they'd nurse Bibi until her paw heals and as it's their house, Alex knows he can't win the argument. Apparently he went off in a mood to buy it a flea collar – he claimed he could see little creatures jumping about in its fur.'

Bill snorted. 'Sorry, shouldn't laugh. Have you and Chloe got any pets back home?'

'No. Dad had a little dog, Bobby, but it died shortly before he did. I would have liked a cat myself but Alex would never countenance it.'

'And what about what you wanted?'

Abi looked away. It was hard to explain, even to herself, why she'd always gone along with Alex's wishes.

'You could have got yourself a pet after Alex left, especially as Chloe seems so keen,' Bill added.

'It seemed such a big responsibility,' Abi muttered.

'A cat?' She could hear the surprise in his voice.

Abi took a deep breath. 'Sometimes I've struggled to look after myself and Chloe.' She looked down at the shadow of lemon leaves patterning the foot of the lounger.

'But you seem so capable.' Bill's voice was softer now.

Abi chewed her lip. 'I haven't always managed that well.'

Bill's blue eyes met hers. He didn't say anything, waiting for her to go on.

'Since my dad passed away . . .' her voice cracked. To her embarrassment she felt tears pricking her eyes. 'When Chloe was at school, I spent hours just sitting around in sweatpants, eating rubbish, not even washing my hair . . .' Abi swallowed. She'd never spoken so frankly to anyone before, not even to Cherry.

Bill moved to sit on the end of her sun lounger, his hand closed over hers. 'And your best friend, she couldn't help?'

'I put on a front, even to her, thinking that if I was miserable all the time, she'd get fed up with me, though deep down I knew she was too good a friend for that. But forcing myself to go out of the house and meet her helped. If I hadn't had Cherry, I don't know what I'd have done.'

Bill squeezed her hand. 'You're lucky to have a friend like her.'

'Yes,' Abi sniffed. 'And to meet you.' She felt the heat rise in her cheeks. Why had she said that? Bill had seemed in two minds when she'd called him her friend that day on the boat.

'And I've been lucky to meet you,' Bill said. 'Even if it was in rather unfortunate circumstances.'

Abi laughed in spite of herself. 'I haven't forgotten you made me fall in the pool.'

Bill smiled ruefully. 'I think you'll be reminding me of that for the rest of my life.' Now it was his turn to go red. 'Well, what I mean is . . . Ah, there's Loretta, shall we get those coffees?'

'Yes, let's,' she said quickly.

Abi requested her usual cappuccino in a business-like voice that belied her swirling emotions. Loretta took their order with a ready smile and tottered towards the pool bar on her tangerine heels.

Abi moved her book and sunglasses case from the folding table between the two loungers so that there would be somewhere to set down their drinks. 'Don't you think Loretta seems very happy today?'

'She's very chirpy. I wonder if it's due to a certain someone.' Bill inclined his head towards the high tables surrounding the pool bar where a solitary Italian gentleman of a certain age was flicking through his copy of *Il Mattino*.

'You mean Salvo? I got chatting to him the other night, he seems like a nice guy. Do you really think Loretta likes him?' Abi whispered, even though there was no chance that the object of their conversation would overhear them.

'I'd put money on it. Haven't you noticed she goes all fluttery whenever he comes near?'

'She did look a bit coy when I mentioned his name the other day. She confessed they had known each other a long time ago.'

173

Bill raised his eyebrows. 'An old flame?'

'Oh, no. Salvo was just a schoolfriend and he was the best friend of Giorgio, someone Loretta was very fond of a long time ago. I shouldn't really say any more . . .'

'It's okay, I don't expect you to break any confidences. I've noticed you and Loretta talking together from time to time.'

'Yes, I was surprised at first but I guess sometimes it's easier to talk to a stranger. It must be a lonely job running a place like this, always having to put on a smiling face and making connections with people you'll probably never see again.'

'And it's a lot of responsibility. I wouldn't fancy running a hotel at all,' Bill said. He stood up as Loretta came back over. 'Here, let me take that tray.'

'Thank you, Bill. *Molto gentile*, very kind.' Loretta flashed him a smile. Her lips were loaded with a pinky-purply gloss that matched her iridescent fingernails.

'Lovely manicure,' Abi said.

Loretta rotated her wrist; a stack of shiny jewelled bangles sparkled in the sun. 'Thank you. They do a good job at Sempre Bella, Flavia's such a perfectionist.'

Abi gasped.

'Something wrong?' Bill said.

'I've got that appointment there later today. I almost forgot. I'll have to leave soon, or I'll miss it. Loretta, you remember I met Flavia because Chloe's staying with her. She offered me a manicure at Sempre Bella.'

'That's kind of her.'

174

'She seems a nice lady.' Abi took a sip of her coffee, savouring the rich aroma.

'Yes, Flavia's a lovely person. I mentioned she's been doing my nails ever since she and Enzo came to Procida, didn't I?'

'I thought you said they'd always lived here,' Bill said.

'That's the impression I'd got from Alex, but when I mentioned Marisa's childhood when I visited their apartment, she and Flavia looked really uncomfortable, almost like they were hiding something.'

'Flavia doesn't like talking about the past, but I don't know why,' Loretta said. 'I believe they lived somewhere on the Amalfi Coast when Marisa was a child but I couldn't say for sure. Anyhow, I'll leave you to enjoy your drinks. I must go and find my guidebook, I promised to lend it to Salvo.'

Bill winked at Abi as Loretta departed. 'Did you see how she blushed when she mentioned Salvo?'

'Honestly! What a gossip you are,' Abi teased.

'Just showing an interest!' Bill's eyes sparkled. 'I'll keep an eye on the two lovebirds today, it'll give me something to do while you're gone.'

'I'll expect a full report,' Abi joked. 'And don't think you can spend the rest of the morning working on that laptop of yours. Loretta will tip me off if you're not relaxing.'

Bill swept his arm across the foot of his sun lounger. 'Look – no laptop, no work, it's all shut away in my room. I've even got a book to read, I started it last night.' He held up a thick paperback with two cowboys on the front cover.

'Is it any good?' Abi asked.

'Yes, but I don't imagine it's your sort of thing.' He held the book out towards her.

Abi turned it over and read the blurb on the back jacket: '*Death, glory, honour and a gun fight you'll never forget.*'

'Boy's stuff.' Bill grinned.

She flicked open a page at random. *Long-legged Jim gripped Sonny's shoulders. 'This town ain't big enough for the two of us,' he snarled.* 'You're right. Definitely not my thing.' As she handed the book back, a small white rectangular card fluttered onto the tiles between the loungers. 'Sorry,' she said. 'I've lost your place.'

'No problem, I'll find it soon enough.'

She bent to pick up the business card.

'There's your bookmark. Hey, wait a moment, this is beautiful.' The sketch of a lidded tureen on the back of the card was exquisite.

'It's a wonderful design,' Bill said.

'*Ceramica Nuova Ondata* – is that one of the companies you deal with?'

'New Wave Ceramics? Unfortunately not, but I'd certainly like to. The pattern on this dish is so unusual, though I'm not too sure the blues and greys are quite right.'

'Umm.' Abi studied the card for a moment longer whilst she sipped the rest of her half-drunk coffee. 'I think raspberry with a splash of something citrus, maybe lime green, would work, perhaps with the edging in terracotta just to ground the bright colours.'

'I would never have thought of that but you're absolutely right. I said you were naturally artistic.'

'Oh, get away!' Abi squirmed. 'So, where are these ceramic people based?'

'The address says they're in Vietri sul Mare but I've never come across them. It was pure luck I found their card tucked in the back of this book. There's no phone number or website, which is a bit odd for a business card. I tried googling them but I can't find anything at all. It's very strange.'

'That's a shame. Will you look for them next time you're on the Amalfi Coast?'

'I'm not planning to return to Italy until much later in the year. I know I'm supposed to be relaxing and not thinking about work but I can't get this design out of my mind. There are several independent shops I deal with that would love something slightly quirky like this. I'm really tempted to take a trip back to the mainland to see if I can find the place.'

'Would you be gone long?' Abi tried to keep the disappointment out of her voice.

'I can take a ferry over to Pozzuoli. From there it's just a train ride to Vietri sul Mare. I can easily get there and back in a day. I really ought to make the effort.'

'You don't sound terribly sure.'

Bill picked up his coffee cup, raised it to his lips and put it down again without taking a sip. 'I know this might be a big ask, but would you consider coming with me?'

'What, me?'

'It's a pretty place. I think you'll like it.' Bill hesitated. 'And, well, I've kind of got to like your company. If you've nothing fixed, we could go tomorrow.'

'If it's just a day trip I guess Chloe will be okay.'

'So, you'll come with me? That's fantastic.' Bill grinned. His blue eyes gleamed. 'We'll talk about it later; I don't want to make you late for the salon.'

'Oh! I must go!' Abi scrambled to her feet. 'I'll just about get there in time if I hurry.'

She grabbed her bag from the end of the lounger, waved a goodbye to Loretta and set off towards the town. From the Piazza dei Martiri she turned into the road that led towards the port. Above her head washing hung from shallow balconies and pigeons perched on junction boxes from which streams of grey electric cabling snaked along the walls. Cars and trucks rattled over the pavement-less, dark lava-stoned road; an approaching van forced her to jump onto a stone step and flatten herself against a doorway. A boy yanked his bicycle away from the vehicle just in time, shouting something in Italian, swearing she supposed.

She had to force herself to concentrate on where she was going. It wasn't just the fear of being late for her appointment at Sempre Bella that was making her palms sweat and her heart beat a little faster. Her head was full of thoughts of tomorrow's outing with Bill.

The road ahead sloped gently downwards, bringing into view the dome of San Leonardo against the bright blue sky. She turned right at the butterscotch-coloured church, catching a glimpse of chequerboard floor and a flower-bedecked altar through its half-open door. Via Vittorio Emanuele was busy with people strolling to and from the port or visiting the launderette, the tobacconist and the hairdresser's. By the time she arrived at the salon, Abi's legs felt heavy and her damp fringe was sticking to her forehead.

She pushed open the glass door, a tinkling bell alerting the young girl behind the shiny reception desk. The interior was pleasantly cool; a fresh floral scent filled the air. On the corner of the desk sat a substantial orange and grey striped vase filled to bursting with a dizzying multitude of flowers in at least a half-dozen shades of pink. Blush-coloured walls and fuchsia leather upholstery on the salon's comfortable-looking chairs completed the look.

'*Prego, s'accomodi*,' the girl said.

Abi hesitated.

'Welcome, come in. Please sit,' the girl said in English. She moved a computer mouse across the desk. 'Abi Baker?'

'Yes, that's right.' Abi hovered. She wasn't sure if she was expected to sit on the couch by the desk or one of the spindly-legged gilt chairs near the door.

'Please.' The girl stepped out from behind the desk revealing a thigh-length, gold-buttoned tunic top in a sugary shade of pink worn over narrow black trousers. She guided Abi towards a high-backed leather chair. 'If you like to remove your sandals, I will bring the bowl to soak the feet.'

Abi remained standing. 'I am here for a manicure with Flavia.'

'A manicure. *Si*! A pedicure also.'

'There must be a mistake,' Abi said.

'No mistake. Flavia herself, she made the booking, a present for you. Now, your shoes off please, I will fetch the water.'

Abi bent down and fiddled with the straps of her sandals. She sank down into the comfortable chair. Water was gushing from the basin in the corner, a strong aroma of lavender filled the air. The girl returned and placed a white plastic foot bath on the floor. Abi eased her slightly swollen feet into the foamy water and inhaled the sweet scent. A pleasant gust of cool air came from a large ceiling fan. The telephone on the reception desk rang.

'Excuse me one moment,' the girl said.

Abi let out a breath; her shoulders dropped. She leant back against the padded fuchsia headrest and let her eyes close. Her mind drifted back to her conversation with Bill by the pool. *I've kind of got to like your company.* His blue eyes with those gold flecks meeting hers. Abi felt a great big smile stretching over her face.

'Abi,' a voice said. It was Marisa.

Abi's head jerked up so suddenly she felt a burning in the back of her neck.

Marisa was standing in front of her dressed in black jeans and a slightly too big gold-buttoned tunic with the Sempre Bella logo embroidered on the pocket. 'I'm afraid Mamma cannot be here. She has asked me to do your treatment instead.'

Abi's mouth opened and closed. Her throat felt too dry to speak. No way was she going to sit in this chair for two hours, one-to-one with Marisa. She couldn't possibly relax with Alex's fiancée filing and painting her fingers and toes.

Abi stood up. She lifted one foot out of the warm, fragrant water and jiggled it about. 'I need a towel,' she said.

'No! Abi, please wait,' Marisa said. 'For Mamma's sake, please stay. She will be so upset if you leave.'

The girl on reception was giving them a quizzical look. Reluctantly, Abi sat back down. She looked longingly at the door, wishing she had the guts to grab her sandals and flee.

'Is Flavia unwell? Please tell me she's okay,' Abi said. She shifted on the padded leather seat. It had seemed so comfortable a minute ago but now it felt as rigid and unyielding as a block of granite.

'Mamma's fine,' Marisa said. She pressed her lips together. Close up, she didn't look so perfect. There were dark shadows beneath her eyes and her skin looked pale and dull under the salon's bright lights.

'I've only met your mother once but I am already very fond of her,' Abi said.

'She was so happy to meet you. You are Chloe's mother, to her you are family.' A slight blush suffused Marisa's wan cheeks. She turned her head slightly so that she didn't have to meet Abi's eyes.

'It is very good of your parents to have Chloe for such a long visit. I know they have been very kind.'

'They're enjoying having Chloe and Elsa. Mamma loves having children to spoil. She's very happy. Now, let me start on your toes.' Marisa sat down at the end of Abi's chair. 'If you could put one foot here?' She spread a small pink towel over the low stool in front of her.

'Are you sure you're going to do it yourself? You're a lawyer, not a beauty therapist.'

'I trained with Mamma originally but then things, umm, changed.' Marisa dropped her head and began carefully drying Abi's toes. 'I've done dozens of manicures and pedicures, hundreds probably. Do you want to choose a colour from the bottles on the trolley whilst I'm doing this?' She picked up a rectangular buffer and worked it backwards and forwards across the back of Abi's heel.

'Sure.' Abi found it hard to focus on the rows of pinks and reds, neutrals and funky blues and greens when Marisa was so near that Abi could smell the fresh scent of her hair conditioner. Marisa used both hands to massage a rich cream into the soles of Abi's poor tired feet. It was disconcerting to feel such pleasure from the hands of the younger woman she so despised.

Marisa seemed to be finding their close proximity as hard as Abi was. Perhaps harder. A tiny vein jumped at the corner of one of her brown eyes and damp patches were appearing under the sleeves of her pink tunic. Abi was sure there was something Marisa was holding back.

'Are you sure Flavia is okay?' Abi said again.

Marisa stopped easing Abi's cuticles back. She raised her head. 'She says I'm imagining things but she tires so easily these days I can't help worrying.'

'I do understand, I hope there's nothing wrong.' Abi was concerned for Flavia and for Chloe as well. Her daughter had already faced the upheaval of Abi and Alex's divorce and the death of her beloved Gramps. Chloe had settled into Flavia and Enzo's Procida apartment without a care and bonded with her new Nonna Flavia. She seemed so resilient but deep down, the events of the last few years must have affected her. If anything happened to Flavia it could be the final blow that could cause Chloe to break.

'Have you chosen your colour? How about one of these brighter shades as you're on holiday.' Marisa snapped back into professional beautician mode complete with a smile that didn't quite reach her eyes. She picked up a bottle of clear liquid. 'I can apply the base coat whilst you decide.'

'I'll go for peacock blue,' Abi said. She wondered if Bill would think it looked artistic. The thought made her smile.

'Lovely. And what about your fingernails? One of the pinks would make a nice contrast unless you want them to match.'

'That mid-pink, please,' Abi pointed. Blue or green fingernails would be fun, but she had a feeling Chloe would find Abi 'so embarrassing'.

Marisa carefully applied the base coat, then two coats of the peacock blue whilst she chatted on about the island and the little gems Abi had yet to discover. Despite her concerns about Flavia, and the awkwardness of having Marisa so near, Abi began to relax. Having the younger woman tend to her feet wasn't quite how she'd anticipated spending a sunny day on Procida, but it was surprisingly enjoyable to lean back in the leather chair, nod and smile and lift each foot up and down in turn.

'I'll just rub in a little oil,' Marisa said. She used her thumb and forefinger to massage the glistening drops in and around the nail beds. 'All done.'

Abi twisted her foot this way and that. 'They're perfect. You're wasted being a lawyer.'

Marisa laughed, her face softened. 'We'll move over to the desk by the window for your manicure if you don't mind. It'll be easier to apply the colour if you rest your hands on the table.'

'This is so kind of you,' Abi said. She was determined not to forget her good manners, no matter who she was dealing with.

'It's nice to realise I haven't forgotten my training. And I'd never let Mamma down. She's done so much . . . sacrificed so much.' A cloud moved over Marisa's pretty features. She paused as if lost in thought.

Abi stood up. She slipped her pampered feet back into her sandals. 'That chair over there?' she asked.

Marisa started. She blinked as though she'd forgotten who Abi was. 'Oh, yes, that desk over there, please. It was this pink, wasn't it?' She picked up the bottle Abi picked out.

Abi perched on the revolving leather chair, trying to resist the temptation to spin herself around and around. She rested her hands on the white glossy table.

'I'm really enjoying that book by the way,' Marisa said.

'Which book?' Abi's mind had drifted away, pondering what to wear for tomorrow's outing with Bill.

'The Hollyhock Cottage one; I downloaded a copy.'

Abi stiffened. There was no need for Marisa to patronise her by pretending to read the books Abi liked just because Abi didn't read great fat classics in the original French. Or in English.

'Really?' Abi said. She deliberately kept her voice neutral.

'The part where Jessie's rescue dog runs wild at the village fete had me in stitches.'

'But that's near the end,' Abi said.

'I've been racing through it; I've only got a couple of chapters to go,' Marisa said. She gave Abi a genuine smile. 'I'm dying to read the rest in the series.'

'I can lend you a couple when you get back to London.' The words spilt out automatically, as if she and Marisa were friends.

'Umm . . . thanks,' Marisa said awkwardly.

'No problem,' Abi said. She studied the chip on her fingernail.

Marisa unscrewed the top of the nail polish remover and swiped a cotton pad across Abi's old varnish. Abi wrinkled her nose at the strong aroma of pear drops.

'I hear you and Chloe went on a wonderful boat trip the other day,' Marisa said.

'It was fantastic, seeing the island from the sea, and Francesco, the guy who owns the boat, made the trip so interesting.'

'Chloe told me she saw shoals of fish swimming under water.'

'It was magical.'

Marisa swapped the cotton pad for a nail file and began to shape Abi's nails. 'Chloe said a man from your hotel treated you. That was very generous of him; it costs a lot to hire one of those boats this time of year. He must like you an awful lot.'

'Bill just wanted some company. He was planning to go anyway.' Abi felt herself flush.

'Really?' Marisa's eyes met Abi's and held her gaze.

'Bill's a bit of a workaholic. He had to force himself to leave his laptop at the hotel and get on the boat and relax for a while. It was easier to do that if he had company.'

'That makes sense.' A smirk played on Marisa's lips. She laid down the nail file and picked up one of Abi's hands. 'Happy with the shape?'

'Yes, great.' Abi was half glad Marisa had changed the subject, half disappointed. Mentioning Bill's name gave her a little frisson of pleasure. Even though he was just a friend.

'So, this Bill, what does he do?' Marisa said. She frowned a little as she carefully applied the base coat.

'He imports ceramics.'

A big drop of clear liquid landed on Abi's finger. 'Oh, I'm sorry,' Marisa said. Her hand shook as she picked up a cotton pad to swipe the excess away.

'He's tagged this holiday onto a business trip. He deals with several suppliers on the Amalfi Coast.'

'Does he arrange the shipping?' Marisa asked. The vein at the corner of her eye was jumping again.

'I suppose so. He doesn't talk to me about his work; he says it would bore me.'

'Or he doesn't want you to know.'

'I can't imagine he's doing anything top secret!' Abi laughed.

Marisa didn't laugh. Or smile. She finished painting on the base coat in silence. The only sounds were the blast of a horn from the street and the tearing of cardboard as the receptionist unpacked a box of products and arranged them in a pyramid on the shelf behind her.

Marisa took the pink polish and began to apply it with exaggerated care. Her brown eyes scanned Abi's face. At last, she spoke: 'Abi, please be careful.'

'Oh, did I knock a nail?' Abi peered at her new polish.

'Not your nails. This man Bill.'

'Bill? What do you mean? He's a nice guy and anyway he's just someone staying at the same hotel.'

'Don't kid yourself, Abi. There's something more. I can tell by the way you say his name. I don't think you should get involved with him – he could be anyone.'

Abi felt a surge of annoyance. 'What right have you got to tell me what I should and shouldn't do?'

Marisa gave her head a little shake. 'I know I've no right, but it's easy to rush into a relationship with someone only to find they're hiding something.'

'Like they're married,' Abi snapped.

Marisa put down the polish. 'I know you won't believe me, but when I met Alex, I had no idea about you or Chloe.'

'Actually, I do believe you. Alex never wore a wedding ring and I'm sure he was quite capable of giving you the impression he was footloose and fancy-free.' Abi paused, it was the first time she'd admitted, even to herself, that it hadn't all been Marisa's fault.

'I honestly didn't know. We didn't mean to fall in love.' A tear glistened in the corner of Marisa's eye.

Abi bristled. Marisa had nothing to cry about; she had everything she wanted. 'I said I believe you, but you must have found out soon enough. You could have put a stop to it. You could have done the right thing.'

The receptionist stopped arranging her pyramid of products. She turned and stared.

'I'm sorry,' Marisa murmured. 'I never meant . . .'

Abi lowered her voice too. 'It's too late to apologise. But I don't see how this has anything to do with Bill. His ex-wife went to Canada taking their kids with her. He's had a tough time.'

'So, he says. Look, Abi, I know I've no right to interfere, but you don't really know if this man is telling the truth. I know from the past how charming some men can be when they have something to conceal. They blind you from reality, showering you with compliments and little gifts, so you don't think to question them when they disappear for hours or days. They become defensive or hazy when you ask for details of their jobs or their past, brush off your questions, pay for everything with cash. Bill says he's in ceramics but you don't really know what he's up to.'

'For goodness' sake, Marisa! Bill's not some mafia hitman, he's a genuine guy! I do know him, and I'll know him even better after tomorrow. We're taking a day trip to Vietri sul Mare. There's a supplier Bill wants to meet. He thought he'd try and see them before he heads back to the UK.'

'Doesn't sound like much fun for you.' Marisa held Abi's hand still and stroked a wide band of pink down the middle of her thumbnail.

'Bill says it's a lovely town. We're going to have a look around and a nice lunch. It's going to be a wonderful day.'

'I hope you're right, but do be careful, Abi.' There was a strange expression in Marisa's eyes.

Chapter Nineteen

Loretta closed one eye, leant further towards the mirror and drew along her upper eyelid with her black kohl pencil, finishing the line with her trademark feline flick. This morning her reflection pleased her. Her yellow frock had a flattering frill at the neckline and emerald-green crystals cascaded from her ears like miniature chandeliers. She usually saved these earrings for celebratory occasions but today felt like a special day: the sky was a cerulean blue and the birds were singing. Love was in the air at the Hotel Paradiso.

Abi and Bill were off on a trip to Vietri sul Mare today. It was supposed to be a business trip, Bill said, but Loretta couldn't help feeling that another whole day together might work its magic on the pair of them. But the reason Loretta was humming to herself as she tied the laces on her green high-heeled wedged espadrilles was nothing to do with the blossoming romance between her two guests and everything to do with last night. Something akin to a miracle had occurred: the feeling that she might love again.

She and Salvo had sat up late talking for hours, long after the lights had dimmed in all of the other rooms.

And the feeling that they could one day become more than friends had hung in the air between them as surely as the picture-book crescent moon in the dark sky above. When they finally retired to their respective rooms, Salvo had kissed her on the cheek. An invisible barrier between them crackled with energy like an electric fence. They hadn't crossed it but Loretta had no doubt that they soon would. It seemed extraordinary that she was experiencing the dizzy feeling of falling in love, something she hadn't felt for over forty years. She corrected herself: something she hadn't *allowed* herself to feel, for there had been moments when she had felt herself falling for someone and forced herself to pull back, turn away and harden herself to the inevitable pain. There was Paolo, who owned the boat yard before Ernesto, a kind and lovely man, and a few years later the wine importer, who was a regular guest at the Paradiso until he confessed that it was Loretta rather than the vineyards that brought him back to the island time after time. She'd closed her heart to both of them.

Salvo was different. He'd seen her at her best. And her worst. Throughout her childhood he'd been there, steadfast in his friendship yet she'd barely noticed him in the shadows cast by Giorgio's bright light. How differently she now viewed him, as if a grey caterpillar had turned into a glorious butterfly bringing colour to her life. She dared to believe the strange coincidence that had brought him to the Hotel Paradiso had given her a second chance of love. She brushed on an extra coat of mascara for luck and walked out to the terrace to serve breakfast, singing as she went.

No one lingered for long over their pastries and coffee that morning. For one reason or another, all her guests had plans for the day. The Dutch couple were taking a boat trip to Capri, the Americans had booked a tour of the old prison up in the Terra Murata and a writer researching Catholicism in Italy was planning to visit some of the island's many churches. Salvo would be out too, visiting old friends of his parents he hadn't seen since he was a child, who lived on the far side of the island. Loretta and Ada would split the cleaning of the rooms between them so that afterwards they would have time to enjoy a rare half an hour sitting by the pool enjoying the sunshine whilst everyone was out.

Loretta worked briskly, cleaning the three garden rooms that led out onto the pool. Soon they were full of the aroma of furniture polish and the scent of fresh lavender-washed linen. Despite the music coming from her portable radio, she could still hear Ada knocking the vacuum cleaner against the bed legs overhead, something that usually made Loretta grit her teeth and tut to herself. Today she was too happy to care.

Once she was satisfied that the rooms were spick and span, she opened the pool bar and switched on the coffee machine so that she and Ada could enjoy a cup. She loaded a tray with two tiny espresso cups and a couple of glasses of water, carried them over to the pool and chose two loungers in a shady corner, knowing Ada would be hot and flustered after finishing her chores. At last her employee appeared, walking a half stride faster than her normal gait.

'Ah, there you are. I've made the coffee and got us a couple of iced waters as well as it's such a hot morning,' Loretta said.

Ada sank down onto one of the loungers, her face grim.

'Whatever's the matter?'

'I found this,' Ada said. She was clutching a sky-blue sheet of notepaper in her hand.

'Oh, Ada, there's nothing to worry about,' Loretta said. She cursed herself for not disposing of Amadeo D'Acampo's letter straight away, but why would Ada go rooting around in the bottom drawer of the reception desk; it was where Loretta kept her spare make-up bag and personal things.

'So, you know about this? How could you, Loretta? I may be just a cleaner and maid but you know how much this hotel means to me. How could you plot to sell it without saying a word?' Ada blurted out. Her voice was harsh, tears of anger gathered in the corners of her eyes.

Loretta stiffened. She and Ada had worked together for years and yet on the flimsiest evidence of an unanswered letter, Ada was accusing her of selling the hotel behind her back. 'Perhaps if you didn't look through other people's possessions you wouldn't find things that offend you,' she answered coldly.

Ada sat up straighter. She thrust her chin forward. 'I wasn't looking through anything. I knocked some papers off his bedside table and some fell to the floor.

I couldn't help that this bright blue page caught my eye. Or perhaps you would prefer me to leave a mess when I clean the rooms.'

Loretta put her hand to her forehead. 'What bedside table? You're not making any sense. I left that letter in the bottom drawer of the reception desk.'

'Maybe you should speak to *him* about looking through your things. He must have wanted it back.'

Loretta took a long draught of her iced water. 'Who's "he", who's "him"?' But even as she said those words, a horrible suspicion was beginning to form.

Ada folded her arms. She looked Loretta in the eye. 'Your old friend Salvo.'

'Give it to me.' Loretta reached for the letter. Her hand was shaking.

Ada thrust the blue paper at her, but her voice softened. 'I thought you said you knew about this. You said there was nothing to worry about.'

Loretta scanned the letter. It was from Amadeo D'Acampo but this time it wasn't addressed to her. It was addressed to Salvo. A pain gripped her as if someone had reached a hand inside her stomach and twisted it. Then stabbed her through the heart.

Dear Salvo, Loretta read.
I enclose the various property details and paperwork as promised. As I previously advised, I regret to report that we have still had no response from the Hotel Paradiso. Therefore, if you are able to visit the establishment during your planned break you could

perhaps make an informal survey of the building and
gauge its potential profitability. If it still meets your
criteria, we might approach the current owner with a
more detailed proposal.

Wishing you an enjoyable holiday,
Sincerely yours,
Amadeo

Loretta fanned herself with the blue paper. Despite her seat in the shade, she felt as hot as if she were holding her face over a bubbling pan of spaghetti. Everything Salvo had told her had been a lie. He had been 'surveying' her beloved hotel, 'gauging its profitability', ferreting out information. The stories they'd shared about their respective businesses had been a way of breaking down her defences; the conversations about her hopes and dreams engineered to uncover how likely she was to sell, to see how low an offer he could propose. The thought of the confidences she'd shared made her stomach heave.

Worst of all, Salvo had used his knowledge of her past to exploit her vulnerabilities. He knew that deep down there was a part of her that still yearned to be loved. The side of her that she had kept hidden away for so long was exposed like an open wound. She would have sworn last night that the look of love in his eyes was for real. What an actor he was!

She wanted to tear the covers from the sun loungers, up-end the folding tables, rip down the parasols, hurl the beach towels into the pool. And scream and scream. How stupid she'd been. How naïve. She should have had the confidence to know that the decision she'd made more than forty years ago was right. She'd vowed that she would never trust a man again. And she never would. Not with her beloved hotel. And certainly not with her heart.

Ada reached out and gently unballed one of Loretta's closed fists. She held Loretta's hand in hers. 'Oh, my dear love. You didn't know.'

Loretta swallowed. She struggled to get the words out. The humiliation of knowing that she'd done little to conceal her affection for Salvo from Ada made it hard to look her employee in the eye. She blinked away the tears forming in her eyes. She sniffed and rubbed her nose before she could speak.

'I received a letter like this before; several letters, in fact, from this Amadeo D'Acampo looking to discuss the sale of the hotel on behalf of his anonymous client.'

'Salvo,' Ada said.

'Yes, so it seems, although when I received Signor D'Acampo's letters I had no idea that Salvo was involved. I threw the first letter away, the second I didn't bother to open. The third is still in the reception desk drawer, the one I foolishly thought you'd found. Please forgive me – I know that you would never look through my things.'

'I know you did not mean it,' Ada said.

Loretta sighed. 'For some time now, I have been contemplating the future. The Hotel Paradiso is my life but since turning sixty, I have wondered how long I can go on as owner and manageress.'

Ada bit her lip. 'So, you might sell,' she said quietly.

'Not for a long while. Receiving those letters made me realise what a wrench it would be to give up this place and yet . . .'

'Running a hotel is hard. I know that.'

Loretta sighed. 'I didn't answer this man's third letter but I didn't throw it away either. I began to wonder if it was foolish to toss away a potential opportunity to get a good price for the hotel. But if I gave up, what would I do with myself then?' Loretta spread her hands apart. 'Of course, if I had taken the matter further, I would have spoken to you but I saw no reason to fill your head with unnecessary worries.'

'I could have helped you come to a decision. We could have talked it over.'

Loretta shook her head. 'Oh, Ada. You don't know how much I appreciate your support but I've got so used to making my own decisions.'

'Of being alone.'

'Yes,' Loretta whispered. 'Then Salvo arrived. He was an old friend from the past; I thought I could trust him. And with all his years at that fancy hotel in Capri, I thought he would understand. I was about to confide in him about my dilemma. I would have taken his advice and he would have advised me to sell. Thank goodness you found this letter. To think how I've been taken in by him.'

Ada sighed. 'He seems so charming. And when I've seen you together, I thought . . .' Her face reddened.

Loretta put her head in her hands. 'Oh, Ada. I thought it too. What a foolish old woman I am.'

'No. You are just turned sixty. That is not old at all.'

'But I am no longer young.' Loretta instinctively touched her hair extensions. Her hand brushed against her dangly crystal earrings. She'd been another person when she chose those pretty green earrings just a few hours ago. A person whose life was brimming with possibilities. Now she just felt tired.

'What will you do?' Ada asked.

'I don't know. I suppose I should go to this evening's mass at San Leonardo's to thank the Holy Mother I have found out the truth. I suppose I've had a lucky escape. But right now, all I can do is carry on as normal – there are plenty of jobs to do.'

'Don't I know it.' Ada levered herself up from her sun lounger. 'I'll check on the linen cupboard.'

'Thank you, Ada, I meant to do that earlier.'

Ada hesitated. 'You can always talk to me, Loretta. You're my boss but we're also a team.'

'A good team, Ada. I don't know how I would manage without you.'

Loretta stood up to clear away the coffee cups. She would tidy up the pool bar and wipe down all the bottles. She would keep herself busy focusing on the hundred and one humdrum unglamorous tasks that lay behind the smooth running of the hotel. And she would try to forget the contentment she'd felt these past few days. Before a few lines on a piece of blue paper destroyed her newfound happiness.

Chapter Twenty

Bill patted his jacket pocket. 'Phew! I thought I'd left these on the train.' He put on his sunglasses.

'Looks like you're going to need them.' Abi was already wearing hers. The sun was fierce even though it was only halfway through the morning. She rummaged in her shoulder bag and fished out the scarf Loretta had lent her. Orange lilies on a turquoise background wasn't a pattern Abi would normally choose but the cotton weave would do a better job of protecting her skin than Cherry's lightweight purple scarf; her shoulders were still rather pink from their day aboard the *Dina D*.

'All set?' Bill asked.

Abi's eyes followed an old white Fiat Panda as it negotiated a bend in the zig-zag road. 'It looks quite a walk down to the town.'

'Lucky there's a lift,' Bill said.

'Good to know.' Abi grinned. She was already regretting shunning her trainers in favour of a pair of silver sandals but her impractical footwear looked ever so pretty with her old blue dress that Bill had already admired and it was a shame to hide her new pedicure away. She tore her eyes from her neat peacock-blue toenails and followed Bill a few yards to the lift where an elderly couple stood waiting patiently.

'Aah, here it is.' Bill moved out of the way to let the old man help his wife inside. The lift inched slowly downwards. It clunked to a halt; the doors opened. Abi and Bill followed the couple out, emerging straight onto a busy road. A young woman in a peaked cap and short-sleeved blue shirt was directing the traffic. She waved them across to the other side where a statue of a smiling mermaid reclined on a stone plinth amongst bobbing daisies, delicate pink gaura and a host of different-coloured flowers that Abi couldn't identify.

'Welcome to Vietri sul Mare,' Bill said.

'I like it already. I didn't realise we were still going to be so high up. Just look at that view! The sea's so blue!'

'The coast leads around towards Cetara, it's a little fishing village famous for its anchovies. Down below us are Vietri's beaches and you can just see Salerno, the big port where the container ships dock.'

'And up there?' Abi gestured to some small white houses clinging to the rugged cliffs.

'Vietri has several tiny hamlets. There's a proper road now but originally the only way up was by donkey and cart.'

'I can't imagine living somewhere so precarious.'

'Fortunately, we don't need to go by donkey today.' Bill smiled.

'Pity, that might have been fun,' Abi joked.

'You'll have to make do with admiring that one, over there by the water fountain.'

Abi stepped towards the green and white animal mounted on top of a wall decorated with painted tiles. Its mouth was open, presumably braying, its green glazed ears were comically large and it sported a ceramic basket planted with fresh flowers on either side of its painted saddle. 'How cute!'

'The iconic *ciucciariello*. The town has been producing little souvenir donkeys modelled like this since the 1920s. The donkeys have become the symbol of Vietri, though funnily enough it was visiting German artisans who first created them.'

'They're adorable. Do you import them?'

'No, but maybe I should – they're supposed to be lucky mascots,' Bill laughed. 'My company specialises in more practical things: tableware, dinner services and such like. I buy from a few of the outlets over the road; it's where some of the best manufacturers showcase their wares. See the old wall panels – beautiful, aren't they? Shall we take a look?'

'I've not seen anything quite like this,' Abi said.

Decorative designs of landscapes and seascapes covered the tiled façades of the lower parts of the tall, three-storey buildings that lined one side of the street. Above the shopfronts, the two upper floors were stark in comparison, simply decorated in white with elegant windows giving onto small balconies. A woman paced up and down on one jiggling a baby. Lines of washing were stretched over others.

'I was blown away the first time I came here – so much talent in one small town. There's a whole tradition of designs to choose from but always something innovative too.'

'Your job must be so interesting – you must tell me more about it.'

'This part of it is fascinating but there's a lot of tapping on my calculator, chewing my pen working out shipping costs and profit margins. If I told you any more about it, I'd end up boring you to tears.'

They become defensive or hazy when you ask for details of their jobs or their past. Abi shook her head to get rid of Marisa's voice. Abi knew Bill wasn't being secretive. He was just being thoughtful. Not every man was like Alex, talking about his boardroom triumphs.

'There's a pedestrian area up ahead. I thought we could find a nice spot for coffee and a pastry before we do anything else,' Bill said.

'Great idea, but hang on a mo, I think there's some guy waving at you from one of those balconies.'

Bill turned his head. He raised his hand in greeting.

'*Ciao*, Bill! *Aspetta*! Wait, I am coming!' the man shouted down. He stepped back from the open window and disappeared inside.

'I'm afraid we're going to get waylaid,' Bill said. 'That was Mario, he runs *Ceramiche Ravellini*. Lovely fellow but he can talk the hind leg off a donkey.'

'Even a ceramic one?' Abi giggled.

'I wouldn't put it past him. Come on, let's go in.' Bill led her through the doorway of the shop below the balcony on which Mario had appeared. The interior was bright, lit by dozens of hand-painted lamps and every wall and most of the floor space was crammed with richly decorated benches, sundials and giant pots. Although modest in width, the space stretched back far further than she would have imagined.

'It's like an Aladdin's cave!' Abi gasped.

Bill tapped the top of a four-foot urn decorated with gold scrolls and fat bunches of cobalt-blue grapes. 'Very popular over here, but somehow they don't seem to look right back in England. I did try importing a few garden ornaments back in the day but I soon realised I should stick to something I know.'

'Plates and bowls,' Abi said.

'Exactly. And soup tureens and platters. Ah, here's Mario.'

A short black-haired man in a striped shirt emerged from the back of the shop, arms held aloft. 'Bill! What a surprise. I did not expect to see you back in town.'

'I hadn't planned to return . . .'

'But you could not stay away.' Mario slapped Bill on the back before pulling him into an embrace.

Bill broke away. 'This is Abi.'

'Abi?' Mario raised an eyebrow and chuckled. He leant towards Abi and kissed her on both cheeks, his beard brushing roughly against her skin. He took both of her hands in his. 'Abi, *piacere*. Pleased to meet you.'

'And you.'

'This is Abi's first time in Vietri sul Mare.'

'I'd never been to Italy before this week.'

Mario threw up his hands in mock horror. 'But now you are here. And you have learnt to drink the proper coffee, *si*? We shall have some, shall we not? I think it is a little early for limoncello.'

'Coffee sounds good,' Bill said.

'Come this way, we will sit at the back of the shop, I do not want to distract my customers with the delicious aroma! We are very busy this time of year, you can see, though with tourists rather than professional buyers like yourselves.'

'I'm in Italy on holiday,' Abi explained as Mario unfolded a spare metal chair that had been leaning against the wall. He called to a young lad who was busy applying sticky tape to a cardboard box. 'Three coffees please, Filippo.'

'How's it going?' Bill asked.

'*Bene*, good. Busy.' Mario sat down. He moved a stack of unpainted spoon rests aside to clear a space on a low table.

'Busy is good,' Bill said. 'And Adelina, how is she?'

'Very well. Knitting for our new grandchild. Did I tell you Elena had another girl?'

Bill was right. If someone organised a world-wide talking marathon, Mario could enter for Italy. But far from being bored, Abi felt a strange, warm feeling of contentment as she perched on the not terribly comfortable chair sipping her bitter espresso and crunching into a *sfogliatella* pastry, stuffed with ricotta and candied peel still warm from the oven.

Mario elaborated on the health and well-being of his extensive family for quite some time. Bill caught her eye and smiled. His relaxed demeanour told her that he was happy to give her this insight into his working life and the people he dealt with. She couldn't imagine why she had let Marisa's silly comments bother her. Bill had nothing to hide.

Eventually Mario drew breath long enough to drink his coffee. He wiped the *sfogliatella* crumbs from his beard. 'And now we come to business. I was not expecting you, so I do not have much to show you yet. We have only created one of the samples for the colours you had in mind for our new Falling Leaves design. Filippo! You have the new plate to show Bill?'

'The leaves?'

'*Si, si*, the leaves, of course. Just put it on the table for me – and be careful with it.' Mario gave a little tut and shook his head. The boy placed a small side plate on the low table with trembling hands. 'Okay, Filippo, you can carry on with the packaging,' Mario said. 'These young people,' he murmured.

Mario held the plate towards them. It was heavily patterned in shades of teal, rust and strawberry. The leaves were executed with such realism that Abi could make out every vein. They seemed to be twisting and turning as though they were blowing across the white background, which was dotted with buds and berries.

Bill gave a low whistle. He turned to Abi. 'You like this?'

'Very much. It looks as if the leaves are moving.'

'All hand-painted by Mario's artisans. This design is very busy so we are using it only for the serving platters and some of the smaller pieces like this. The main dinner plates will be left mainly white with a decorative border.'

'But we will make it look as though a few leaves have fallen onto the plates.' Mario smiled. 'We still need to trial some different colours, especially for this thin line we paint around the rim.'

'Mario has suggested the darker teal, but I am wondering if we should choose something more playful like the brighter strawberry pink,' Bill said. He turned to Mario. 'Abi's good with colours, she's got an artistic streak.'

Abi fiddled with her empty coffee cup. 'Oh, I really don't know.'

'Tell me what you think. There is no right answer but it is always interesting to have another opinion,' Mario said. He took her coffee cup and handed it to Filippo along with his.

All eyes were on her. 'Perhaps this custard yellow.' She pointed to one of the berries.

'The last colour I would have picked out,' Mario said. 'But I do believe that could be interesting. We'll trial that one as well as the teal and the strawberry pink.'

'If you think it might work . . .' Abi mumbled.

'Sometimes the unusual choice is the right one. You must work in the arts, Abi. What is it that you do?'

Abi shifted on the metal chair. 'I, er, don't really do anything. I mean I'm, um, a full-time mum.'

'Then you have my admiration – you do the most important job of all.'

Abi stiffened but there wasn't a hint of sarcasm in Mario's voice. He looked at her with his kind brown eyes. 'I look forward to seeing what you will do when your children are no longer small.'

'How long have you had this shop?' Abi quickly changed the subject. She didn't want to admit that Chloe was practically a teenager. And she definitely didn't want to think about how intimidated she was at the thought of one day going back to work and struggling with a computer all day. Fortunately, Mario didn't need any further encouragement to talk about the four generations of the Ravellini family who had owned the business before him.

After another half an hour of chit-chat, Bill managed to wind up the conversation. He rose and folded up his chair. 'Good to see you again, Mario. I'm so looking forward to the new designs.'

'This range – I think it will be one to be proud of,' Mario said. 'I wish you a good day and I am so happy to meet you, Abi. I hope the rest of your day is pleasure, not work.'

'This has been both,' Abi said. '*Grazie mille! Alla prossima volta!*'

'*Complimenti*! To the next time indeed! I think you know more Italian than our friend Bill has learnt in all these years.' He slapped Bill on the shoulder.

'Thanks again, Mario,' Bill said. 'Oh, just one more thing.' He took his wallet from his back pocket and handed Mario the business card he'd shown Abi by the pool.

Mario turned the card over in his hand and frowned. 'What is this? The design is most unusual. I must know

207

every factory and shop in town but this this firm, Nuova Ondata – no. Where did you get this card?'

'I found it quite by accident. Someone had been using it as a bookmark! I wondered if you knew of them.'

'No, I am afraid not, but you know we could create something like this dish if you like.'

'I have no doubt you could. You will always be my most important supplier but I was curious to find out what Nuova Ondata do.'

'And now I am too,' Mario said. He studied the card. 'Via Diego Taiani, but no number and no website. I have walked down that street a thousand times. I am certain there is nothing of the kind there. Let me know if you find them.' He handed the card back to Bill.

Bill slipped it back into his wallet. 'I will do. *Ciao*, Mario, thanks again.'

Bill waited until he and Abi were a little way down the road before speaking. 'I'm sorry if that went on a bit long. I hadn't planned to drag you into a meeting with Mario.'

'We couldn't very well just walk by once he'd spotted us,' Abi said. 'And anyhow, it was interesting to find out more about your work.'

'Perhaps in small doses. I promise not to bore you with the details. By the way, that blue dress is lovely, it brings out the colour of your eyes.'

'Um, thanks.' The thought of Bill looking into her eyes made her feel quite light-headed. She cast around for something neutral to say. 'I do like this town. Which way do we go next? It looks like the road forks.'

Bill stopped by a striped ceramic urn bursting with frothy pink gaura and looked at his watch. It had a plain dark brown strap and simple Roman numerals, so different from Alex's flash Rolex.

'It's nearly lunchtime. I was going to suggest we take that pedestrianised road to the left; there's a restaurant on a rather nice tree-lined piazza where I thought we might have lunch, but after Mario's pastries I'm not really hungry right now. Are you?'

'I'd rather wait a while. I'm quite full to be honest and it's a waste to have lunch in Italy if you're not really hungry.'

'My thoughts exactly. We'll eat later and maybe now I could show you around the older parts of the town. I can't guarantee we won't get lost. It's a bit of a maze but I'm sure you'll find it interesting.'

'I'd love that. But what about finding the ceramics place?'

'Nuova Ondata? I thought we'd look for them later on, then even if we fail to find them we'll still have had a good day.'

Abi moved a little closer to Bill to let a woman walking a pair of dogs pass them. 'I'm already having a good day. I love what I've seen so far. I'm so glad you brought me.'

'I'm glad too.' He paused, blue eyes roaming over her face. 'Meeting you has made such a difference to my stay on Procida. I've had a great time with you, and with Chloe. I like you a lot, Abi. You're, um, different.' He dipped his head slightly; she caught the citrus scent of his aftershave mingling with his sun-warmed skin. He reached out and gently touched her cheek. Her heart was pounding. She swallowed hard and licked her dry lips.

'*Permesso!*' a man shouted. 'Excuse me!'

Abi turned. A short red-faced man in a baggy orange T-shirt was puffing over a trolley laden with cardboard cartons balanced precariously half on and half off the pavement. Reluctantly, she stepped aside.

'Let's go before we get in anyone else's way,' Bill said. He put his hand under Abi's elbow to guide her around the man's load.

'Sure.' Abi was keen to explore the town. And she was even keener to uncover Bill's feelings for her. Had he really been about to kiss her here in the street? *Different*, he'd said. Not *beautiful, sexy, funny* or *kind*. Was *different* a good thing?

'This way, I think. And then perhaps up to the church of San Giovanni Battista.'

She followed Bill along a narrow street, leaving behind the large ceramic outlets, the chattering tourists laden down by their unwisely heavy purchases and the buzz of mopeds and tooting of cars heading down to the coast road. They wandered up steep staircases where washing hung overhead and the hum of conversation and clatter of cutlery came from behind closed doors; ducked under arches where mopeds and small cars were parked and found shady corners where the odd cat lounged amongst terracotta planters brimming with flowers.

Around every corner, more painted ceramics awaited them: decorated door jambs and staircases; single tiles above doorways, larger designs forming murals spread over dozens of tiles on walls and down passageways. The Vietri artists employed every colour imaginable and every type of subject. One minute Abi was admiring a stylised vase of flowers, the next a soft-faced Madonna and child or a monk poring over his holy books. Whichever way she turned, there was something new to see.

Every so often they got a little lost, doubling back on themselves, but they could hear the distinctive chimes of San Giovanni Battista. Bill stopped near the church and refilled their water bottles at a tiled fountain painted with a chubby character munching on slices of green and pink melon. Abi adjusted Loretta's scarf and they took a quick peek into the church.

'There's something unusual I could show you next, the site of the Wheel of Foundlings,' Bill said. 'It's an interesting bit of history. A desperate poor or unmarried mother could anonymously deposit her baby there, turn the wheel and it worked like a revolving door, leaving the child in the church's care. I thought these dated from the Middle Ages but I believe the one here is more recent.'

Abi glanced at a laughing family taking up half the width of the street. 'Imagine leaving the house with your baby concealed beneath your clothing knowing you were going to give it away and you'd never see him or her again.' She shivered. 'How horrible, I can't bear to think of it. Losing Chloe still scares me now, her going off with Alex and Marisa and not needing me.'

'She'll always need you.' Bill hugged her close. She snuggled into his shoulder breathing in his comforting smell. How safe he made her feel. 'We won't bother with the wheel. Shall we go and find that place I mentioned for lunch? I haven't ruined your appetite, I hope.'

'Unfortunately not, it takes an awful lot to do that.' Abi tweaked the flesh at her waist. 'I should really start eating more healthily and tone up a bit.'

'Don't put yourself down – you've got a great figure, Abi. Come on, let's go.'

Abi followed him down the street with a spring in her step. Today's outing promised to be special. *A great figure*, he'd said. Two compliments today, an almost-kiss and they hadn't even had lunch!

'We'll head to the far end of Corso Umberto, there's a nice place there,' Bill said. He slipped his arm through hers. Her heart gave a little skip.

Corso Umberto was busy with crowds of tourists delighting in the shopping opportunities afforded by the lively thoroughfare. Brightly coloured jugs and plates hung from exterior walls and trays of goods were piled up by doorways. The shops were interspersed by restaurants and cafés with outside seating shaded by elegant cream awnings. Enticing aromas of garlic and herbs drifted over, sharpening her appetite despite Mario's pastries.

As she paused to admire yet another decorative mural, Abi's eyes were drawn to a half-opened door decorated with a curly metal lattice. Beyond it lay a wide passageway where an old red Fiat 500 was parked on an intricate mosaic floor. An iron lantern hung from the arched ceiling and beyond that the passage widened into a courtyard where a tiered stone fountain made an elegant centre piece.

'Oh, that looks interesting, shall we take a walk down there?' Abi said.

'There's not much to see.' Bill didn't even turn to look where Abi was pointing.

'But the fountain looks so pretty and those tiles on the wall behind – aren't they leaping horses?'

'There are much nicer murals further down the street,' Bill said.

'Couldn't we . . .' she began, but the expression on his face deterred her. His easy smile was gone, his troubled eyes focused on some distant point.

They walked on. All around them people were laughing and chatting. A toddler threw himself on the pavement ahead of them kicking his legs in a huge tantrum. Abi couldn't help catching Bill's eye. They both started laughing; Bill was back to his old smiley self. They continued up the road, past a shop window full of the town's lucky donkeys arrayed in several different sizes and colours though most were glazed in the traditional bluish green.

'You can tell they're hand-painted from the way they all have slightly different expressions,' Bill said.

'I can't believe they can sell so many.'

'You can't have too much good luck, I guess. Look, there's the trattoria I was thinking of, but I'd like to show you something first. That's if you don't mind.'

Abi rubbed the back of her leg. 'Does it involve steps?'

'Luckily not, flat as a pancake. In fact, we're right here.'

The end of the street had widened into a pleasant piazza paved in simple grey slabs. Leafy pollarded trees on three sides of the square created a shady canopy for the benches below where people were resting, escaping the afternoon sun. Bill led Abi behind the row of trees.

'I just wanted to show you the view, it's probably my favourite spot in the whole town.'

She leant against the waist-high railings. The sun was sparkling on the blue sea below. For a moment she thought he might kiss her. Despite her fears of getting involved with another man, she couldn't help feeling she'd rather like it. She could feel her resolve slipping away.

'It's just beautiful, I'm having such a good day,' Abi said. She smiled up at him encouragingly.

'Lunch?' he said.

'Sure.' She did her best to hide her disappointment.

Bill quickened his pace as they approached the trattoria. He pulled out a chair for Abi at the last remaining outdoor table. 'Good timing! Shall we have wine? The food's so good here it deserves a proper accompaniment.'

'Please,' Abi said.

Bill opened the leather-bound folder lying on the table.

'What do you think? Something white? Shall we get a bottle or are you happy with a glass as it's lunchtime?'

'Just a glass for me,' Abi said. It was nice to savour a glass of wine but she didn't want to get all giggly.

'What do you fancy to eat? Their pasta with aubergine and swordfish is particularly fine.'

'If that's what they're eating over there, I definitely want to try it.' Abi's mouth watered at the aroma coming from the next-door-but-one table.

'We could share some fried anchovies to start with.'

'Now you're talking.' Abi unwound Loretta's scarf and slipped it over the back of her chair. She let Bill do the ordering. Even though she caught a raised eyebrow from the waiter at Bill's pronunciation, she couldn't help admiring his stumbling attempts at the language and his calm, quiet manner, so different from the way Alex spoke loudly in English to the waiters in Spain.

The man cleared their menus away and returned with their wine. Bill waited for the man to leave. He picked up his drink.

'*Cin cin!*' Their hands brushed as he gently knocked his glass against hers. Abi had never considered her knuckles to be an erogenous zone. Until now. She took a sip of the wine, hoping the cold liquid would help cool her rapidly rising temperature.

Bill slowly brought his glass to his lips. The tip of his tongue caught a rogue drop of wine glistening on his upper lip. Her hand tightened around the bulb of her wine glass. She swallowed hard.

'Try one,' Bill said.

She hadn't even noticed the waiter place their starter on the table.

'Thank you.' Her teeth sank into a warm, crispy anchovy.

'Like it?' Bill asked.

Her joyous laugh caught her by surprise.

The pasta was even better than the appetiser. Neither of them spoke much whilst they were devouring it. Abi put down her fork. There wasn't a morsel left on her plate.

'They do amazing ice-cream sundaes,' Bill said.

Abi's hand automatically crept to her stomach. 'I couldn't.'

'Maybe you could fit one in later on. Let's try to find our mystery ceramic folk first,' Bill said. He reached into his trouser pocket, pulled out a roll of notes and plucked off some euros. Abi reached for her purse. Bill put out a restraining hand. 'No, I invited you today. This is my treat.' He handed the money to a hovering waiter and told him to keep the change. *They pay for everything with cash and shower you with compliments.* She wished she could forget about Marisa and her stupid comments. Why were they sneaking back into her head on such a perfect day?

Abi pushed back her chair. 'Thanks, Bill. That's very kind of you.'

'My pleasure.' Bill picked up Loretta's scarf from the back of Abi's chair. 'Better not forget this.'

'Thank you.' She draped it over her shoulders. 'Do you think we'll find this ceramics place?'

'To be honest, I'm not that confident. I've walked down via Diego Taiani before and all I remember is a barber, a fishmonger and a greengrocer. And if Mario has never heard of them . . .' Bill shrugged.

'It's worth a try though,' Abi said. She increased her pace to match Bill's longer stride.

They'd lingered so long at lunch that the shops were beginning to reopen after the afternoon siesta, though the road was still quite quiet compared to the throngs of people they'd encountered earlier. Outside the fruit shop, huge sun-ripened cantaloupe melons piled high in wooden crates gave off their distinctive scent. A stooped elderly lady with black hair scraped up in a bun was giving some apricots a good squeeze whilst her younger companion was picking through the cherries to select the most appealing punnet. Abi bent down. Why was it that even tomatoes smelt so much better in Italy than they ever did back home?

They walked up along one side of the street and then the other, checking every building and doorway but there was no sign of Ceramica Nuova Ondata. And brandishing their business card produced nothing but blank faces.

'Seems we've come on a wild goose chase.' Bill turned the card over in his hand before tutting and slipping it back into his wallet. 'I know Mario said he could create these sorts of designs but I would love to meet the people behind this. I guess it will just have to remain a mystery. I've dragged you away from Procida for nothing.'

Abi looked at his crestfallen face. 'I've loved visiting a new place; it's just a shame for you that you've had a wasted day.'

He rested his hand briefly on her shoulder. 'I don't think a day with you could ever be wasted . . . Shall we get that *gelato*?'

She followed him back up the road to an attractive little café. Funnily, she felt she could just about squeeze in an ice-cream after all. She picked out a strawberry and mango sundae straight away and left Bill pondering the menu whilst she slipped inside to use the bathroom.

'What did you choose in the end?' she asked, sitting back down.

'I didn't. I just ordered an ice-cream for you and our two coffees.'

'Oh, I'm going to feel terrible eating one by myself. You're going to have to taste a bit.'

The waiter had anticipated Abi's suggestion, bringing two long-handled spoons along with the two espresso cups and her dish of ice-cream. Bill reached across the round marble tabletop and tried a little.

'Mmm, delicious . . . thanks.'

'Has that made you change your mind?' Abi asked. She couldn't help feeling a bit awkward eating her way through a giant sundae whilst Bill toyed with his espresso.

'No, I'm fine with this.' He tapped the handle of his cup. 'You're happy with yours, aren't you? I've just got to run a quick errand. I won't be long.'

By the time Abi had swallowed her large mouthful of mango sorbet, Bill was already on his feet. 'Don't worry, I'm not doing a runner. I've already paid,' he quipped.

Abi stared in disbelief at his disappearing back, his empty espresso cup the only sign that just moments ago they'd been sitting down together. It was obvious that he'd deliberately timed his departure to leave her sitting alone with her ice-cream. What was he playing at?

The minutes ticked by. The ice-cream was melting despite the café's striped awning, its shape gradually shifting from peaked mountain to spreading lake. Her appetite had vanished along with her companion, but she pushed her spoon around the glass bowl, forcing herself to eat some more; she hated waste. She sipped her coffee then swallowed another spoonful of the strawberry flavour. Her teeth sang in protest.

With every mouthful, her irritation increased. Bill had set off in the direction of the main ceramic outlets. Why would he need to do that when their route back to the railway station would take them in that direction later? She shovelled down more of the sundae, barely conscious of the sorbet's sharp fruitiness and the vanilla's luscious creaminess, Marisa's warnings now echoing in her head. Could Bill really be up to something dodgy? Might he even be going to the mosaic-floored passageway, the one he'd avoided going down that led to the pretty tiered fountain?

She gulped down the last spoonful of ice-cream too quickly. Little hazelnut sprinkles caught in her throat. She started coughing; her nostrils burnt. She reached into her bag for a tissue. There was a new message on her phone from Chloe.

Abi opened the message – there were three photographs attached. Chloe looked so happy in them, Abi felt the tension of the last ten minutes ebb away. Even the sight of her daughter in that too-grown-up pink bikini couldn't rile her. She used her fingers to expand the screen. Chloe had said she was going to the beach with Elsa, but this wasn't the volcanic sand of Chiaia Beach where the family usually went. It looked rather stony. She wondered where they had gone.

Abi typed her reply with one finger, the way that made Chloe sigh and roll her eyes. *Glad you're having a good day. Vietri sul Mare is beautiful.* She added a couple of photos, smiling to herself as she chose a snap of the quirky green donkey on its plinth – that was sure to elicit a reply.

She felt someone approaching from behind.

'Hi!' Bill looked relaxed and happy, like a guy who'd been for a pleasant stroll, not some dodgy cash-flashing businessman returning from goodness-knows-where. Why had she filled her head with Marisa's nonsense? In a minute Bill would tell her why he'd left so suddenly and where he'd been. She waited for him to explain.

'Sorry I took so long. You were okay, weren't you? Looks like you enjoyed that sundae.' He glanced at the empty bowl and laughed.

'It was delicious.' Abi gave him a tight smile.

'Okay to make a move?' Bill asked.

He chatted inconsequentially about the weather and the ceramics – yet more ceramics – as they walked down the very road he had just walked up.

'So where did you go?' she said at last.

'It's a secret — all will be revealed later.' Bill tapped his nose.

Abi's mood darkened. Why was he being so secretive? Why had she been so quick to trust a man after her experiences with Alex? Had Bill's business card for the non-existent Nuova Ondata ceramics company been a ruse to put her off the real reason he had come to Vietri sul Mare? But why then had he brought her along in the first place? None of it made any sense.

They drew level with the entrance to the mosaic-tiled passageway. The doors with the metal curlicued decoration were now closed.

'Was that where you went?' she asked.

'Where?' Bill's eyes were focused straight ahead.

'In there! Down that passageway, the one you didn't want me to see,' Abi snapped.

'What? Where that fountain is? Why would I want to go there? I told you there was nothing worth seeing.'

'Nothing for *me* to see,' Abi said. 'Nothing you *want* me to see.'

'What do you mean? Why are you acting so strangely?'

'Me?' Abi's voice rose. 'I'm not the one disappearing off, tricking someone by buying them an ice-cream so they wouldn't follow you.'

They stood in the middle of the street facing each other, Abi's muscles tensed like a boxer's.

Bill gave a little laugh. 'Tricking you? I was going to suggest we just have coffee after all, but your eyes lit up when you saw that list of sundaes. And when yours turned up and I saw how large it was I thought it would give me time to run a quick errand. I was only gone a few minutes.'

'At least ten,' Abi said.

Bill sighed as though she were the one causing the problem. 'I didn't expect you to be sitting there with an empty dish when I got back. I thought I'd only be gone five minutes.'

'So, what took you so long?' Abi said coldly.

'What's going on, Abi? Why are you quizzing me like this?'

Abi raised her chin and looked him straight in the eye. 'Maybe I'm right to be suspicious.'

Bill put one hand on his hip. 'Suspicious about what?'

'Your work: product delivery, packaging and all the other stuff you don't want to talk about,' Abi said.

Bill's face darkened. 'You're suspicious because I don't want to talk about *product delivery*! What the heck, Abi!'

Abi felt a surge of anger. 'I'm not stupid, Bill. If you're doing something dodgy . . .'

'I import ceramics, Abi,' Bill said slowly. 'Mainly from Italy and most of those I source here in Vietri sul Mare. This morning you met my biggest supplier, Mario, and sat down with him in his own shop. What do you think I'm doing in Italy? Running the Procida branch of the Naples mafia?'

'I . . .' Abi began, but Bill was already striding on ahead, his back stiff and upright. 'Bill, wait!' she called.

Bill slowed down and allowed her to catch up. She glanced sideways at his tense jaw. Her accusations did sound silly when she spelt them out. Marisa's stupid suspicions were probably unfounded, but if Bill had told her where he was going, they wouldn't have argued. It was all his fault.

They walked side by side, Bill made the odd remark, but the air between them was thick with tension. The lift up to the railway station seemed to take an eternity and its jolly fish-patterned tiles did nothing to lighten her mood. In the train carriage she took the seat next to him; it was easier than having to look directly at him on the stop-start route back to Pozzuoli. She stared at her phone. Chloe had replied. *Hope you're having fun too! Love you, Mum.* Abi felt a little tension ease from her shoulders. Her daughter was happy. Abi wished she could feel that nothing else mattered.

Bill squirmed in his seat. 'You might as well have this. There's nothing else I can do with it.' He took a small peppermint-green paper bag from his trouser pocket and put it on her lap. It was tied with a pink satin ribbon.

Abi stared at it, a sick feeling creeping over her.

'Go on,' Bill said.

She struggled with the ribbon, all fingers and thumbs. Inside the bag was a knobbly tissue-wrapped parcel. Small paper hearts spilt over her lap as she peeled back several layers of paper. 'Do you think they used enough wrapping,' she quipped.

Bill didn't smile. 'That's what took me so long. The woman in the shop was quite insistent on making it perfect.'

She knew what the gift was as soon as she glimpsed the first flash of bluey-green glaze. A *ciucciariello*, the lucky little donkey of Vietri sul Mare. She ran a finger over one of its smooth green ears.

'Thank you, he's adorable.'

'That's why I disappeared. I wanted to surprise you by giving it to you over dinner tonight. I wanted to do something nice.'

'I'm so sorry. I feel terrible. I don't know why I accused you of such stupid things.' Abi's voice was small.

'I also spent too long choosing the one with the nicest face,' Bill said flatly.

'Sorry,' Abi said again. It was all she could say.

The train journey seemed endless. At last they pulled into Pozzuoli.

'We'll have to walk quickly if we're going to catch that ferry,' Bill said.

Abi picked up her bag and reached for her scarf. 'Oh no! It's not here!'

'What?'

'Loretta's scarf.'

'It hasn't fallen on the floor, has it?' Bill started peering around.

'No, it's not here.' Abi threw a pointless final glance behind her as they stepped off the train. She knew exactly where she'd left it: at the café in Vietri sul Mare, on the back of her chair.

She struggled to keep up as they hurried to the jetty. Her bag was heavy on her shoulder as if the little donkey had doubled its weight. One of her toes was rubbing against the strap of her stupid, impractical silver sandals; it felt like there was a stone in her other shoe. What did it matter if they missed the ferry? The day couldn't get any worse.

They reached the dock just as the boat was loading. Abi slid into the seat next to Bill. He made a few remarks about the journey but their once easy conversation and banter was punctuated by long silences.

Abi's phone pinged: another smiling photograph of Chloe; she was obviously having a great time without her. Abi should never have come to Procida. Chloe didn't need her; she had Elsa, fun-dad Alex and perfect Marisa. And now Bill was angry with her. Abi was useless: she couldn't hold onto a man; she couldn't even hold onto a scarf. It had been so kind of Loretta to lend it to her and now she'd lost it. She felt tears pricking her eyes. She let them fall; it didn't matter what Bill thought. It was too late to worry about that.

She rummaged in her bag, pulled out a tissue and blew her nose loudly. Bill turned. His eyes softened when he saw her tears.

'Abi, what is it?'

'Everything,' Abi sniffed. 'I've lost Loretta's lovely scarf. Chloe's having a great time here without me. You're totally fed up with me.'

'Hey!' Bill put his hands up. 'I'm not fed up with you, you daft thing. I was angry though. I just don't get it – what happened back there?'

'It was Marisa,' Abi snivelled. She wiped her nose with the back of her hand.

Bill handed her a clean white handkerchief. 'Go on.'

'She said I was too trusting. She planted all these doubts in my head. I know it sounds stupid, but she made everything you did sound suspicious.'

'Like what, for heaven's sake?'

'Like when you didn't want to talk about your work, saying I wouldn't be interested.'

'You'd be the first woman who was,' he said wearily. 'If I don't talk about my work, it's because I don't want to bore you. *A boring, obsessed workaholic* – that's what Gemma called me. She hated me taking work calls out of hours and cut me off if I ever sought her advice, though she liked the things she could buy with the money I made. She said I didn't need to travel; I could hold all my meetings online. But you can't do it like that, Abi, not if you want to feel the quality of a bowl in your hand and understand the people and the processes.'

'You need to see those incredible saturated colours for real.'

'Exactly. Gemma just didn't get it or didn't want to. She started to make me feel like I had to choose between my family and the business. It seemed so ridiculous I couldn't believe she meant it. Until she left.'

Abi touched his arm. He flinched.

'My work cost me my wife and my two daughters. Is it any wonder I don't want to talk about production costs and shipping schedules with every woman I meet?'

'I'm sure your two girls know how much you love them.'

'Sure. From thousands of miles away.' He turned his head and stared out of the window. The blue of the sea was dulled by the thickened glass.

'I'm sorry,' Abi said quietly. 'I don't know why I listened to Marisa. It was crazy to doubt you.'

'You're right. You shouldn't have listened to her. *Friends* trust each other, Abi.' He took his phone from his pocket and started composing a message.

'We are still friends, aren't we?'

He sighed. 'Don't worry about Loretta's scarf. Mario will go to the café and see if they have it. He can send it to the hotel; I'll reimburse him next time I'm in Vietri.'

'Thanks, that's very kind.' Abi swallowed hard. Next time *he* was in Vietri – why had she ever imagined there would be a 'we'? She stared across the aisle; a young woman on the adjacent set of seats was resting her feet on a pink holdall. A baby sat on her lap, grasping her tangle of silver necklaces in his small brown fist. The woman's partner was leaning over both of them, playing peekaboo with his son. The baby gurgled, the woman laughed. Abi looked away.

At last, the ferry docked. Abi shuffled along behind the stream of disembarking passengers. An elbow knocked against hers; the wheel of a toddler's pull-along case bumped over her toes.

'I'm still full after that lunch,' Bill said. 'I think I'll just get a snack from the mini bar rather than eating out tonight.'

'Sure.' Abi bit down on her lip. 'Actually, I think I'll take a stroll around the port; I've been sitting down too long.'

'See you later then, have fun.' Bill turned and walked away. She stood by the water's edge watching him until he was out of sight. He didn't look back.

She walked slowly along the seafront amongst the holidaymakers arriving from Naples, the daytrippers returning to their hotels, the shoppers emerging from the minimart with carrier bags clanking with bottles and cans. Two drivers shouted at each other through open windows, a child grizzled. But the sounds couldn't block out the noise in Abi's head.

She walked towards the tolling bells of Santa Maria della Pietà, passing behind the church to the marina and on to the jetty where she, Bill and Chloe had boarded their round-island trip with Francesco. There was a gap where the *Dina D* had been moored. A man with his trouser legs rolled up was hosing down the wooden deck of his glossy white yacht. Where would he sail to next? The boat owners had a thousand potential adventures, sailing over the open sea. Abi's own life had never felt smaller.

She kept walking until she came to a café mounted on wooden stilts that stood at the entrance to La Lingua Beach. She ordered a lemon granita and sat at an empty table overlooking the gritty sand; the late afternoon sun dappled the surface of the sea. She sucked her tangy drink through a straw, elbows resting on the wooden table. Her tastebuds sang with the hit of sweet-sour lemon. If only the rest of her felt equally alive. She and Bill had been on the cusp of a relationship. And now it was over. But she couldn't regret meeting him

– he'd blasted away the last pieces of Alex that had been clinging to her heart. Abi now knew she couldn't go back to London and carry on her life as she'd done before. She loved Chloe so much but being her mum was no longer enough. She needed something else; she needed some*one* else. There was an empty space in her life that no amount of Sanjay's bargain wine boxes could fill.

She wished she had a book in her bag to make her look less conspicuous. Instead, she fished out a rather chewed biro. She plucked a paper napkin from the metal box on the table and began copying the image of a sailing yacht from a poster on the wall. Using long strokes, she shaded in the hull and added waves around the napkin's edge. On a whim she added a rudimentary octopus and a comical rubber duck just for fun.

A piercing shriek from the beach distracted her from her doodling. Below her, a slim, tanned teenage girl in a well-filled Day-Glo bikini was screaming with laughter. The girl was sitting on an orange beach towel squeezed up against a boy of about the same age, but she wasn't laughing at something the boy said, she was laughing at another girl bent double coughing and spluttering, holding a cigarette. Abi guessed the silly young thing had just tried her first puff. A third girl, a scrawny, knock-kneed little thing, was sitting next to the wannabee smoker, her arm draped over her shoulder to comfort her.

A second boy took the cigarette from the girl's hand. The girl stopped spluttering, but she was still looking down at the sand. Her bikini was sugar-pink, just like the one Marisa had bought Chloe and she was wearing a pink bucket hat like the one Abi had bought. The girl turned her head in the direction of the café. It *was* Chloe.

Abi threw down her biro, pushed her chair back, grabbed her bag and stormed down the wooden steps towards the beach. Her ankle turned on a stone. She swore. Wincing, she advanced on the little group.

'Chloe!' Abi bellowed.

'Mum!' Chloe gasped. Her hands went to her mouth.

'What are you doing? Where's Elsa? Who are these people?'

'Marisa took Elsa to the play park, and these are my friends, I told you about them.' Chloe's chin was raised but there was a tremble in her voice.

'You told me about two *girls*. And you said you were going to the beach with Elsa today.'

'I changed my mind, so what?' Chloe bit her lip.

'It's okay,' one of the boys said. Abi caught the sweet sideways glance her daughter gave the scruffy-looking kid. She felt the blood rise to her face; her stomach was knotted with anger.

'It's not okay! You were smoking! Smoking can kill you!' Abi knew her voice was rising. People were turning to look.

'Not if you only have one puff,' Chloe muttered.

'Don't you talk back at me!'

The girl with the stupendous figure giggled. The scruffy boy smirked. 'Don't worry,' he whispered. He touched Chloe's arm.

'And you, you can take your hands off my daughter!' Abi yelled. She knew she was losing it but right now she didn't care.

Chloe stood up and glared at Abi, eye to eye. 'You can't talk to my friends like that.'

'I can say what I like! I'm your mother! Say goodbye to these people and come with me.'

'I'm not going anywhere. You can't make me.'

'I've had enough!' Abi raged.

She reached for Chloe's arm. Chloe span away. Abi grabbed at Chloe's bikini strap. The thin strip of material pinged away. One side of the bikini top flopped open, revealing a soft curve of flesh, a pale imitation of its padded twin.

Chloe screamed. Abi froze. The buxom girl covered her face, whether in horror or to mask her giggles, Abi wasn't sure.

'Go away!' Chloe shrieked. The skinny girl was handing her a T-shirt.

'I'm sorry,' Abi said. Her voice was quieter now.

Chloe's head appeared through the top of the T-shirt. Tears were spilling from the corners of her eyes.

'Look what you've done. I hate you!'

Abi stepped forward. 'Chloe, love . . .'

'Don't speak to me! Go away! You've ruined my holiday. Stay away from me!'

'I came out here to see *you*,' Abi said.

Chloe put her hands on her hips. Her eyes narrowed. 'I don't want you here, Mum. Go back to your hotel and hang around with your new *boyfriend*.'

'I don't have a new boyfriend,' Abi said.

'Whatever.' Chloe sighed. 'Go and hang out with your new *friend*. I hate you, Mum! You're ruining my life!'

The buxom girl glared at Abi. The skinny one giggled nervously. Chloe turned away, she grabbed the two girls by the hands and ran off into the sea. Abi stumbled away up the beach, her vision blurred by tears. She crumpled onto a bench overlooking the rows of white yachts. How happy she'd been that day sailing on the *Dina D*. Now she'd wrecked everything. Alex, Bill, Chloe – one by one she'd destroyed all the relationships that mattered to her. She sat staring out to sea as the sky darkened.

Chapter Twenty-One

The Dutch couple were back from their trip to Capri.

'Did you have a lovely time?' Loretta asked.

'Fabulous,' the wife replied. She rested her red sunhat and handbag on the ledge of the reception desk whilst Loretta retrieved their room key.

'We snorkelled amongst the fishes. Sun's hot out there on that water though.' The husband lightly touched a sunburnt patch on his nose. 'We had lunch at the place you recommended then afterwards we just lay on the beach before we dragged ourselves back here.'

Loretta smiled politely and nodded.

'We took some marvellous pictures. Here, I'll show you,' the wife added. She pulled out her mobile phone. There was a photograph of a pug in a bow tie on the cover.

'Oh no, sweet pea, Loretta won't want to see our photos. She must have been to that old island a hundred times. Let's get to our room. I need a shower, I'm kind of hot and sweaty all over.'

Too much information, Loretta thought, but she was glad he'd spared her from looking through the photographs. It was hard to pretend to be interested when all she wanted to do was curl up in a corner and howl.

'See you later, Loretta!' The wife picked up her hat and followed her husband up the stairs.

Loretta smiled a professional smile. Her head felt as though she'd been banging it against the smooth white surface of the reception desk. She used the pads of her fingers to try and smooth out her scrunched-up forehead.

The keys in the cubby holes behind her were gradually claimed as more guests came and went. The Dutch couple reappeared in matching white jeans to take a wander down to the marina for a plate of squid stuffed with anchovies and came back happily sated. Now only three keys remained: Abi's, Bill's and Salvo's. This morning they would have been the three people Loretta was most looking forward to seeing. Now she slumped in her seat wishing she didn't have to face any of them. What a difference a few hours made.

Loretta was certain Abi and Bill's outing to Vietri sul Mare would be the catalyst for her two guests' friendship to evolve into something more. She imagined them tumbling back into the hotel after stopping off in the marina for a romantic dinner. Bill's shirt would be a little wrinkled but his face lit by a huge smile. Abi would be glowing with newfound happiness, a little pink in the face, her blonde hair tousled by a day at the seaside, albeit one with a visit to a ceramics outlet thrown in. She wanted to be happy for them but their contentment would make her own disappointment even harder to swallow.

She could have sworn Salvo's feelings were genuine. The connection between them had seemed so real, as if she could reach out and touch it. But she had been blind; he had played her for a fool. She dug her nails into the palms of her hands hoping the physical discomfort would trick her brain into ignoring the aching in her heart.

The door opened. She sat up straight on her stool, patted the combs in her hair and put on a bright smile. Bill's feet fell heavily on the tiled floor.

'*Buonasera*,' she said.

'*Buonasera*.' Bill looked as though he'd come from a tense meeting about cashflow and investments rather than a happy day out with a vivacious woman. The words 'where's Abi' died on Loretta's lips.

Bill jiggled his foot. 'My key, please.'

Loretta took the hint. She handed it to him without further pleasantries.

'*Grazie*,' Bill said. He walked wearily through the glass door to the garden. He didn't turn towards the pool bar for his customary evening drink but headed straight to his room.

Loretta waited a few moments before making a last check around the sun loungers and parasols. Someone had left a sunglasses case on the tiles under one of the folding tables; they would be searching for that tomorrow. She locked the shutters on the pool bar, went back to the reception area and waited.

How the time dragged on, each hour seemed to last an eternity. Although Bill had long since gone to his room, the sadness he had brought with him had failed to dissipate. Even the flamboyant display of bright pink roses on the corner of the reception desk looked miserable, though their heady scent perfumed the air as sweetly as ever.

Loretta changed the soft music piped through the sound system for something more upbeat. Her foot began to tap. Above the strains of '*Quando, quando, quando*' she could just make out voices on the steps leading up from the marina. Abi was back and she wasn't alone.

'Loretta, *buonasera*!' Salvo's voice boomed across the room. Although Abi was just as tall as Salvo, standing beside him she looked pale and small.

'Hi, Loretta,' Abi said. She looked around the room, avoiding Loretta's eyes.

'How was Vietri sul Mare?' Loretta asked. She knew Abi was unlikely to be in the mood for small talk but the longer Abi stayed by the reception desk, the less time Loretta would spend alone with Salvo.

'I liked the decorative tiles everywhere, but I'm really rather tired.' Abi yawned. 'May I have my key?'

'Of course.' Loretta reached into the cubby hole and took out Abi's room key. She was tempted to dump Salvo's on the desk beside it.

'Good night, Loretta, see you at breakfast,' Abi said. She trudged out towards her garden room, shoulders slumped.

Salvo leant against the reception desk. Loretta moved her chair a little further back but not far enough to evade the warm, gingery fragrance she would now always associate with him. A momentary flicker of surprise crossed his face.

'I bought you this,' he said. 'I noticed you have rather a collection of cacti by the door.'

Now she noticed the glazed pot he was holding, tied with a pink satin bow. It was a strawberry cactus. Her mother had had a near-identical one. It couldn't be a coincidence – he had remembered from all those years ago.

Salvo smiled at her. She felt her treacherous heart lurch. If Ada hadn't found the incriminating letter in his room, she would have been bowled over by his gift. And she would have sworn she saw love in his eyes.

'What is the matter? Don't you like it?' he said.

Loretta hesitated. No matter how much she despised his underhand tricks, Salvo was a guest at the Hotel Paradiso. She would maintain a façade of polite professionalism. She would cope with his betrayal. She had coped with worse before. And in a few days he would be gone.

She gathered herself together. 'Thank you, you are very kind. It will make a lovely addition to my collection; this mauve pot is very attractive too.'

'I hoped you might approve, though perhaps roses would have been more appropriate.' His soft brown eyes sought hers.

She dropped her gaze. 'No, I wouldn't say that. This is most appropriate.' She gently touched one of the cactus's spines. It looked vicious enough to pierce her heart.

'I remember how your mother loved these plants. It is nice that you continue the tradition here.'

Loretta turned the pot in her hands. She couldn't help admiring the gently curved shape and the quality of the glazing. 'The cacti help me feel that in some small way my parents are still with me. I feel their presence here. I am determined to remember all that they taught me. Every day their advice has helped me to make a success of the Hotel Paradiso. This place honours their memory. I shall never sell it.' She put the potted plant down on the desk with a thud.

Salvo started. 'Loretta, are you okay?'

'Very well, thank you.' She forced a smile. A muscle in her jaw twitched.

'I think I'd better have my key — I need to freshen up,' Salvo said. 'Those old friends of my parents were very hospitable, too hospitable perhaps if that is possible. They have an extensive family, each child married at least twice and yet all the exes are still friends.' He laughed. 'Our casual lunch was in reality a seven-course feast. Every time I rose to take my leave, some other neighbour or friend or ex-husband or wife dropped in. It's been a very long day. Perhaps for you too.'

She handed him his key without another word.

'Thank you.' He hesitated before turning away. The door to the upstairs bedrooms swung shut behind him. He was gone.

At last she could shut the hotel up for the night. Her limbs were heavy, her head still ached. She longed for her bed but she dreaded falling asleep. After all she'd discovered today, she couldn't imagine experiencing the blissful sleep she'd enjoyed since Salvo's arrival and in the absence of her happy dreams there would be a space in the dark for her old nightmares to return.

She picked up the cactus Salvo had given her, untied the satin bow and opened the front door. The outside light illuminated the eclectic mixture of potted cacti that surrounded the hotel's entrance and lined the edge of the first few stone steps leading towards the marina. She could smell the sea on the night air.

She crouched down, balancing awkwardly on her spindly high heels, wishing she'd thought to bring out a cushion to kneel on. Carefully, so as not to risk chipping or breaking her immaculate ruby nails, she dragged several of the pots around, shifting them into different positions until there was room to place the new cactus in a position that pleased her. She straightened up, rubbing her back. She was satisfied with her handiwork; the plant suited its new location. And when she stood behind the reception desk tomorrow, she wouldn't have to look at it.

Now she was ready to go to her bed. At least she would be able to rest her body ready for the next day, even if her mind was bound to whirr all night trying to make sense of the last few days. She pushed open the front door to the hotel. Someone was standing in the reception, leaning against the newel post at the foot of the stairs. Salvo.

Loretta let out a gasp.

'I'm sorry, I did not mean to startle you; I thought it better to wait here than to creep up on you whilst

239

you were outside. I could see you rearranging the plants from my bedroom window. Why don't we sit down and share a drink together? I don't want to be impertinent but I couldn't help noticing that when I returned to the hotel you seemed a little tense.'

Loretta took a breath. Salvo was a guest – had she not resolved to treat him like any other? 'I have already shut the pool bar but of course you are welcome to take a seat on one of the sofas here and have a nightcap. What would you like?'

'Whatever is to hand. *Foglioli* perhaps, if it is no trouble. You will join me, won't you?'

Loretta retrieved a half-open bottle of the lemon leaf liqueur from the small selection kept in one of the storage cupboards behind the reception desk. She took two crystal glasses from the shelf and placed them with the bottle on a bamboo-handled tray. She didn't want to have a drink with Salvo but the *foglioli* might help calm the nerves that were hopping around in her stomach like a colony of rabbits. She took a step across the lobby. The glasses rattled.

'Here, let me take that.' Salvo's hand brushed hers as he took the tray. He set it down on one of the glass-topped coffee tables. '*Prego.*' He gestured to the three-person button-backed couch.

Loretta sat in the adjacent armchair instead. It meant she had to look directly at Salvo but it was better than sitting side by side where she would feel the warmth of his body. She was already unsettled by the fluttering she'd felt when his hand touched hers.

Salvo raised his glass. 'To your good health and to the prosperity of the Hotel Paradiso.'

Loretta swallowed a large mouthful. She usually made it into a refreshing spritz but tonight it seemed appropriate to savour its bitter taste. The drink tickled her nose; warmth spread through her veins. 'To the Hotel Paradiso,' she said.

His eyes roamed over the upholstered couches, framed art-deco posters and the blue and pink Murano glass chandelier with its dozens of candle-shaped bulbs.

'You have performed miracles here,' he said.

'It's my life's work.' Loretta looked him straight in the eye. She could feel the tension in every muscle in her face.

'I can see that.' He leant towards her, cradling his tumbler in both hands. 'And the Blue Parrot has been mine, though of course as general manager I have only ever been an employee, never an owner. But lately I have come around to thinking that life must be about more than work, however joyful and all-encompassing that work has been. Don't you agree?'

Loretta squared her shoulders. 'I can't think what you mean.'

'A devotion to work such as ours leaves no room for relationships. A time comes when one begins to realise the sacrifices one has made.' He sighed and drained his glass.

Loretta couldn't avoid his gaze. His eyes were full of such genuine sadness; she had to force herself not to reach out and take his hand. She had to be strong and remember the real reason he was here sharing this nightcap, buttering her up with his soft words and fake friendship.

'You think this applies to me? You imagine perhaps that I might be planning to sell this hotel in order to have an easier life, one where I might have more time to pursue these personal matters.' She couldn't help a bitter little laugh escaping.

He frowned, picked up the dark bottle and topped up both their glasses. She didn't try to stop him; the alcohol was making her braver.

'I am interested in your dreams and plans, of course I am. Otherwise, why would I be sitting here?' His eyes were no longer sad. They communicated something quite different. Was it hope?

'So, you admit it,' Loretta said carefully. 'You admit that you are here to uncover information about me and my plans for the Hotel Paradiso.'

His head jerked backwards. 'Admit it? That is a rather strange choice of words. Is it not natural to be interested in an old friend?'

'A friend?' She raised her chin and regarded him steadily.

He tipped his glass, apparently examining the colour of his drink. He cleared his throat before he said: 'These last few days, I felt perhaps . . .' He didn't complete his sentence, instead he looked up at her as if searching for a sign that he should continue. She folded her arms across her chest, wishing her heart would stop hammering. She willed him to finish his drink and go. The silence grew.

Eventually he got to his feet. 'It is a beautiful night. I think I will take a last short walk along the marina. I think it will help me to sleep. I would like it very much if you would join me.'

She picked up the tray and held it in front of her. 'I'd rather not.'

'Of course, I understand. As you wish.' He walked towards the door.

Loretta stowed the bottle back in the cupboard and left the two empty glasses on the ledge for Ada to find in the morning. Habitually, she straightened the papers on her desk below the counter even though she'd tidied everything into neat piles earlier. The letter from Amadeo D'Acampo that Ada had found was amongst them. She itched to feed it into the shredder, but she knew she must keep it. The sheet of sky-blue paper would serve as a warning in case one day in the future she was tempted to unseal her heart.

She opened the front door, letting in the fresh night air. Somewhere below the hotel, Salvo was walking through the marina. She stood for a few moments looking up at the crescent moon. Gently, she closed the door but left it on the latch; she knew Salvo would have the sense to shut it firmly behind him. It was unprofessional not to wait behind the reception desk for his return, but she couldn't face him again tonight. Perhaps Salvo still thought her ignorant of his plans and would be surprised to find her gone. Perhaps he would work out the reason why. It didn't matter either way – as long as she stayed strong and didn't dwell on the hurt in his eyes.

Chapter Twenty-Two

Cherry's face appeared on Abi's phone screen half hidden amongst folds of white fabric. Her eyes were bleary, her cheeks marked by pillow creases.

'Sorry to call you so early, I know it's only seven,' Abi said.

The top part of Cherry's nightdress appeared from under a heap of bedding. She propped herself up against the headboard. 'Six. You're an hour ahead.'

'Oh!' Abi gasped. 'I'm such a terrible friend.'

'You've done worse.' Cherry gave a throaty laugh. 'But it's a good thing you've phoned. I couldn't make head nor tail of that message you left last night. I did try and call back later but it went straight to answerphone.'

'Yeah, sorry. I needed an early night,' Abi lied. She'd switched her phone off in case Bill called, though there was fat chance of that.

Cherry rubbed her eyes. 'So, what's going on? All I could make out was something about Chloe hating you – and you know that's not true.'

'She *does* hate me.' Abi felt tears well up. Again.

'No, no, no, she does not! Come on, what happened?'

Abi sniffed and snuffled through the story of her confrontation with Chloe. Cherry listened in silence adding just the odd 'uh huh' so Abi knew she was still listening.

'I wish I'd never come to Italy,' Abi sobbed. 'If I'd stayed in London, Chloe might have missed me. Now she's going to end up even closer to Marisa than if I'd stayed at home.'

'Sure, Chloe's mad at you right now. She's bound to be – you embarrassed her in front of her new friends. And when you're a soon-to-be teenage girl, that's the worst sin of all.'

'I shouldn't have said anything. I should have pretended I hadn't seen her with that cigarette, then none of this would have happened.'

'Are you *kidding* me? My mum caught me with a packet of fags once, said if she smelt so much as a whiff of smoke on me again, she'd tan my hide so I couldn't sit down for a month of Sundays.'

'I'd forgotten that,' Abi said. For a moment she was back there: the two of them sitting cross-legged in the park in their brown blazers, their school skirts hitched up round their thighs. Cherry had smoked like a pro; Abi had been too chicken to try.

'Remember when we met those boys and got drunk on that bottle of my uncle's rum? We were only thirteen.'

'I was so sick, put me off drinking for years. Oh, Cherry, I had to let Chloe know I was cross but I went over the top, didn't I? I can't imagine how I would have felt if my mum had come down when we were with those boys and dragged me away.'

'She would have saved us both a hell of a hangover,' Cherry laughed.

'Seriously, Cherry, I've messed up so badly.' Abi's voice caught. 'Chloe hates me now. I don't know what to do.'

'Chloe doesn't hate you – she just thinks she does. Send her a message to say you're sorry, then give her some space. She'll come around, I promise. Now you get yourself dressed and go eat some breakfast.'

'I will,' Abi lied. She took a sip of the peach juice from the minibar. It was thick and fragrant but it wasn't doing much to quell her hunger; she hadn't eaten since yesterday's ice-cream sundae but she couldn't face seeing Bill over breakfast.

'Bet it's nice weather you've got over there,' Cherry added.

Abi levered herself off the bed. Cradling the phone under her chin she padded across the tiled floor and eased the curtain that covered the glass doors to the garden back an inch. 'Glorious,' she had to admit.

'You forget about Chloe and do something nice today because when I'm emptying bedpans, I want to think of you out in the sunshine with a big smile on your face. Get that nice Bill to take you out somewhere.'

'Oh, Cherry,' Abi said. 'We had a lovely time in Vietri sul Mare then everything went wrong.'

'Hold on a moment.' Cherry's face was replaced by a blurry image of her kitchen tiles. Abi could hear water gushing. 'Sounds like we both need a cup of tea; you got a kettle in that fancy room of yours?'

Tea in hand, huddled in her bathrobe, Abi poured out the sorry tale.

'What!' Cherry shrieked.

Abi held her phone a few inches further away from her ear. Cherry was turning the air blue, calling Marisa every name under the sun.

'But it's my fault I listened to her,' Abi said. 'It's my fault I doubted Bill because of what she said.'

'She's always been jealous of you.'

'What?' Some of Abi's tea sloshed onto the bedcover. She dabbed it with the belt of her dressing gown. 'Marisa – jealous of me? She's so beautiful, nearly seven years younger and she's so successful and smart; she even reads books in French.'

'Books in French?' Cherry snorted. 'Surprised she finds the time between preening and titivating herself.'

'She doesn't need to preen – she's naturally beautiful,' Abi sighed.

'Not what I see.' Cherry's tone brooked no arguments.

'And she took Alex.'

'Sure, Marisa's got Alex but you had him first. You were the first woman he fell in love with; Chloe's his first child. Alex has put a ring on her finger, but he's not married her yet, has he? I reckon he's got cold feet. Maybe he's still in love with you.'

'Well, I'm not in love with him. I wouldn't want him if he was the last man on earth.'

'Hallelujah!' Cherry high-fived the screen. 'I've waited years to hear you say that.'

'I can't believe it's taken me so long to realise how much better off I am without him.'

'Whatever's gone wrong this holiday, it's been one good trip if it's got that man out of your system. I reckon that Bill's got something to do with it.'

'It's too late. I've messed everything up. Oh, Cherry, how am I going to put it right? Bill's the best thing to happen to me in years.' She hadn't realised until she said it out loud.

'Bill's not a stroppy soon-to-be teen like Chloe. He's a grown man, you'll patch it up.'

'Maybe.'

'I tell you what I'd do if I were you.'

'What?'

'Go and see that Marisa. Tell her to keep her nose out of your business and ask her what the hell she was playing at.'

'Okay,' Abi said, though she knew she would never have the nerve. 'Thanks, Cherry, I don't know what I'd do without you.'

The call ended but Abi didn't put down the phone. She opened her airline app. Buying a last-minute flight wasn't going to be cheap but she no longer had any reason to stay on in Procida. There were seats on the afternoon flight from Naples. She typed in her credit card details.

Chapter Twenty-Three

A motorboat was moving across the bay trailing a white streak through the blue water. Abi stretched out her legs and leant back against the bench. She should have been on her way to the airport by now but she couldn't leave the island without saying goodbye to her daughter. Chloe still wasn't answering her calls and when she'd tried phoning the apartment, Flavia told her that the family had already left for the beach. It looked as though Abi was going to have to stay on the island for at least one more day.

From her vantage point in the belvedere, she could just see the smooth sands of Chiaia Beach. Chloe was down there somewhere, frolicking in the sea without a care, happier with Marisa than she ever was with Abi. Alex would be messing about, playing the fun-loving father. Did he scare Elsa by pretending to be a shark the same way he'd done when Chloe was little?

They had had fun, her and Alex, once upon a time. He could be a bit abrasive, a bit flashy and brash, but he wasn't a bad man and he was a good father. But they were too different to make it work – she could see that now. He and Marisa fitted together the way she and he had never done; it was no wonder they'd fallen in love so quickly. Alex had cried when he'd told Abi about his new love, begging her to understand. And now, although she couldn't forgive him for his adultery – or for walking out on Chloe – she was no longer bitter. Abi had been so young when she met Alex, tying herself up into knots trying to please him. He had never been right for her – coming to Procida had shown her that. And meeting Bill. With Bill everything was easy – *had* been easy – until she'd thrown it all away.

She reached into her bag to find something to distract her, but her phone wasn't there; she must have left it lying on the bed where she'd been lounging listlessly until Ada the maid knocked on the door. Abi sighed. Half-heartedly she took a stub of pencil from amongst the crumbs lying at the bottom of her bag and picked out a leaflet about a guided island tour she once thought she and Bill might take.

Searching for inspiration, she turned towards the yellow bulk of Santa Maria delle Grazie. She drew a curved line; the shape of the dome began to materialise on the back of the leaflet. Her drawing wasn't bad at all; perhaps her art teacher had been right when she'd accused Abi of squandering her talent. Lost in the moment, an hour passed, every inch of blank paper filled. Feeling surprisingly satisfied, she lowered her sunglasses and closed her eyes. Just for a moment.

The chimes of the church bells woke her; she blinked in the still-bright sun. A glance in her handbag mirror confirmed her face was as flamingo-pink and shiny as she feared. Her throat was parched; she hoped she hadn't been sleeping with her mouth open. Desperate for a drink, she headed for the nearby café.

She stopped for a moment to fumble in her bag, checking she hadn't forgotten her purse. Relieved to find it there, she looked up. A familiar figure was strolling up the road towards the piazza.

Marisa's eyes were shaded by outsized tortoiseshell-rimmed sunglasses; a woven straw bag with leather handles was hooked over one of her slender arms. Although she was coming from the direction of the beach, her white linen dress was uncreased and her long hair bounced as though she was auditioning for a shampoo advertisement. Abi ran a hand through hers; the ends felt crispy and dry.

Marisa drew level with the drinking fountain. Abi stepped out in front of her.

'Oh, hello, Abi. How are you?' A slight frown creased Marisa's otherwise line-free forehead.

'Where's Chloe?' Abi said. She wasn't in the mood for pleasantries.

'What do you mean?'

'Exactly what I said. Where's my daughter? Flavia said you were all at the beach. Together.'

'Chloe *is* at the beach, with Alex and Elsa.'

'And you couldn't be bothered to join them?'

Marisa took a step backwards. 'What do you mean? I've been with Alex and the girls all day.'

'Like you were yesterday? You're supposed to be

looking after Chloe, not leaving her running wild with a pack of random teenagers getting up to all sorts.'

'She's made friends with a couple of local girls. Isn't that a good thing?'

'They were hanging out with boys!'

'So what? There are boys at her school. You're too anxious, Abi. That's the problem with single parents.'

'And whose fault is that?' Abi snapped. 'Chloe was smoking, Marisa. She's twelve years old!'

Marisa gathered up her long hair and smoothed it over one shoulder. 'I don't want her smoking any more than you do, but so what if she had one puff of a cigarette? You're making too big a deal of it. All kids experiment and do stupid things.'

'When there's no one there to watch them.'

Marisa stiffened. 'Chloe's thirteen next month, not three. Now if you don't mind . . .' Marisa stepped to one side.

Abi put out her arm. 'I haven't finished yet.'

'Please let me pass, I've got things to do. And there's no point having a go at me. You could have spent yesterday with Chloe but you swanned off to Vietri sul Mare with that bloke from your hotel. How did it go by the way?'

'Fine.'

'Not well then? You're better off without that man. Don't say I didn't warn you.'

Abi had never hit anybody but she yearned to smack Marisa's smug face.

'Actually, our day was perfect until I let your poisonous bile spoil it. You did it deliberately, didn't you, planting doubts in my head.' Abi's voice rose. 'You're not content with wrecking my marriage, you had to sabotage my chances with Bill as well. What is it with you, Marisa? How many lives do you want to destroy?'

Marisa didn't speak. A tear trickled down from behind her sunglasses.

'I don't know what you're crying for! It's my life that's ruined, not yours.' Abi turned to walk away. She needed to sit down, needed that cup of tea. Or something stronger.

'Wait!' Marisa grabbed Abi's arm. 'I was trying to help you, trying to stop you making the same mistakes I made.'

Abi shook her off. 'What do you care?'

Marisa kept level with Abi's stride. 'I care about Chloe.'

'Hmph!' Abi snorted but she slowed her pace a little.

'She's Elsa's sister, and I love her too, whatever you may think. I couldn't bear it if anything happened to her.'

'What do you mean?' Abi said. She stopped walking. They stood facing each other at the top of the steps leading down to the Marina Corricella.

'Don't rush into anything, Abi. It might seem romantic to fall in love in Italy but you don't really know anything about this Bill. You don't know if he's who he says he is. Some men . . . once you're in their grip, it's hard to get free.'

'Look at me,' Abi said.

Marisa pushed her sunglasses up so that they nestled in her mane of glossy hair.

Abi fixed her gaze on Marisa, like a collector pinning a butterfly to a board. Marisa's dark eyes stared back, full of fear.

'Something happened to you, didn't it? Some man treated you very badly. I'm right, aren't I?'

'It was a long time ago,' Marisa mumbled.

'I think you're going to have to tell me.' And before she could stop herself, Abi said: 'I think we should go for a drink.'

'Okay,' Marisa said.

'I know a good place.' Abi strode down the steps. Marisa followed her, meek as a lamb.

Abi grabbed them a couple of seats at Bar Arturo. The waiter seemed to sense their urgency and the bottle of white wine and plate of *bruschette* that Abi ordered materialised almost immediately. Marisa ignored the food, intent on glugging back her wine. Abi munched her way through the crunchy garlic-rubbed bread, waiting for Marisa to speak.

Marisa took another huge gulp of wine. 'I know you hate me, Abi. I know what you think of me.'

'I don't hate you,' Abi said automatically, but she was surprised to find it was true. Cherry had used dozens of choice words to describe Marisa that morning, but now none of them seemed to fit this wide-eyed young woman who sat opposite Abi, trembling like a baby bird fallen from the nest.

'I was young and foolish,' Marisa said. Her voice was barely a whisper.

'I won't judge you, I promise.' Abi folded her arms and waited.

The couple at the next table paid their bill and left.

'What happened?' Abi prompted. 'Who hurt you, Marisa? Who was he?'

Marisa leant forward. 'My ex-husband . . . Ciro,' she said.

Chapter Twenty-Four

A little wren was hopping around the terrace, pecking at crumbs in the gaps between the paving slabs. Breakfast was over, just a smattering of cups needed to be cleared away. The other guests were long gone but Salvo remained, his face hidden behind *Il Mattino*. Loretta waited, willing him to get up and leave.

He laid down his newspaper but instead of getting up, he leant back in his seat and called her name. She crossed the terrace, her wedge-heeled sandals feeling as unsteady as her highest stilettos. It was early morning but her yellow blouse felt damp beneath her arms. He nodded to an empty chair.

'Please, do sit down. It seems I have some explaining to do.'

He ran a finger across his moustache. A speck of blood marked a scrap of tissue paper clinging to his neck. 'I hardly slept last night,' he said.

'Guilt, I expect.'

'Yes, I am sorry, so sorry to cause you such distress.' He turned a page of the newspaper over. Inside was a piece of sky-blue notepaper. 'When I realised you had found this letter – I caught sight of it as I took my key from behind the desk last night – your cool behaviour towards me suddenly made sense.'

'I would hardly welcome your betrayal with open arms,' Loretta said. Her voice was remarkably steady. 'You used our old friendship to your advantage, to make me feel that you and I were some kind of kindred spirits to gain an advantage for your plans. You wanted to discover my weaknesses and find a reason to persuade me to sell this hotel. I never would have thought you could be so underhand.'

'My dear Loretta . . .'

'I am not your dear Loretta.' She pushed back her chair.

'Please, do not go. Spare me just two minutes and I think you may understand.' His brown eyes beseeched her. 'Please.'

'Very well, but you will need to be brief – I have a hotel to run. And I will continue to run it long after you have left.'

Salvo spread his hands. 'Oh, Loretta, I understand your anger, but you have everything upside down. I was scared to reveal the true purpose behind my visit but not for the reasons you think. But now I will have to tell you, however hard that may be. I would rather risk you laughing in my face than to leave this place with you thinking ill of me.'

'Go on, I'm listening.' She sat straight and upright in her chair.

He cleared his throat. 'I have been thinking of retiring, as I told you before, but the thought of a life without work, a life without a hotel to run, has been too hard to contemplate. I decided to think about running a small place of my own, somewhere that accommodated a dozen or so guests rather than the two or three hundred we have at the Blue Parrot. But when I started to investigate such a possibility, I realised I had no idea where to begin. So, I mentioned my dilemma to an old friend, Amadeo.'

'The writer of the letters I have been receiving.'

'Exactly. Amadeo has bought and sold commercial property in the past and suggested that he might be able to assist me, as an old friend. He would source the details of a couple of dozen hotels and approach them on my behalf. Once he had gauged the likely interest from the owners, he would prepare a shortlist for my consideration and I might visit those that most appealed to me. I was intrigued by the idea of perhaps running a hotel on this island and disappointed when he reported that he had identified a potential hotel here but that the proprietors were not interested in opening discussions with us.

'Imagine my surprise when I realised the Hotel Paradiso was the place where my beloved niece spent her honeymoon. She'd made such a good report of your hotel I thought it worth carrying out my own investigation during my break from my duties.'

'So, you admit that is why you came.' Loretta struggled to keep her voice steady.

'Yes, at first that was the reason, but the day before I was due to leave, my niece rang to wish me a good trip and during that phone call she talked a little more about her visit here. It was then that she mentioned your name. I asked her a few discreet questions and realised it could be you, my dear friend from many years ago. Thoughts of buying the Hotel Paradiso were banished from my mind. It was now something else entirely that motivated me. My heart leapt at the thought of seeing you again, as thrilled as a schoolboy off to meet his footballing idol. How excited I was packing and preparing for the trip!'

'After forty years? I am surprised you remember me.'

'You never forget your first love,' he murmured.

'No, you can't be serious . . .' Loretta began. But the look in Salvo's warm brown eyes stopped her.

He linked his fingers together. 'You may laugh now, but how painful it was for me. I knew you were so in love with Giorgio. I had to witness the two of you together day after day. You and my best friend. The night he proposed to you was the hardest of my life. I tried to persuade myself I was glad to see how happy you were with him. I believed he deserved you and would treat you well. And then, the day before the Capri to Naples swim, I found out he was cheating on you with Adriana. I was so angry. I wanted to tell you, but I could not bear to be the one to bring you such devastating news, fearing you would hate me for it. And when you emerged from the sea that day, it was too late. You saw them for yourself.'

'You were so quick to comfort me. I was so glad you were there.'

'And I was glad to assist, even if it was just my friend-ship you needed that day. But with Giorgio out of your life, I was still unable to make my feelings known. I believed that a beautiful girl like you wouldn't look twice at me. Even so, when you left the island, my heart was broken. I cut off all contact with Giorgio. I could not bear to look at him. Perhaps if you and he had not been together, I might somehow have found the courage to ask you on a date but now it was too late. How could I compare with the lover you had lost? And so I threw myself into my career and the rest, as they say, is history.'

'I had no idea.' Loretta shook her head. But as she spoke, memories were gently taking shape.

'How could you know? When a star shines as bright as Giorgio's, it throws everything else into shadow.'

And made her blind to the kind, decent boy who had hoped to love her.

'But when I came to this hotel and saw you again, I realised how little my feelings had changed,' Salvo continued. 'I thought perhaps . . . oh, well . . . once a fool, always a fool.'

'You were a fool. But only a fool not to throw that letter from Signor D'Acampo away.'

'So, you believe me.' Salvo pulled out a white hand-kerchief and dabbed his eyes. 'Please excuse me for being so sentimental. But to know that you haven't lost your regard for me means the world to me.'

'I was too quick to judge.'

'On the contrary, you had all the evidence you needed right in front of you.' He picked up the blue notepaper.

'Shall you do it, or shall I?' Loretta asked.

'Be my guest.'

She tore the blue paper in two. Right down the middle.

'Tomorrow is my last night here. I would love to take you out for dinner for old times' sake. Perhaps we could go to I Due Gabbiani down in the marina. I have the impression your Ada would be happy to look after the hotel for the evening.'

'One of the many impressions you've gleaned.' Loretta raised her eyebrows.

'I was asking for that comment, I suppose.'

'Indeed you were,' she laughed. 'I would be delighted to have dinner with you tomorrow. And perhaps tonight we might have a drink together at the end of the day.'

'Like we did the night before last?'

'Picking up where we left off?' She flushed furiously as she spoke.

His face lit up. 'I shall count the hours. But now I must leave you to look after your guests and get on with your day.'

She picked up the remaining coffee cups and loaded them onto a tray. When she returned to reception, she opened the front door and surveyed the display of succulents. She rearranged a few of the pots to give Salvo's gift pride of place.

Chapter Twenty-Five

Tears ran down Marisa's cheeks. Abi waited. A white cat prowled by. It looked rather like the pictures of Bibi that Chloe had shown her, except this cat was plumper with a heart-shaped mark on its nose.

At last, Marisa spoke. 'I was only fifteen when I met Ciro, my ex-husband. Our family was living in Atrani back then, a little place near Amalfi. Ciro came from the fishing village of Cetara further along the coast. He was so handsome, loving, attentive – every young girl's dream. He charmed Mamma and Papa too at first. It was only my younger brother Nico who saw what we didn't want to. "How does he afford that fancy car he drives? The presents he gives you?" he asked. I told Nico he was jealous because he was a school kid and Ciro had a good job distributing ceramics to various retailers around the coast.

'It wasn't long before Ciro showed his possessive side, controlling what I wore, who I saw, where I went. Naïvely I believed it was because he loved me so much. My friends dropped away and Mamma was worried, but I was so determined to prove I was right I married him as soon as I was able. Mamma and Papa attended our tiny wedding but their faces were grim.

'Ciro bought us a beautiful top-floor apartment. He filled it with fancy furniture; money did not seem to matter to him. When I questioned him, he became defensive but I assured him I would love him no matter what. Eventually he confessed he was involved in a racket smuggling counterfeit watches and the like. They brought them in via the docks in Salerno and concealed them inside ceramic urns and figures from down the coast at Vietri sul Mare. I was horrified – this wasn't the life I wanted. I begged him to stop but he laughed in my face.

'Eventually I plucked up the courage to leave but that morning I was sick. I thought it was nerves; I couldn't go through with it that day. The next day I was sick again.'

'You were pregnant?'

Marisa was silent. Voices rose from some children skipping past the bar. A gull cawed from its perch on a heap of fishing tackle. Abi didn't mind waiting; she could do with a moment to process everything she was hearing.

'Yes, I was pregnant. A little boy, so it turned out.' Marisa's voice shook. 'I told Ciro, hoped the baby would provide the impetus for him to change his ways but he stepped up his activities, saying any son of his would live like a little prince. One night I overheard Ciro planning a bigger job. We had a massive row. I rushed out of the door, saying I was leaving him, I didn't want my child to have a criminal for a father. Ciro knocked me to the ground, kicking

263

and punching me. Oh, Abi, the blood . . . I'll never forget the blood.'

Instinctively, Abi reached across the table. Her hand closed around Marisa's.

'I lost my baby that night. When I left the hospital, Mamma and Papa were waiting for me. I never saw or heard from Ciro again until he filed for divorce, but I feared I'd see him around every corner. My parents could see what a state I was in; they sold our beauty salon at a loss so we could leave quickly and we moved to Procida and set up Sempre Bella to make a new start. Nico had to switch schools halfway through term and leave all his friends behind. He blamed me for the upheaval and our parents for standing by me. As soon as he could, he quit his studies and moved away to the north. We hardly hear from him anymore; it breaks my parents' hearts.

'I'd always planned to work in the beauty salon with Mamma, the way I had in the school holidays but all the upset left me yearning for a new start. I'd done well in my exams so I applied for a place to study law in England, but I felt so guilty leaving my parents after all they'd been through.'

'I'm sure they are proud of you. It's not so easy starting over.'

'I suppose so, but they've always hoped that I'd return to Italy.'

'I'd understand if you wanted to return. It's so beautiful here.' Abi lifted her eyes to the dome of Santa Maria delle Grazie.

'I know how Mamma and Papa suffer having both me and Nico living so far away. But I'll never move back; just being here for the summer has made me all jittery.'

Abi rested her chin on her hand. 'I'm so thankful. I've been so worried you and Alex and Elsa might move here for good, then Chloe would want to live with you and I'd lose her for ever.'

'Oh, Abi! How could you think that! I know how strong a mother's love is. I loved that first child I lost even though he wasn't yet born, and I couldn't bear to live without Elsa. I would never take your child away from you.'

'You took my husband.' Abi couldn't help saying it.

'I never planned for any of this to happen,' Marisa sniffed. 'Alex and I had only been together for a few weeks when I found out about you but by then I was already pregnant. I admit I didn't care about you, Abi; I didn't care about Chloe. I was blind to everything but the life growing inside me. It seemed like a miracle, that after losing Ciro's baby God had given me a second chance.'

'And Ciro, whatever happened to him?'

'He went from bad to worse; I heard he died of a drug overdose in prison. I'm free of him, Abi, but it's made me scared to get married again. I know it sounds silly but I didn't even want to get engaged. I told Alex I was a modern woman who wasn't interested in that sort of thing, but he proposed anyway. I couldn't turn him down; I thought he would doubt my commitment to him and I couldn't let my child's father walk away. I've always found an excuse to put off the wedding: waiting for Elsa to be born, waiting for the next promotion, waiting to finish moving house . . .'

'Surely Alex understands.'

'I never told him what happened. I was so ashamed. If I'd left Ciro straight away, my little boy would have lived.'

Abi put her hand on Marisa's arm. 'You can't live like this, hiding what happened for ever. For all his faults, Alex is a good man. He loves you, Marisa. He deserves to know the truth.'

'I know you're right. In a way it will be a relief. I'm glad I've told you, Abi, even though I know you hate me.'

'I can't hate you, Marisa.' Abi shook her head. 'Not anymore.'

Chapter Twenty-Six

'Coffee?' Loretta asked. She was already making Salvo's caffè macchiato. The aroma of the freshly ground beans smelt so good.

He laid his folded newspaper on one of the aluminium tables. 'Thank you. You look busy.'

'Most of the guests seem to have decided to stay by the pool this morning, so I'll be running back and forth with drinks.' She smiled.

'I don't blame them, it's a perfect day for it. I myself am planning nothing more taxing than reading the paper then perhaps taking a dip. If you get a few moments free perhaps you could join me.'

Loretta tensed. 'I told you I don't swim.'

'I didn't mean in the pool. I'd rather not have your eyes on me whilst I thrash around like some sort of ungainly penguin.' He laughed. 'I meant you might like to take a coffee or cool drink with me, take a few minutes to take the weight off your feet, have a chat, or of course just relax and not even speak.'

She put his coffee down in front of him. 'Thank you, I would love to join you a little later when all the guests are settled with their drinks.'

'For now, I shall content myself with last night's *Corriere della Sera*.' He spread out his paper.

Loretta moved around the pool, collecting orders and delivering drinks, adjusting parasols and dispensing advice on how best to see and enjoy the treasures of the island. Despite the heat of the morning, she felt fresh and energetic, her skyscraper green heels as comfortable as a pair of old plimsolls. Happy guests enjoying the Hotel Paradiso always gave her a boost, but knowing she would soon be drinking a coffee with Salvo was the reason for her ear-to-ear smile.

To sit with him, feeling his comforting presence, observing his oh-so-familiar gestures and seeing his warm brown eyes seek hers, she couldn't think of anything she'd rather do. She would be happy to sit in silence but she knew that inevitably they would talk. Neither of them wanted to waste an opportunity to find out more about the lives they'd led since she'd left Capri. She wanted to hear all his new plans and dreams, and she believed he felt the same – he always listened to her with such genuine attention. And she couldn't help imagining that their once solitary plans for the future might now include each other. They had so much in common, they fitted together so well, she could talk to him about anything. Anything but the day after the Capri to Naples swim. She wished she could shrug off the memory of her cowardice like a pair of ill-fitting shoes. But every time she thought she could move on, it surfaced like a piece of debris carried back by the tide.

Loretta cast a long glance around the pool area. The man who'd been exploring the island's churches was swimming up and down in a slow front crawl. Drinks were being sipped, pages of books being turned, the only sounds an Italian couple exclaiming over a game of cards and the splashing from the pool, where the Dutch husband had joined his wife on their hibiscus-print lilo, which sagged alarmingly. Loretta could safely take a break and spend it with Salvo.

She poured herself a glass of mineral water, too impatient to spend precious moments making a coffee, and approached his table. He laid his newspaper aside, ran a finger across his dark moustache and smiled. 'You have a few moments – I'm glad.'

'Yes, all the guests seem happy for now and Ada will keep an eye on reception though we are not expecting anyone new today.' She hopped up onto the stool; the table between them was small, he was so near she could catch the scent of his cologne. Today's linen shirt was light blue; how well it suited him compared to the bright colours he'd sported in his youth. His hair was still thick, cut neatly into the nape of his brown neck. He must have been just as handsome all those years ago, yet she hadn't noticed, dazzled by Giorgio's flashy looks. How lucky she was to be gifted this second chance.

She realised he was looking at her curiously, waiting for her to speak.

'I said, "you must remember him",' he said.

'I'm sorry, my mind drifted away for a moment.' Loretta smiled. 'Remember who?'

'Marco – I can't believe that little kid with the Pinocchio T-shirt is running for mayor.'

Loretta gripped the tabletop. Of course Salvo would talk about Marco. Why had she been so stupid to think that he wouldn't mention his name. Salvo knew what a coward she was – everyone did. How could she have kidded herself that he might be ignorant of that shameful night.

'You must remember him,' Salvo repeated. 'His mother worked in the *pasticceria*; they had that cheeky white dog.'

'Little Tino,' Loretta murmured.

'He was always getting up to mischief, wasn't he? I remember how he used to sneak into the *macellaria* to steal sausages and drove old Signor Manuelli crazy.'

'Such a sweet dog.' Loretta's voice cracked.

Salvo started. 'Loretta, what is it?'

She could not speak. There was nothing she could say to make things right. Yet she so desperately wanted Salvo to say he understood what had happened to her that night, to hear that he didn't despise her. His opinion meant so much to her.

'Loretta.' Salvo spoke, louder this time.

Voices drifted over from the sun loungers; a splash as someone jumped into the pool.

'I'm so sorry . . . I've never forgiven myself. Marco could have drowned that night. I have asked myself "why" so many times but I still don't know why I didn't try and save him.'

'What do you mean?' Salvo frowned. 'How could you have helped? It was the day after the Capri to

Naples swim. You were at home, exhausted, I know you were. I called on you to see . . . to check if you were okay, after Giorgio and . . . well, your mother said you were not to be disturbed, that you weren't seeing anybody, that you hadn't the energy that day.'

'I did spend all day in bed but later I sneaked out for a walk alone. It was dark and late and the wind was whipping up a squall but I went down to the beach confident I would not meet anyone. Maria and Marco were there, Tino their little dog was struggling in the water and I know I could have saved him. For me it should have been easy but I just stood there frozen whilst Marco screamed. I wanted to run into the sea but my feet wouldn't move. Instead, it was Marco. He broke away from Maria and dived into the water. Maria was helpless, I knew she could not swim. She was begging Marco to turn back, but even if he had heard her, he wouldn't have taken any notice, he loved that little dog so much.

'Maria turned around, she saw me, Salvo; she saw that I, *il delfino*, the girl who could swim all the way to Naples, was standing on the shore, doing nothing, letting their little dog drown and her son risk his life. And then Marco began flailing his arms shouting for help. He wasn't a bad swimmer, but he was only eight years old, he didn't have the strength. Again, I tried to move but it was as though I were sinking in quicksand. It was a miracle that Lorenzo, the petrol pump attendant, appeared. He dived into the water and pulled Marco to safety. But it should have been me. I should have done it. I knew then that I couldn't stay on Capri. Maybe I could have coped with people pitying me for losing Giorgio, but people despising me for my cowardice – I couldn't bear it.'

'But Maria said there was no one on the beach that night except her and Marco. Lorenzo and the headmaster's daughter were having a late evening stroll when they heard screams coming from the shoreline, or so they said. Perhaps Maria did turn in your direction, but she couldn't have seen you there in the darkness. I'm sure if she had, she would have called your name.'

'I suppose you're right, but I was there. And I know Lorenzo and Barbara must have seen me.'

'Lorenzo didn't mention seeing anyone else, though perhaps he kept quiet, not wanting his old headmaster to ask too many questions about what he might have been doing with his only daughter down on the sand. No one ever knew you were there, Loretta.'

'But *I* know. And I have to live with the guilt and shame, not knowing why I acted as I did.'

Salvo's soulful eyes looked at her with such genuine concern it took all her strength not to cry. He took her hand in his, it was warm and strong. 'My dear Loretta, do you not realise there is no need to feel guilt. Barbara's father was so impressed by Lorenzo's heroism, he cast aside all his misgivings about his lack of prospects and welcomed him into the family. He and Barbara were married by the turn of the year, and only a few weeks ago they visited the restaurant at the Blue Parrot to celebrate the birth of their fourth grandchild.'

'I am glad to hear that; I remember how those two had to sneak around behind her papa's back. But what about little Tino and please do not say "he was just a dog". Tino was part of their family; I remember how Maria bought him to distract the children from their grief after their beloved nonna died. They loved that little pet and I could have saved him. It was unforgivable.'

'I would never say "he was just a dog"; I remember how devastated I was when the old cat who lived at the Blue Parrot died. But Tino didn't drown, Loretta. He turned up a few days later, thirsty and hungry, with just a few scrapes and cuts. He must have made it back to shore somehow and curled up exhausted somewhere.'

Loretta gasped. 'Are you sure?'

'I saw him myself. I went to the *pasticceria*, running an errand for Mamma and there he was, curled up in the corner, snoring away.'

'I can't believe it!' Loretta began to shake. The tears she'd been holding back began to fall.

'Tino recovered fully and he lived to a ripe old age, stealing from Signor Manuelli right to the end. Nothing terrible happened that night. Marco didn't drown and Lorenzo was thrilled to be thought of as a hero. Oh, Loretta! Have you tormented yourself all this time?'

Loretta nodded. 'I was so ashamed I never spoke about it, not even to my parents. If only I had told them, they would have passed on the news that Tino had been found. And I had no idea about Lorenzo and Barbara's happy news; I expect Mamma thought that telling me about their engagement would make me pine for Giorgio.'

'I'm no psychologist but perhaps your subconscious mind linked diving into the sea with the shock of Giorgio leaving you and tried to save you from further trauma. But whatever happened, now you can be free of it. None of us can change the past. We can only go forward, still making mistakes, still muddling through life, just trying our best.'

'With good friends by our side,' she said quietly.

Salvo's eyes softened. 'Friends, and I hope, something more. I am glad I have found you again, Loretta.'

'Oh, Salvo . . .' she sniffed. She felt too choked up to say anything more.

The smoky-grey cat was sitting at the base of a lamppost washing itself, one leg lifted at an awkward-looking angle. Abi stood watching the crew of the *Mamma Lucia* disembark, the first man ashore lighting a rolled-up cigarette. The tables outside Bar Arturo were filling up, reminding her that she'd missed breakfast for a second day.

'Good morning!'

She spun around. 'Oh, hi, Bill.' Her hand went to her hair; she hadn't bothered to wash it that morning and her T-shirt was the least flattering thing in her case, but there was no point worrying that Bill thought she looked a mess. That ship had sailed.

'I missed you at breakfast these last two mornings.'

'I haven't been hungry,' Abi lied. She could swear she caught the scent of warm pastries wafting on the breeze.

'Are you sure? I'm going to sit in one of the bars for a while with a coffee. Why don't you join me? You look like you could do with a *lingua di bue* – they say the ones at Bar Arturo are almost as good as Da Maria's.'

The thought of the island's signature puff pastry made her stomach rumble. 'I would love one, thank you.'

'There's a couple of spare seats over there. I'll see if I can catch the waiter's attention.' Bill pulled out her chair and gave the waiter a nod. 'I was going to have a coffee at the pool bar but Salvo was hanging around sneaking looks at Loretta from behind his newspaper, so I thought I'd leave them to it.'

'That was thoughtful. And so's this.' Bill was such a kind man; she'd been foolish to avoid him just because she had killed off their romance-that-never-was before it had had a chance to begin.

'No problem.' He turned to the waiter. 'Two coffees and a *lingua di bue* please.'

She took a sip of bitter espresso and bit into the pastry's flaky layers, savouring the lemon cream filling. 'Thanks, Bill, I needed this more than I knew.'

'I'm glad to see you eating. I was concerned about you, you know. I saw you come back yesterday; you looked like you'd seen a ghost.'

'I had the weirdest afternoon.'

'Tell me.'

She flicked away a flake of pastry that was clinging to her T-shirt. 'I hardly know how to begin.'

Bill sat in stunned silence as Abi repeated Marisa's story. 'Phew! No wonder she got freaky with you when you told her I imported ceramics from Vietri sul Mare.'

'It must have brought back all those bad memories. Losing a baby like she did – I can't imagine her pain. And feeling responsible for the rift between her brother Nico and the rest of her family – that must be hard to live with. You know, Bill, I've hated Marisa for so long but seeing her crumple like that, it was as if all her power over me has gone. It feels like I can finally move on.'

'I'm glad. You're a nice person, Abi. You deserve to be happy.'

But not with you. He had made that clear.

She wiped her fingers on a paper napkin, put on her sunglasses and stood up. 'I thought I might go for a walk. Thanks ever so much for the coffee and pastry, Bill.'

'Sure, have fun.' He didn't offer to go with her.

'Bye, then.'

She started to walk in the direction of the boat repair shop, past the statue of the Virgin Mary. Leaning against the plinth that supported the old fishing boat planted with flowers was a familiar figure puffing on a cigarette. Alex. A button on his designer shirt was undone, his jaw unshaven, his eyes bloodshot.

'Alex! Are you all right?' She could not think when she'd last seen him so dishevelled and he'd given up smoking not long after Chloe was born.

'Marisa's divorced! She told me I was the only man she'd really loved but she's been married before to some petty criminal, would you believe it!'

'Have you two had a row?' Abi said.

'Of course we have! How can I marry someone who's lied to me?' Alex stormed.

'You of course have zero tolerance for lies,' Abi couldn't help snapping.

'And I've said sorry I lied to you about Marisa a million times. This is different, Abi – I don't know if I can stay with her.' He took a drag on his cigarette.

Abi took a deep breath. 'I can't see what's different except that you're on the receiving end for once. But that's not what matters. Marisa's your fiancée. You have a child, Alex, a little girl who's not yet five! You walked out on me and Chloe. Are you going to walk out on Marisa and Elsa too?'

'Please, Abi, don't be like this. Tell me what to do.' Alex's voice cracked. He dropped his cigarette stub on the paving and crushed it with his shoe.

'Marisa's a victim, Alex, can't you see that?' Abi said quietly. 'She met Ciro when she was a naïve young girl, just three years older than Chloe. She got herself into a situation she couldn't handle. She lost her baby too – can you imagine how that must haunt her? And she blames herself for her brother Nico moving away. Of course, she was wrong not to tell you she'd been married before but maybe she wanted to try and put her marriage to Ciro out of her mind. She doesn't need you flying off the handle, Alex, she needs your love and support. And so does Elsa. If you want to leave Marisa, fine, please yourself, but I'm not going to make you feel better by telling you you're doing the right thing.'

'So, you knew about this! Why didn't you say anything?'

Abi shrugged. 'It wasn't my story to tell.'

'I still love Marisa, I loved her as soon as I met her, but I don't know what to do. You've got to help me.'

Abi put both hands up. 'I'm not getting involved and it's not fair to ask me.' She turned to walk away.

Alex grabbed her arm. 'Please, Abi, I'm no good at explaining how I feel.'

She tried to shake him off. 'Let go, Alex – you're hurting me!'

His fingers tightened.

Bill was beside them in an instant. He must have stayed nearby, watching her as she walked away.

'You heard the lady. Let her go.'

'Who the hell are you? You can't interfere between me and my wife!'

'She's your ex-wife, I believe,' Bill said pleasantly.

Alex took a step towards him. Bill was no taller than Alex and he didn't have Alex's gym-toned muscles, but he seemed to have grown in height. And width. Alex hesitated.

'Just go, Alex,' Abi said. 'Go and sort things out with Marisa.'

'Thanks for nothing, Abi,' Alex said.

'And, Alex, one more thing – pick up that cigarette.'

Alex's mouth opened and closed. He picked up the butt and strode away.

'Abi, are you okay? My God, you're shaking. Come here.' Bill drew her into his arms. She felt so comfortable and safe. She didn't want to let him go.

Eventually, he stepped away.

'Thank you,' Abi said.

'It's nothing – that's what friends are for. We *are* still friends, you know.'

'I'm glad of that.' She turned to go.

He touched her lightly on the arm. Her skin still came alive at his touch.

'I've missed having dinner with you,' he said. 'Would you join me tonight?'

'Yes, I'd love to.' Abi's brain understood Bill was just being friendly. But her fluttering heart hadn't got the message.

Chapter Twenty-Seven

Abi sliced through the crunchy pistachio topping; the ruby-red just-cooked tuna yielded easily to her knife. She raised her fork to her lips. The flavours exploded in her mouth.

Bill smiled. 'Looks like you made a good choice.'

'The food's amazing. Thanks for suggesting dinner tonight.'

'My pleasure. Loretta recommended this place to me; she loves the seafood and particularly that tuna dish but I didn't realise she and Salvo would be here.'

'They're so wrapped up in each other they probably haven't noticed us,' Abi laughed. She wasn't surprised, it was such a romantic setting: tiny tea lights flickered on each table and the soft glow of the streetlamps cast streaks of light across the dark water. The plump white cat with the heart-shaped mark on its nose was dozing on the deck of a motorboat tied up nearby, reminding her of their trip on the *Dina D*. If only she and Bill . . . She tried to push the thought away; she'd enjoy tonight for what it was: two friends having dinner together. She wouldn't fret about what might have been. And for a few hours she would try to forget that she and Chloe still weren't speaking.

'I heard from Mario today,' Bill said.

'About the new designs?'

'Yep. He made up a plate using that colour scheme you suggested.'

Abi coughed on a mouthful of wine. 'You're kidding? He trialled the custard yellow around the rim?'

Bill slipped his hand into the pocket of his jacket hanging on the back of his chair. 'I don't like to get my phone out at dinner but I thought you'd want to see this . . . Look!'

Abi leant forward. The new design was really striking; she couldn't believe how perfect her suggested colour scheme looked. Maybe there was something she was good at after all.

'I like it, but do you?'

'I love it. Mario's going to mock up a couple of other items to see how the colours work across the set. I'll be going over to his showroom to take a look before I go back home. He's persuaded me to stay overnight and have dinner with his family then I'll head to the airport from there.'

'Tomorrow?' She couldn't help feeling disappointed. She had hoped she might spend part of her last day with him.

'No, they won't be ready that quickly. It will probably be after you've gone back home. I'll send you over some pictures if you like.'

'Thanks.' She painted on a smile.

Bill cut a piece of squid, lifted his fork then put it down again.

'Abi, I have a confession to make.'

'I trust it's not as dramatic as Marisa's.'

Bill laughed. 'No, nothing like that, it's more of an explanation, really. It's about that day in Vietri sul Mare.'

'It's okay, Bill, you don't have to tell me. Friends don't need to know everything about each other.'

'But I want to tell you – I wish I'd explained before.'

'Okay, I'm listening.'

Bill poured a little more wine into both their glasses.

'You remember I told you that Gemma, my ex, resented all the time I spent working?'

Abi gave an encouraging nod.

'Just before we broke up, I had a trip to Italy planned. I was desperate to view some new designs but I had an inkling that going away again might be the last straw for us. I persuaded Gemma I could get the business done in a day or two and that if we came out here together, we could turn it into a holiday. I was bowled over when she agreed. She even said she'd come to one of the ceramic showrooms with me, "to see what all the fuss was about" were her exact words.

'We stayed in a beautiful hotel in Amalfi. I thought things were going well but according to Gemma, my mind was always on work and perhaps it was. But funnily enough once we arrived in Vietri, she seemed to cheer up. She loved the murals and the colourful shopfronts everywhere. We walked down that tiled passageway you wanted to see, the one with the fountain at the end . . .'

Bill stopped. He ran his forefinger around the rim of his wine glass. 'I remember her studying the mural in the courtyard as clear as can be. My meeting had gone well, the sky was an intense blue, I felt stupidly optimistic. Then she told me, right there, she wanted to leave. At first I thought she meant leaving Italy. But of course she meant leaving me and our marriage.'

His eyes showed the old hurt and bewilderment.

'Oh, Bill. I'm sorry,' Abi said.

Bill reached across the table. His hand closed over Abi's. 'I should have explained, but I didn't want to dredge up the past. We were having such a wonderful day. Abi . . . I've been thinking . . .'

A burst of 'All About That Bass' came from Abi's bag.

'I'm so sorry, I should have put it on silent.' She rummaged in her bag and fished out the phone. 'Oh, it's Chloe.'

'Answer it. I want you to relax and enjoy your meal, not fret about why Chloe was phoning you.'

'You know me too well,' Abi laughed. She spoke into the phone: 'Hello, love.'

'Mum!' Chloe's voice was urgent.

Abi's stomach clenched. 'What is it?'

Chloe's words came out all in a rush. 'Mum, it's Elsa. She's missing!'

'What do you mean? What's happened? Where are you?'

'In the marina.'

'So am I, with Bill at I Due Gabbiani, the place with the seagull sign and the bright blue tablecloths.'

'I know where you are. Don't move!' Chloe rang off.

Abi stared at the phone. 'Bill, Elsa's missing . . . I'm sorry, I . . .'

'Forget about the meal. Finding Elsa is more important. Look, here's your Chloe!'

Chloe skidded to a halt by Abi's table, panting. 'Mum! Mum!'

'Tell me what happened – slowly.'

'Nonna and Nonno took me and Elsa for a pizza at that place by the boat repair yard. Nonno fell asleep after eating his. We were all giggling, then Nonna's friend came past and they started chatting. I started looking at my phone . . .' Chloe paused and bit her lip. 'I looked up and she was gone, Mum. Elsa's gone. She's not anywhere.'

'It's going to be okay, love, we'll find her.'

'It's all my fault.' A tear ran down Chloe's face.

'Of course it isn't. No one's to blame.'

'Sometimes I wished Elsa would go away so I could have Dad to myself . . . and now she's gone. But she's my little sister . . . What if we never find her?'

'That's not going to happen. We'll all look for her, but where's your dad? Where's Marisa?' Abi could see Flavia and Enzo approaching, their faces grim.

'Dad and Marisa had a row this morning and Dad stormed out then he came back and they made it up. They went off for a meal in Chiaiolella Marina, just the two of them looking all lovey-dovey.'

'What does Elsa look like?' Bill said.

'Like this.' Chloe thrust her phone in front of him.

'Oh!' Bill gasped. 'I think I saw her run past a minute ago. Look! Doesn't that look like her over there on that yacht?' He pointed towards the smart white motor yacht tied up by the harbour's edge where the plump white cat had been sitting. The cat was still there, perched on the stern. A small curly-haired girl was wobbling along the side rail, her hand outstretched towards it.

'Mum!' Chloe shrieked. 'It's Elsa!'

Abi leapt up; her wine glass caught on her sleeve, it smashed to the ground. In a few strides she was at the marina's edge.

'Elsa!' Abi shouted.

Elsa made a grab for the cat; it swiped at her with its paw. The little girl lost her balance and toppled into the water. Everything happened in an instant, but Abi felt as though she were watching in slow motion. She braced herself to jump in.

Bill was beside her in an instant. His arm pulled her back. 'No, Abi. I'll get her.'

'Are you mad? You can't swim!'

Bill kicked off his shoes. So did Abi. But they were both too late.

An orange stiletto flying through the air, a flash of lime-green chiffon, a last glimpse of scarlet toenails . . . Loretta dived into the water. She resurfaced inches from the thrashing child.

'Just look at her!' Salvo said.

Abi gasped. 'But Loretta doesn't swim!'

Salvo chuckled. 'Not swim? The girl they called *il delfino*!'

285

'Oh, Mother Mary.' Flavia clutched the cross around her neck. 'It's all my fault. My precious grand-daughter . . .'

Enzo stood by her side, gripping the top of his walking stick, murmuring words of comfort.

In a matter of moments, Loretta was swimming back towards them holding the spluttering Elsa above the water. Abi bent down and took the wet child from Loretta and held her in her arms. Elsa clung to her, gulping and crying. Abi rubbed her back. 'There, there.' She took the striped beach towel one of the waitresses from I Due Gabbiani was holding out to her and wrapped Elsa up tight.

'She's fine,' Bill said. 'Thank God.'

Abi wiped her eyes. She used the same tissue to wipe Elsa's nose before handing her to a tearful Flavia. Enzo crossed himself, mumbling a prayer of thanks.

'Elsa, you silly thing, what were you doing?' Chloe said.

'I wanted to play with the cat, like with Bibi,' Elsa sniffed.

'We must get hold of Alex and Marisa,' Bill said.

'Oh yes, and thank Loretta properly,' Abi added. She'd almost forgotten about Loretta in all the melee.

'I'll call Alex – his number is in your phone, isn't it? But you can't thank Loretta yet, she's still in the water,' Bill said.

'You're kidding,' Abi said, but Bill was right. Loretta was swimming back and forth across the harbour in a strong front crawl, her head dipping up and down.

Something dark and glittery was bobbing in the water: Loretta's hairpiece and fancy clips had floated away.

'Just look at her, go,' Salvo said. There was pride in his voice and the glimmer of a tear in his eye.

The customers in the restaurants and bars had fallen silent, watching. People were gathering at the water's edge. Chloe was now standing next to the curly-haired boy who had been with her on La Lingua Beach.

Abi put her hand on Chloe's shoulder. 'Are you okay?'

'Yes, I'm so happy Elsa's okay,' Chloe sniffed. 'Mum, this is my friend Luca.'

The scruffy boy smiled.

'Hi,' Abi said.

'I've missed you, Mum. I'm sorry. I should have answered your calls. I know it was silly to try that cigarette.'

Abi hugged Chloe tightly. 'I'm sorry too. But, oh, love, none of that matters now. We're all here safe and sound and that's what counts.'

Chloe's body relaxed into Abi's arms. 'I love you, Mum.'

'I love you too.'

'Look!' Bill said.

Reluctantly, Abi separated from Chloe. Everyone was staring at the breakwater marking the entrance to the harbour.

Loretta was clambering up the volcanic rocks. She reached the highest of the lot, balancing on top of it; her torn chiffon dress, now soaking wet, moulded to the outline of her body. A huge cheer rose from the crowd. Loretta raised both arms aloft. Like an Olympic swimmer on the winner's podium.

Bill put his arm around Abi's shoulders. 'Let's all go and sit back down.'

'Come on, Chloe, you too, Luca,' Abi said.

The waitress from I Due Gabbiani managed to push two tables together. Flavia sat down cuddling Elsa, one hand toying with her crucifix. Enzo ordered a coffee and a grappa for his nerves. Abi was tempted to ask for a fresh tuna steak; her half-eaten meal had been cleared away, but she settled for a slice of lemon cake. No coffee for her; her heart was still hammering. Chloe chose an *affogato* – vanilla ice-cream with a shot of espresso poured over – such a grown-up choice! Her scruffy friend Luca ate his way through a giant slice of chocolatey *torta caprese* as if he hadn't been fed for a week. Elsa poked her fingers into a towering mound of *gelato*. It dripped onto Flavia's lap but Flavia didn't care a jot.

Chloe jumped up. 'Elsa, here's Mummy and Daddy!' She scooped her half-sister off Flavia's lap.

Alex and Marisa were running towards them hand in hand. Marisa's hair was wild; her cheeks streaked with mascara. Alex grabbed Elsa. 'Daddy's here, darling! Daddy's here!'

Marisa flung herself on Abi, pressing her against her bony body. 'Oh, Abi, oh, Abi. Elsa's safe!' she blubbed.

'My girls! I love them all so much,' Alex said. He kissed Chloe on the head.

Abi caught his eye. He had the grace to look embarrassed. 'Sorry about this morning,' he said quietly. 'You were right – I needed to sit down and talk to Marisa, not fly off the handle. And I shouldn't have been so rude to you.'

'I've forgotten that already,' Abi said briskly.

'I do love Marisa, you know,' he whispered.

'Be kind to her, Alex. You two are good together. You're far better suited than you and I ever were.'

'Thanks, Abi, I really appreciate that.'

'Where's the puddy-cat?' Elsa wailed.

'There she is, over there by the big pile of fishing tackle with her kitty-cat friends,' Marisa soothed. 'Now let's go home and see your own special cat, Bibi.'

'I'd better message Tania,' Chloe said. 'She put a picture of Elsa on her socials as soon as I told her. Look, Mum.'

Abi took her daughter's phone. A photo of Elsa and a couple of lines of text filled the screen.

'It says "missing" in English and Italian,' Chloe said.

'That was very good of her. Thank goodness we didn't need to use it.' Abi let out a breath. The drama of the evening was still sinking in.

'Come on, Chloe, let's go,' Alex said.

Chloe shoved her phone in her pocket and shovelled down her last mouthfuls of dessert. She and her friend Luca stood up.

'Bye, Mum. Bye, Bill, see you, Luca!'

'Thanks for the *torta*, *ciao*, Chloe, *ciao* everybody.' Luca ran off in the direction of the boat repair shop, shoelaces flapping.

The commotion on the marina was dying down; people were drifting away. Loretta was out of the water, wrapped in a tablecloth, a spare towel and Salvo's arms.

'What an evening!' Abi sighed. She suddenly felt exhausted.

'Just you and me, again,' Bill said.

'*Limoncello*?' The waitress proffered two shot glasses.

'*Si, grazie*,' Abi said. Bill nodded his assent.

'I'm rather glad I didn't have to jump in. Thank goodness for Loretta,' Abi said.

'Same here. But I wouldn't have let you do it – there could have been rocks or anchor chains or anything down there.'

'I would have been fine.'

'Probably,' Bill said. 'But I couldn't take that chance. If anything happened to you, I don't know what I'd do. When Alex told you about his row with Marisa, I couldn't bear to think there was a tiny chance you might go back to him if he and Marisa split up, however unlikely that was. Even then I still wouldn't admit to myself how I felt about you. But seeing you about to jump in, it gave me the kick up the backside I needed. I've finally stopped kidding myself. We're friends, Abi, but I don't just want to be your friend.'

She held her breath. Bill's blue eyes locked onto hers.

'I think I'm falling in love with you, Abi.'

She felt a smile spreading across her face. 'Oh, Bill. I'd jump into the harbour a thousand times to hear you say that.'

★

Loretta's heart rate gradually returned to normal. The rush of adrenaline had ebbed away. She touched the back of her head; her hair extensions had gone. Her eye make-up claimed to be waterproof but she doubted it had survived the battering of the sea.

'What on earth can I look like?'

'A panda?' Salvo suggested with a smile.

'What must you think of me?' She put her hands to her face.

He gently prised them away. 'Loretta, you've always been beautiful, ever since you were a little girl with untamed eyebrows and bruised knees. Then, as you grew up, I was almost too scared to look at you – I couldn't see a single flaw. And forty years on, when I saw you again, you were just as lovely as I remembered. But tonight . . .' Salvo paused. 'Your hair's a tangled mess, your dress is torn and there's make-up smeared all over your face. But you came alive out there in the sea; the sparkle is back in your eyes. Believe it or not, to me you've never looked more beautiful.'

Loretta's hand squeezed his. 'Oh, Salvo, think of all the years we've wasted.'

'No, darling Loretta, think of all the years ahead of us. Let's get you back to the hotel, you're shivering. Put these on, the waitress has lent them to us.'

He held up a pair of rubber flip-flops.

'Never!' Loretta said. 'My sandals are lying just over there.'

She leant on Salvo to steady herself as she tied the criss-cross ankle straps on her four-inch heels. Holding his arm, she tottered back through the marina towards the steps leading to the Hotel Paradiso, smiling all the way.

Chapter Twenty-Eight

Chloe perched on the cannon swinging her legs; the bells of Santa Maria delle Grazie were chiming. Abi watched a huge white gull swoop overhead, heading towards the port. In a couple of hours, she and Chloe would be boarding the ferry there to take them to Naples for the night. And the next day they'd be catching the early flight home.

It was sad to be leaving the island. Yesterday she and Bill had spent a lazy day together wandering aimlessly – it had been magical. And this morning she and Chloe had walked up to the Terra Murata. Abi's legs still stubbornly refused to tan but they'd carried her easily. She felt fitter and stronger. Stronger in so many ways. Tomorrow she'd be eating dinner perched at her kitchen island in London knowing Bill was hundreds of miles away, but their separation was only temporary. They'd arranged to meet up next week – she could hardly wait.

'Chloe, are you sure you want to come home early with me?' Abi said. 'I know we changed your flight, but we can change it back again. I know how much you love it here.'

'I've had a great time but it's Tania's birthday soon and I promised her we'd do something together.'

'That's nice of you, love, but won't you miss it here?'

'A bit, especially Nonno and Nonna. I love Nonna Flavia and Nonno Enzo . . . You don't mind about that do you?'

'Of course I don't; I'm happy you've got other people in your life who love you too. But I am a bit worried about Flavia. Marisa told me she's been getting ever so tired lately.'

'Flavia's fine, Mum. Marisa made her go to the doctor; he's pretty sure she's just anee – something or other, it's like when you don't have enough iron.'

'Anaemic.' Abi let out a breath. 'So it looks like it's nothing serious, thank goodness.'

'Nonna says no one has to worry about her – she's going to be around for years and years and I can stay with her next summer. We will come back to Procida next year, won't we? Please say yes.'

Abi's eyes strayed towards the pastel houses tumbling down towards the Marina Corricella. 'Of course we can, as long as it doesn't clash with school or college.'

'College is ages away.'

'Maybe for you, but not for me. I'm thinking of applying for a design course, but I'm going to take some local art classes first to get back in the swing of it, just a couple of mornings a week. I'm finally going to do something with my life. I'm going to make you proud of me.'

'I'm already proud of you – you're the best mum in the world! But who cares what I think, you need to do things for yourself, Mum, not for anyone else, that's what Tania says.'

'There are days when you girls sound more mature than me.' Abi sighed. 'Come on, we'd better get going if you're going to get your packing done. Do you need me to come and help you?'

'Of course not! I can do my own packing, I'm nearly thirteen!' Chloe skipped down the road, swinging her arms as they left the Belvedere dei Cannoni behind them.

Abi kissed her goodbye outside the door to Flavia and Enzo's apartment. 'See you later, love, good luck with your packing.' She resisted the temptation to add, 'Don't leave anything behind!'

Back at the Hotel Paradiso, Abi's suitcase was already sitting behind the reception desk under Ada's watchful eye. She stepped through the glass door and walked to the pool bar, but Loretta wasn't behind the counter. It was Salvo.

'Coffee?' he said.

'Please.' She hoisted herself up onto one of the tall bar stools. An enticing aroma drifted over from where Salvo was busying himself with the levers on the coffee machine. A bird was tweeting; splashing sounds came from the pool. Abi sent a quick message to Cherry; it would be fun to laugh over a glass of wine with her best friend again.

'There you are.' Salvo placed a small espresso in front of her.

'Thank you. I thought I'd have one whilst I wait for Bill, but I was expecting to see Loretta – isn't she around?'

Salvo chuckled. 'You need to take a close look at the pool.'

Abi slipped down from her perch and walked along the path. She stopped abruptly on the tiled edge, staring in astonishment. Loretta was standing in the shallow end, hands on hips, her hair piled up on top of her head. 'One, two, one, two. *Bravo!*' she called.

In the deep end, hanging onto a polystyrene float and kicking his way through the turquoise water, was a familiar sandy-haired figure in elephant-print trunks.

'Bill!' Abi shouted.

Bill let go of the float. He flailed around in the water before grabbing onto the side. 'Excuse me a moment, Loretta.' He hauled himself up the metal steps. Water pooled at his feet.

'I can't believe it! You're learning to swim!'

'You never know when you might need to dive in,' he laughed.

'You might have to rescue me.' She stood on one leg and did a fake wobble.

'Careful, Abi!'

'You'd better grab onto me, or I might fall.'

'But I'm dripping wet!'

Abi stepped towards him. 'I don't care. I just want you to hold me and kiss me. Again.'

Epilogue

The soothing strains of Claudio Baglioni drifted from the speaker mounted on the wall. Flavia massaged the final drops of facial oil into Loretta's forehead. Its heady scent blended with the aroma of roses from the scented candle burning on the window ledge.

'We're all done,' Flavia said. 'Take your time.' The sound of running water came from the corner basin.

Loretta opened her eyes. Flavia snuffed out the candle; a plume of dark smoke curled in the air.

'Come through when you're ready.' Flavia closed the door to the treatment room behind her.

Loretta swung her legs off the couch and slipped on her violet sandals. Flavia was waiting behind the front desk ready with the card machine. Loretta opened her purse. She spent rather a lot of money in Sempre Bella these days; it was easier to find the time to visit now that she and Salvo were running the Hotel Paradiso together.

Flavia took the payment. 'Thank you, Loretta.' She handed over the receipt then held out a framed photograph, a smile on her face.

'A wedding photo? Oh, do let me see!' Loretta took it carefully.

'London was so busy and crowded, but Enzo and I wouldn't have missed it for the world.'

'Marisa's dress is beautiful, and Alex and Enzo look so smart too.' Loretta nodded approvingly at their matching dark navy suits and carefully knotted ties. 'And surely this must be . . .'

'Nico. Marisa's younger brother.' Flavia's wrinkled brown face lit up as though she'd held one of the Sempre Bella scented candles beneath her chin. 'I always believed that one day the rift between him and Marisa would heal. It was finding out that little Elsa could have drowned that brought Nico to his senses; he couldn't believe he'd almost lost the little niece he'd never met. Since then, he's phoned us all regularly, but to see him and hug him at last – that was a moment I'll never forget . . .' Flavia blinked away a tear. She rubbed her eye with the back of her hand. 'Look!' She reached behind her. 'Here's the other photograph Marisa sent. Don't the two girls look lovely?'

'Beautiful.' Elsa looked so sweet with a pink bow in her hair and her big half-sister Chloe looked ever so sophisticated in palest blue.

'Chloe's fourteen now and thinks she's all grown up.' Flavia smiled.

'I remember being that age,' Loretta said. How certain she'd been about the way her life would unfold. She'd marry her sweetheart Giorgio and live on Capri for ever. Instead, she'd found a wreck of a hotel on Procida and lovingly turned it into a place of hopes and dreams – her own piece of paradise. And just as she was contemplating the next stage of her life, Salvo had walked through the door.

Loretta handed back the photograph. 'It was lovely to see these pictures. Thank you so much, Flavia, I'll see you next week.'

The warm air hit her as she stepped out of the air-conditioned salon and walked up the street. Ada and the new girl who'd worked for Salvo at the Blue Parrot would have finished cleaning all the rooms by the time she got back, except for one of the garden rooms. Loretta wanted to prepare that one herself – for two very special guests. This afternoon, Abi Baker was returning to the Hotel Paradiso and this time she wasn't coming alone.

Salvo had already rearranged the room so that it held two single beds instead of a double, and Ada, despite Loretta's instructions, had cleaned the bathroom until the taps sparkled. There were only a few finishing touches to add. She swapped the bedside lamps for two with prettier shades and put a potted pink petunia on the dressing table. She rooted through the linen cupboard for some cheerful lemon and lime cushions and placed them on Abi and her best friend Cherry's beds. Finally, she arranged a platter of fresh fruit for the two women to enjoy on Abi's mini hen weekend.

Afterwards Cherry would be heading back home to London whilst Abi flew out to meet Bill in Canada. The two of them were determined to see Bill's daughters in person to break the news about their little half-brother or sister who was on the way. Loretta knew Abi was nervous about meeting them, but she had a funny feeling everything would work out okay.

Loretta double-checked the room – everything was as perfect as could be. She slid back the glass door, stepped onto the room's little patio and out to the pool. No one was in the water. She glanced at the dainty watch Salvo had bought her; she could spare a few minutes before any guests were due to check in. She hurried up to her bedroom and changed as quickly as she could.

She stood at the edge of the pool, adjusted the unflattering-but-necessary hat that protected her hair. The sun sparkled on the turquoise water. She raised her arms and dived in.

Acknowledgements

Firstly, thanks to my husband Robert for putting up with me running around making notes during our holiday to Procida, a place we had previously visited on day trips from the nearby island of Ischia. We stayed in a hotel overlooking the Marina Corricella exploring all the places that Abi does in *Invitation to Italy* – but thankfully without the drama. Also, thanks to Robert for his help with the character of Bill and to Eileen and Stella for being my first readers.

Thank you to my agent Camilla Shestopal of Shesto Literary for her helpful suggestions and patience – as always.

I am lucky to have a wonderful editor at Orion, Rhea Kurien. Our off-the-cuff verbal edit over a Bellini put this book on the right track! Thank you also to the rest of the team at Orion.

I would recommend the Romantic Novelists' Association to every writer; it is always good to meet up whether in person or on Zoom.

Most importantly, a big thank you to my readers. I do appreciate all your reviews and comments.

You can connect with me on Twitter: @VictoriaSWrites and Facebook: @VictoriaSpringfieldAuthor.

Take an unforgettable trip to sunny Tuscany . . .

When sisters Cassie and Lisa receive a wedding invitation, the last person they expect to be getting married is Jane, their seventy-year-old aunt! Convinced that she's making a big mistake, the two put their differences aside to travel to the vibrant Tuscan city of Lucca. But there's something magical about Italy . . . and this trip may just change their relationship – and their lives – forever.

Jane knows it's not just a holiday fling. After her husband of four decades passed away, Jane never thought she'd find love again. But Luciano, with his big heart and artistic flamboyance, fills her life with colour. Can she convince her nieces it's never too late for a second chance?

<u>Available to buy now!</u>

Sun, sea and spaghetti . . .

Italy was Bluebell's dream destination but taking her granny's place on the *Loving and Knitting* magazine competition holiday she'd won wasn't quite what she'd had in mind. For one thing she didn't knit and for the other . . . well being single probably discounted her from the love category too. But a free holiday is a free holiday and it's the perfect escape from her lacklustre life.

Michela didn't think she'd be returning home to the Amalfi Coast so soon but a new job at her cousin's restaurant on the harbour of Positano is a dream gig, miles away from the grey London clouds. This time though, she vowed not to fall into old habits. Stefano was the past and now a bright future beckons.

But under the Italian skies a whole host of possibilities await and maybe happy-ever-after is just a plane ride away . . .

<u>Available to buy now!</u>

Under the Tuscan sun, the lives of three women are about to change forever . . .

Donna has been running the Bella Vista riding centre from her rambling farmhouse in Tuscany, taking in guests who enjoy the rolling Tuscan hills, home-grown vegetables and delicious pasta. It's been a decade since her husband Giovanni walked out, convinced she was having an affair. When the truth finally comes to light, can everything return to the way it was ten years ago? Or is it too late to start over?

When self-confessed workaholic Harriet takes an impromptu holiday to Tuscany, she quickly discovers that the relaxing yoga holiday she had been antici-pating will be anything but. She's shocked when she's asked to swap her yoga mat and leggings for riding jodhpurs and a helmet! But the longer she stays at serene Bella Vista, the more she begins to rethink the way she's been living for so long . . .

Shy artist Jess has had a crush on Donna's son Marco from the first moment she saw him. This is her second visit to Bella Vista, and she's secretly hoping to pick up where they left off last summer with an almost-kiss. But is Marco still interested or will this be a summer of sadness?

<u>Available to buy now!</u>